БТ 7/21		

D&P/4261/4.12

Nottinghamshire County Council

Please return / renew by the last date shown.

COUNTERFEIT
MURDER

COUNTERFEIT
MURDER

Inspire
Culture | Learning | Libraries

John R. Dean

ISBN: 978-1-4834-6094-9 (sc)
ISBN: 978-1-4834-6095-6 (hc)
ISBN: 978-1-4834-6096-3 (e)

Library of Congress Control Number: 2016920078

Cover image: Chris Busby
geminitiger@me.com

Lulu Publishing Services rev. date: 12/2/2016

CONTENTS

PREFACE

It was September 18, 1939, two weeks after the start of World War II, in the former Kaiser Wilhelm's Finance Ministry in Wilhelmstrasse, Berlin, a building now under the control of the Nazi Party. A proposal to destabilise the British banking system by sending aircraft to deliver and litter the United Kingdom mainland with counterfeit bank notes, ranging in value from £5 to £50, was tabled at a meeting of senior staff appointed by Adolf Hitler.

The plot was not well received by everyone present, in particular propaganda minister Joseph Goebbels, who openly doubted its value and practicality. However, any lack of support in the scheme was matched by a fervent desire for its success by officers in the SS-foreign intelligence, thus ensuring Hitler's approval for a project code named Andreas.

Following a stop-go start, progress is slow and after a number of executive changes, caused by poor management and incompetency, Andreas founders and grinds to a halt in June 1941. Stuck in limbo and going nowhere the project was reviewed and revitalized in May 1942 when Schutzstaffel Sturmbannfuhrer (SS-major) Bernhard Krueger was handed the task of resurrecting Andreas by Walter Schellenberg, head of the SS-foreign intelligence. Krueger's remit was to concentrate on producing sufficient high quality counterfeit banknotes to undermine confidence in the British banking system on the British mainland and abroad.

The counterfeiting operation was renamed Operation Bernhard, generally shortened to Bernhard, after its newly-promoted leader Major Krueger, a textile engineer with an eye for detail who had already proved his worth in managing the forging of passports and identity papers. At first unsure of this new assignment Krueger was ultimately pleased to be given the opportunity particularly as it kept him away from the Russian front and out of harm's way.

On the orders of SS-Reichsfuhrer Heinrich Himmler, who personally reviewed and authorised the continuation of counterfeiting British pounds, Major Krueger selected talented Jews and other inmates from the ever-increasing number of concentration camps, notably those at Auschwitz and

Sachsenhausen. Krueger harnessed the imprisoned skills of expert engravers, engineers and other professionals.

Printing presses from the original project Andreas' headquarters at Delbruckstrasse 6A, Berlin were dismantled and installed at Sachsenhausen.

Major Krueger improved on the work done by Andreas by producing even better quality printing plates that incorporated almost all of the Bank of England's security marks. He developed a suitable rag-based paper finished with watermarks and by using replicated matching inks the finished counterfeit notes were near perfect. Crucially, the code for generating valid serial numbers was broken, contributing to the ability to mass-produce uniquely numbered counterfeit notes. Printing started in the autumn of 1942 and accelerated to a peak production of 650,000 counterfeit notes per month in June 1943.

Ultimately Bernhard was not implemented as originally intended. The main reason being, as had been feared by its supporters, was that the Luftwaffe did not have sufficient spare planes available to deliver the snowstorms of counterfeit notes onto British soil.

Furthermore, the counterfeit notes were by now of such high quality, accepted as genuine by Swiss banks and others including some British, they were being used to pay for strategic imports and the services of German secret agents working in Allied countries.

By 1943, Bernhard was fully under the control of the SS-foreign intelligence, with Major Krueger still leading the development and printing operations. The newly printed counterfeit money was now being transferred on a weekly basis from Sachsenhausen concentration camp to Berlin, and then most of it into Italy where it was being laundered.

Following the success of producing over 132 million pounds of counterfeit English banknotes, the forgers' skills were now concentrated on the American one hundred dollar bill. The conscripted counterfeiters, who were well aware of their impending fate, delayed progress in any way they could subtly devise. Thus they struggled to make quality counterfeit dollar bills until as late as February 1945. Then, just as mass production was about to begin, the Reich security head office ordered all counterfeiting work to be stopped and the presses dismantled.

The Bernhard counterfeiting team with its plates, presses and lorry loads of crates packed with counterfeit notes was moved out of Sachsenhausen concentration camp. Transported by road and rail first to another camp at Redl-Zipf and finally to Ebensee concentration camp where the prisoners were to be killed.

On the fourth of May a revolt amongst the Ebensee prisoners encouraged by slack security and the sight of fleeing German guards presented the counterfeiters an opportunity to disperse and lose themselves in and amongst the camp internees. None of the counterfeiters were executed there and Ebensee camp was liberated just two days later by soldiers of the US Army's 80th Division on the sixth of May in 1945.

From the first day of his appointment, Major Krueger, having exacted total responsibility for technical and production control, was well aware of the lack of support from Goebbels and other high-ranking officers and advisors in the Nazi Party for Bernhard as originally planned. He also knew that the better quality forged notes, produced by Andreas and now the even better Bernhard forgeries were being used to pay agents and to buy strategic supplies including arms mainly through Friedrich Schwend and brothers Rudi and Oskar Blasche, acting as money launderers operating across Europe.

Nervous and wary of the possibility of the original aim of Bernhard being scrapped and fearing a posting to the Russian front or any front, Major Krueger secretly, with the support of Walter Schellenberg, the head of the SS-foreign intelligence and his superior officer, developed a subsidiary plan known only to a few as Kinder-B (Baby-B or Baby-Bernhard).

Major Krueger's daring plan was to implant large amounts of counterfeit money directly into the British banking system, allowing it to unwittingly spread a virus of forged notes. This virus would precede and complement any later snowstorm of counterfeit paper cash to be picked up like litter off the streets.

A successful Kinder-B would give credence and a boost to Bernhard's aim to destabilise the British banking system and at the same time see off any dissenting voices. In particular, he hoped to win over those vociferous officers and advisors close to Hitler who saw armament and infrastructure destruction as the better option to defeat an enemy that is within touching distance across the English Channel. With the sceptics being won over, Major Krueger felt confident that the necessary planes would be made available to deliver Bernhard as planned.

Kinder-B requires bulk sums of counterfeit five-pound notes to be delivered by air to secret agents and German sympathisers in England. It is necessary for the agents to gain direct access to the British banking system and, by whatever means available to them, deposit or substitute counterfeit banknotes for real ones by the tens of thousands of pounds. A virus of forged notes would be spread between the banks by themselves and amongst their trusting business and private customers.

The ruse would purposely be exposed sometime after Bernhard had been launched to the skies through a series of coded information messages that were expected to be intercepted and deciphered by the British intelligence service at Bletchley Park. This move was aimed at causing the maximum mayhem and loss of confidence in the banking system.

Late in 1942 a Dornier bomber took off from Deelen airfield, Holland, to make a special delivery to German agents operating in England. What happened to Operation Kinder-B and those involved is a story yet to be told.

CHAPTER 1

FRIDAY 11ᵀᴴ DECEMBER 1942

Harry Cole is just about to drop the latch on his backyard gate when out of the corner of his eye he sees a cycle being stood across the far end of an entry passage he shares with his terraced neighbour, it is the postman. Going back into the house, he passes through a dimly-lit kitchen and living room into the front room. A postcard lay at the foot of the panelled green front door on a strip of brown Lino that edged around the room between a ragged carpet and drab brown painted walls.

Cole picks up the postcard. It was the third of three he had received during the past week or so. The card is a picture of a granite scree-strewn hillside with a few trees in the background. There was no dedication and it could have been any side of any of a thousand hills anywhere. The postcard had been posted in London, the other two in Glasgow and Manchester; all were simply addressed by house number and street name. He goes back into the living room to the side of the chimney breast and opens a dummy flue cover to reveal a wall safe. Taking a key from a large key ring and chain clipped to a broad leather belt, he opens the safe and slides in the card alongside the other two. He will come back to them after work.

Dropping the latch on the back gate he turns and pulls on a cloth cap and cycle clips before pushing his bicycle through the echoing entry into Heanor Street, Leicester. Turning right, he sets off to work. Cycling along Heanor Street into Craven Street then Harding Street he passes Lottie's sweet shop on his right. Next he passes the Freeman's Arms public house on his left before cutting through a jitty beneath a vast blue brick viaduct carrying the Great Central Railway snaking its way through the city. Soon he joins the towpath on the Grand Union Canal at the North Lock and a brisk ten minute ride brings him to the foot of some stone steps to climb and crossing a road he is faced by a patch of land surrounded by a fence of eight foot high corrugated metal sheets. Behind the fence is a scrap yard standing abreast some sidings between the road and the Great Central Railway main lines.

The scrap yard is a business Cole has gradually built up between the war years and made easier by changing his name from Kohl to Cole. He chose to stay in England following his release as a German Prisoner of War. In June 1917 he had been injured, captured and interned in England.

Before the Great War, Cole had been a school teacher, teaching English language in Cologne. After his release he took what work he could find, first he worked as a farm hand in Herefordshire before moving to Rugby to work as a platelayer on the railway. He was forced to move on again taking on a labourer's job at a foundry in Leicester. On both occasions he lost his job as soldiers returned home from the war and took up their old employment.

As a foundry labourer he worked hard to become a charge hand and lived a frugal life style saving his money. Ultimately he became self-employed as a scrap metal merchant renting a plot of railway land with access to the railway sidings.

At number 11, Granby Street, Leicester is the Midland Bank and the Assistant Chief Cashier William Markham is letting staff in at the side door around the corner in Bishop Street. Admitting staff is just one of his routine duties as a trusted key holder. The cashier is often dealing with customers' safety deposit boxes or supervising the moving of large amounts of money in and out of the vaults to and from tellers' money drawers or between the Midland and other banks. Additionally, he supervises large sums of cash transfers to local businesses to pay for wages, raw materials and services.

Leicester's industries, like many other towns and cities, have been turned towards the war effort. Boots, shoes, socks and clothing are made for the armed forces personnel and any amount of engineering hardware is manufactured for tanks, artillery and aircraft. Cash payment is often the preferred option.

In Charles Street, the city's main police station settles into a quiet routine as the morning briefing and shift changeover is completed without any undue fuss. Even during war time, crime in Leicester is still a nuisance, being mostly low level disturbances of a breach the peace or petty theft. Incidents were often fuelled by beer and spirits still readily on tap at any of the many public houses, taverns and off-licences strewn across the sprawling city and its suburbs.

Sat squarely at a mahogany desk, the recently promoted Detective Inspector Wallace Clarke checks his diary for the day, Friday 11th December 1942. At ten o'clock he is in the Magistrates Court for remand proceedings against a drunkard for assaulting and injuring a pub landlord. In the afternoon he is to visit Corah's, a local clothing manufacturer, to discuss the collection of cash from the Midland Bank and its delivery to its finance office where staff wages are made up and its sub-contractors paid.

Standing in his puddle ridden scrap yard, December is proving to be unseasonably mild and wet, Harry Cole is sorting scrap metal exchanged for a few coppers or commandeered by the Local Authority on behalf of the Government to support the war effort. Highly valued aluminium, zinc, bronze, brass and copper are separated into individual railway wagons with general iron and other metals thrown collectively into another.

Weekly, or as wagons are loaded to the brim, they are collected, weighed and shunted into the rake of a goods train destined for the foundries in Sheffield via Nottingham on the Great Central Railway.

In June 1917 Harry Cole had been wounded by shrapnel. He and his troop desperately defended its position against the Allies led by the British Second Army in the battle of attrition at Messines Ridge, a prelude to the Battle of Passchendaele. This war injury had left him with a slight limp that proved on more than one occasion to be an acceptable excuse when asked if he would be joining up to fight the Germans.

Since the end of the First World War Cole had lost himself in the English social system assuming an air of Englishness and had covered his tracks well. He knew he would never be called to arms for his adopted country since there was no official record of him existing and his injury was a credible excuse for failing any medical should he ever be challenged.

Having once been a teacher of English he now worked on his accent. He found it easy to settle and had become an accepted and respected member of the community who outwardly supported the fight against Hitler and Germany. Despite his injury, work on a farm, shovelling ballast on the railway and labouring in a foundry had left him as strong as an ox. Cycling to and from work had kept him fit as a fiddle for whatever else may one day be expected of him as a sleeper agent working for his Fatherland, Germany.

It had been patriotic Heinrich Kohl that enlisted in the German Army in 1914. Coming from an educated background and able to speak fluent English he was instantly considered for officer training. However, Kohl spurned the interest of the recruiting officers preferring to enlist and fight amongst the rank and file.

Shortly after completing his basic training and polishing his boots in readiness for the passing out parade, Kohl was summoned to the camp commandant's office. The immaculately uniformed commandant sat at a highly polished rosewood desk and was flanked by two suited gentlemen. Kohl was informed that in spite of his earnest wish to stay amongst the rank and file he was reminded that he was now in the army where he had to follow orders.

Kohl was further informed of other roles he had been selected for to help Germany win the war, yet at the same time he would be allowed his wish to stay amongst the troops on the front line. He was reminded again that it was his duty to do as commanded. Kohl's ability to speak fluent English had been brought to the attention of the German Military Secret Service. The two intelligence officers that sat implacably alongside the camp commandant closely observed Kohl and said nothing.

In the event of any capture of the enemy close to where Kohl was posted he would be required to act as an interpreter during any interrogation, particularly so if an English officer was taken. Kohl's additional role at the front would not be without recognition or reward; he would be allocated a post war position in the military secret service. His new job will require him to fine tune the English reading, writing and oral skills of would be secret agents and others, including embassy staff, before they are posted abroad. Kohl can expect a remuneration of three times of what he could expect as a returning school teacher.

Kohl, being a bachelor with no close family ties, makes him even more appealing to the military secret service. Another role is outlined to him. In the unlikely event that Kohl was himself captured and sent back to England as a prisoner of war he would be required to avoid repatriation and assimilate himself into the English population and become a sleeper agent: an undercover agent for Germany whatever the outcome of the war.

Kohl would only become active once contacted by an established agent code named *Mercury* who was already operating in England.

The possibility of working as a clandestine agent was even more of an interest to Kohl as is a further reward that on his recall to Germany he would receive substantial pension to be paid whether he had become active or not.

Kohl dutifully accepted the additional roles particularly as he saw the interpreter work as a way of honing his knowledge of the English language and the prospect of a higher paid job at the end of the war was not to be sniffed at. Working as a sleeper agent was not without risk, he is aware that being captured in England as a German agent he would be hanged or shot as a spy. He pushed this concern, real as it was, to the back of his mind as he thought of the job teaching English to other intelligence staff at a level of pay that can only be described as a windfall.

What Kohl wasn't told is that now he is part of the military secret service any breach of security on his part, or his cover being blown could mean he could not be safely repatriated. He would then be just as likely to be executed by a fellow agent before the British had time to interrogate him, secure what information they could out of him and then hang him. With a salute Kohl was dismissed from the commandant's office.

Heinrich Kohl re-joined the ranks for the passing out parade. He was proud to be a soldier heading for the front line. However, it was to be another six weeks before he confronted the enemy.

This newly trained soldier watched anxiously as lorry load after lorry load of singing soldiers were dispatched to the western front. Kohl was sent to Berlin where he received intensive training on interrogation techniques and skills in spy working, working under cover and simple code making and breaking skills. He was identified by a number being simply known as agent 1809, it being his birthday.

Following his extra training Kohl was reassigned to another regiment and his six weeks absence was listed as having caught measles and had to be kept in isolation. The one time school teacher from Cologne, at the front line was now someone special: a special agent ready to work as required, as an interpreter or as a sleeper agent for the military secret service.

———◆———

In England, at the Midland Bank in Leicester, Assistant Chief Cashier William Markham, a man in his late forties, is a closet fascist and a Nazi sympathiser. He has not yet been called up nor had he any inclination to enlist in any of the services. He had been easily befriended by Cole during their many cycle rides into the countryside where they could talk freely about the war without being overheard.

Nervously, Markham checks his pocket watch, it is ten past three and he is expecting some one. Harry Cole is ten minutes late as he leans his cycle against the bank's wrought iron railings that have so far escaped government requisitioning. On his way from the scrap yard Harry Cole had made a detour across town to the slipper baths in Vestry Street where he had shaved and bathed making him late for his appointment with William Markham.

"Good afternoon Mr. Cole, usual?"

Both men go down into the basement, passing a uniformed guard at the half way landing and continue through an open oak door before unlocking a heavy metal grille gate and enter a brightly lit ante room in front of an open vault door. Beyond the vault door are the stacked rows of private safety deposit boxes. An attendant clerk is dismissed for a short break as William Markham takes charge and locks the grille gate behind him.

Using two keys numbered the same, one passed to him by Harry Cole and one of his own from a set of bank keys the assistant chief cashier unlocks a correspondingly numbered bronze door and withdraws a snugly fitting metal box. He places it on a table in a small alcove leaving Harry Cole to his own business. It only takes a few minutes for the scrap merchant to deposit a small soft leather pouch of assorted small diamonds, a few gold rings and sovereigns.

Closing the box lid he calls and gestures Markham to come forward and passes the box back to him. Two keys are turned back to the lock position each man pockets his own key.

"Anything else I can help you with Mr. Cole?"

"As a matter of fact there is. I would like to rent two more boxes; the larger ones will do nicely."

"Not a problem, I'll sort the paper work out and they'll be ready for your next visit."

Returning to the ground floor Harry Cole joins a short queue waiting for a teller, one of several sat on high stools along a broad sturdy mahogany bench and protected by a small ornate brass grille.

High above the public space is the cathedral like ceiling with its elaborate cross-beamed clerestory walls and its tracery glass roof forming an arcade. Transferring the weight of the roof to the walls is a girder beam and queen post trusses with curved and arched braces stretching out from polished granite wall shafts set on corbels decorated with heraldic shields. The glass sky lights let in the weak light of a dull day. The building's architecture is a provocative display of the wealth generated by the bank.

Cole doesn't have to wait long to cash a cheque. Among his monies are a few notes, some silver coin and a weighty bag of pennies and ha'pennies.

Today is Friday and pay day. The two old boys, labourers, who help Harry Cole sort scrap, eagerly await the spic and span merchant's return. Not all the cash is for wages, some of the silver coin and mostly the bag of copper coins are for payment for the odd bits and pieces of scrap metal brought in by rag and bone men with their horse drawn carts, or any metal brought in by the public who are often skint and in dire need of a few pennies to supplement meagre incomes. Street urchins drag the canal for anything that is metal and are rewarded with a balloon or a piece of ribbon and on rare occasions a few homemade toffees or humbugs from Lottie's sweet shop in Harding Street.

Turning left outside the bank, Harry Cole walks his bike the short distance to the market and buys a few potatoes and a suspect looking onion. Mounting his bike, he cycles towards the High Street and turns left heading for Applegate Street before carrying his cycle down a flight of stone steps onto the canal towpath at West Bridge.

At the scrapyard labourers are waiting with itching palms and impatient feet are treading dirt, it is almost time to knock off. They spot Cole crossing the road from the canal and act as if still busy and interested in their work by quickly chucking bits of metal into sorted heaps or a nearby wagon.

An hour or so later and alone in his terraced house, Harry Cole sits at a rickety table and dines on a mash of boiled potatoes and onion as logs crackle in an open fire. A flickering oil lamp has its wick adjusted; it burns brighter improving the poor light.

Cole reads and re-reads the three postcards in the order they had arrived. The first card from Glasgow had a sepia coloured picture of the Central railway station and a simple message, *Baby-B and MTD expected home soon*; and signed *B* with two *xs* for kisses. The second card from Manchester likewise in sepia, showed an Edwardian scene in Piccadilly Gardens, its simple message was *VPM on his way* and similarly signed *B* with a single *x* for a kiss. The third and last card with its grainy black and white picture of a hillside had a slightly longer message *LQ and DD to join the rest soon* with three *xs* and is signed *W*.

These simple and innocent looking messages are coded information about a clandestine delivery from Germany. It is to be a delivery of £100,000 of forged £5 notes to be sent by Major Krueger who heads the German counterfeiting project Bernhard, this particular delivery is code named Kinder-B.

The three postcards had been sent to Harry Cole from a German secret agent operating, somewhere in England with access to a radio receiver and transmitter and known only as *Mercury*. Harry Cole has no knowledge of who *Mercury* is or of his or her whereabouts nor has he any need to know. If captured, what he did not know he could not divulge. *Mercury* had sent a message in three parts; each part in itself meant nothing and if any one of the three cards had been intercepted, lost or destroyed this would render the whole message secure as being un-decipherable by anyone, including the British Intelligence Service at Bletchley Park. Now that Harry Cole is in possession of all three cards he is able to decipher the message and act.

Mercury's message being in three inter-dependent parts allows for a simple alphabet code to be used. The message required the capital letters to be substituted with letters from a sequence using a standard typewriter QWERTY keyboard. Harry Cole had been expecting the cards and was informed of the decipher method two weeks earlier as he picked up an apparently discarded newspaper left for him in an empty train compartment as he travelled from Leicester to Nottingham. On the back page someone had circled an advertisement for a second hand typewriter.

Cole makes regular trips to Nottingham on the pretext of selling-on second hand jewellery and items of gold he has legitimately bought, he says, for rock bottom prices at his scrap yard from people who were either hard up or, though he wouldn't admit it, occasionally from members of the criminal fraternity: Harry Cole would oblige anyone.

Cole lifts a heavy Imperial Model B typewriter out of its carrying case onto the table and feeds in a used envelope; he has no luxury of a sheet of paper. The typewriter's three rows of lettered keys are considered as three separate circles joined between the first and last letter of each row. Taking the cards in the order they have arrived he must translate the information from each card to form the whole message.

The letters on card one *MTD* are replaced with letters two keys to the left on the keyboard (or clockwise on the circle) as indicated by the two *xs* for kisses. He types out the letters BEA. For card two, he counts one key, only a single kiss this time, to the left of *VPM* to give CON and he now has a word, BEACON. The last card translates to HILL from the letters *LQ* and *DD*, three *xs* as kisses requiring three keys to the left. He now has a delivery location at Beacon Hill, a rocky outcrop, in an old volcanic region located in the Charnwood Forest area north of Leicester.

For the delivery date he checks the posting dates for the cards: they were posted on the 3rd, 5th and 9th of the month. By adding the dates this gives him a delivery date of the 17th. Harry Cole knows that the delivery will be the next Thursday, 17th December.

The single letter signatures on the first two cards is *B*, a possible reference to Bernhard are ignored but the *W* on the third card, and it being the odd one out is relevant and being the 23rd letter of the alphabet decodes to 23.00 hours.

Harry Cole now knows he is required to meet a delivery at 11pm on Thursday the 17th December, at Beacon Hill. Distracted by crackling wood burning in the fire, his eyes are first drawn to the fire then back to the third card and he takes a closer look at the picture of the hillside, smiles and mutters under his breath,

"Beacon Hill itself, maybe?"

With the stub end of a pencil he jots down Beacon Hill on the back of the card and with an exaggerated flourish scrawls two capital letters inside a circle and places it on the mantel piece above the fireplace. The other two cards are burnt in the log fire, followed by the used envelope and decoded message.

Harry Cole's success as a German agent requires him not to keep any evidence, however small or apparently meaningless, that could link him to the Fatherland or a fellow agent. To do so risks exposure and being caught, with inevitable fatal consequences.

To hide his real identity since being released as a POW Cole had moved around, assumed a different name and integrated himself into communities before finally working as a scrap metal merchant. He even joined a local cycling club to give him an air of social respectability. His joining was readily welcomed in light of the club's dwindling membership as younger members were either called up into one of the services or enlisted voluntarily.

What Harry Cole does keep and being a cycle club member gives him a good reason to have, are a number of road maps used for planning cycle rides, usually for when it was his turn to lead a club ride into the countryside. With pots cleared away he lays out a map and checks the location of Beacon Hill, a high point in the Charnwood Forest area north of Leicester. He knows the location and surrounding area well from cycle club rides in the past and as a coincidence would have it, a club ride is planned for the coming weekend on Sunday the 13th.

The planned ride is out of the city to Cropston Reservoir and into the Charnwood Forest, breasting the lower slopes of Beacon Hill before freewheeling down towards Woodhouse Eaves on the return to Leicester. This planned ride offers an ideal opportunity for him to refresh his memory not only of Beacon Hill itself but also note any landmarks that may be of help. The next time he is there it will be dark and any stranger who is not sure of his whereabouts is bound to arouse suspicion among the Home Guard, the Constabulary and locals should he be unlucky enough to bump into any of them.

Standing outside his front door Harry Cole looks left and right,

"Which will it be?" he thinks.

He turns to the left and heads for The Heanor Boat public house in the neighbouring Rayns Street.

He downs a couple of pints of bitter thinking of the day when he will be downing ale from frothing beer steins back in his home town of Cologne or rather what was left of it following the Allies' thousand bomber raid earlier in the year in May.

———◆———

In Blocks 18 &19 at Sachsenhausen concentration camp Major Krueger is making final arrangements for Kinder-B's £100,000 in counterfeit English £5 banknotes to be handed over to an officer from SS-foreign intelligence who will escort the money to Deelen airfield in Holland where the Kampfgeschwader 2, (German Battle Wing K2), is stationed. Krueger is confident that the forged notes will fool anyone as they are exchanged between hands or dropped into tills or pass across bank counters; he has been meticulous in organising the processes required and using only the best of engineers and engravers he could muster from the concentration camps.

Major Krueger watches on as prisoners with furrowed brows and pursed lips silently pack the wads of counterfeit notes into two canvas bags. One of the senior engravers moves forward and stands between the prisoners and Krueger blocking his view of the wads being packed. The two men make eye contact with each giving the other a knowing look, both are aware that the success of the counterfeits will bring different rewards for each of them: away from the Russian Front and surviving the war for Krueger and even still certain death for the engraver whose shirt back is by now wringing wet with a nervous sweat. With the packing completed, draw cords are pulled to close the canvas bags which are in turn stuffed separately into two steel drums painted in camouflage drab and green.

The engraver and Major Krueger both need to keep the counterfeiting project going, yet for the engraver and his fellow inmates the situation is dire and any early completion is not contemplated. The counterfeiters' only real hope for survival is defeat for Germany and their release by the Allies, but that possibility seems remote. However, each extra day they can survive helps them to hang on to their dream of liberation. A mutual respect builds between Krueger and the counterfeiting team he has amassed. He needs them as much as they need him.

Major Krueger continually urges the engravers to perfect the side by side plates required for the printing of notes in pairs. This process is needed to ensure the rapid and bulk production of notes that will have the recognisable three deckled sides and one straight side once the paired notes are separated by guillotining. He needs to have the bulk production up and running as quickly as possible to ensure sufficient notes will be ready for release from the air by the Luftwaffe to deliver Bernhard's snowstorms of paper money.

The Kinder-B camouflage painted drums are removed by German armaments engineers to a workshop and sealed with a screw lid and secured with a combination lock. These are the same engineers who had previously prepared and armed the drums with booby traps using an explosive petrol-magnesium incendiary device. Failure to open the drums by any other method than using the correct combination will trigger the trap and the forged notes will be soaked in petrol and incinerated as if it were a giant magnesium flare. As another precaution the incendiary device is wired to a secondary timing device that will engage automatically if a drum is not correctly opened within 30 minutes of the parachute being deployed.

The steel drums with their valuable cargo are taken out of the workshop and handed over to the SS-foreign intelligence officer who is ignorant of what the drums contain. He is under orders of the head of the SS-foreign intelligence Walter Schellenberg to take the drums, escorted by armed guards, to the Geschwaderkommodore (Commanding Officer) of the K2 Battle Wing stationed at Deelen.

On arrival at the airfield the steel drums are each fitted with a parachute and to all intents making them look like miniature versions of parachute land mines. The camouflaged drums are quarantined in the armaments store and no one other than the counterfeiters, the armaments engineers, Major Krueger, Walter Schellenberg and the K2 commanding officer has any idea what is inside the sealed containers or are aware of their ultimate destination.

CHAPTER 2

SUNDAY 13TH DECEMBER 1942

As custom dictates the Ratae Convivial Cycling Club congregate in the city centre close to Leicester's landmark clock tower. It is nine o'clock and the low sun casts long shadows, the air is mild for the time of year with a hint of rain to come later.

More intent on socialising rather than serious cycling, taking picnics and calling at hostelries for refreshment the RCCC, or sometimes irreverently called *The Arses,* muster eleven riders on a variety of bicycles. With a few exceptions bicycles are of the cost next to nothing make do and mend home-made hybrids, being either sit up and beg town bikes or are a poor copy of the more sporty drop handlebar type. Among the contingent is the Midland Bank's Assistant Chief Cashier William Markham and a newcomer, Detective Inspector Wallace Clarke of the Leicester City Police. The club's ride leader and navigator for the day makes brief introductions and gives general directions for the 20 mile round trip.

The ride leader mounts his bike and heads the group in single file down Church Gate into Lower Church Gate heading north and out of the city centre. Passing the Woolcombers Arms and Heanor Boat public houses the riders are joined by a twelfth member Harry Cole riding out of Heanor Street tagging on at the rear.

After crossing the Grand Union Canal at Pasture Bridge the group cut across St Margaret's Pasture before dismounting to walk across a footbridge over the River Soar. In the saddle again they press on into Emerald Street before going over Blackbird Road into Anstey Lane.

The wheel whirring string of cyclists of varying body strengths and fitness break into smaller groups of twos and threes with the occasional single struggling on alone. The first rest cum catch up point is Pack Horse Bridge on the outskirts of Anstey village. Before that there is a steady hill climb out of the city along Anstey Lane passing the city's sewage treatment works before relaxing the leg muscles with a freewheel downhill run to the bridge.

Cole and Markham pair up, a questioning look and a nod towards the newcomer DI Clarke brings a shrug of the shoulders from Markham,

"Don't know him, only that he's a copper."

"Well, we'll need to be a little more guarded in what we talk about," replies Cole.

Bicycles are propped against the ancient river bridge; Cole and Markham edge down to the water's edge and with cupped hands sip on the icy cold water, wetted hands are rubbed across faces to refresh the senses.

"Those two safety deposit boxes, I'll be in tomorrow," says Cole in a low voice.

"When's the delivery?"

"Soon, and it's at Beacon Hill."

"Beacon Hill? That's where we off to today."

"I know that, just pure coincidence and no need to panic. No one knows what we are about and it's an ideal opportunity for me to make a recce to refresh my bearings and check out landmarks."

"What about the copper?"

"Just a minor inconvenience him being here, just don't give him anything to think about."

The ride leader goes over the directions for the following sections of the ride; most know the route anyway and pay little heed. It will be a steady ride into The Nook at Anstey then a right turn towards Cropston and its reservoir where there will be a short stop for a cycle check before a continuous hard climb to the west and south sides of Beacon Hill. Here they will take a longer break for drinks and sandwiches.

"More time for those arriving first," quips Markham.

"Aye," agrees Cole with a wink.

Behind them DI Clarke,carrying a few more pounds than he would like, grimaces at the prospect of the impending steep climb and shuffles his slightly overweight six-foot frame between them to collect his bike.

Once again in a bunch, the twelve bell ringing cyclists enter Anstey village square, The Nook, turning right for Cropston. The landlord at the Coach and Horses sweeping the path in front of his pub raises his broom to salute the cyclists' bell ringing chorus. His muttering wife ignores them all and gets on with scrubbing the pub's stone door step.

The club ride reaches the fringes of Cropston at a four way junction where the cyclists go straight over and slightly left down to a level road running for about a third of a mile. On the left is Cropston Reservoir shimmering in the winter sun, to the right is the water pumping house with the road itself stretching across the top of the dam. At the end of the dam a road joins from the right, here cyclists dismount for a short rest in among a triangle of fir trees edged in by a grass verge. Some riders take in the view and admire the sheen on the reservoir while the rest take the opportunity to check tightness of wheel nuts, tyre pressures and the effectiveness of brakes. The hard climb is about to begin.

Since leaving the outskirts of Leicester the narrow roads and lanes meant riders needed to be no more than two abreast. The next section is no different though all know it's likely to be an ever stretching and lengthening single file as each cyclist rides against himself taking in a steady climb of four hundred and sixty feet in approximately three and three quarter miles.

Harry Cole and William Markham soon forge out a slight lead as both men pump hard on fit sturdy legs and draw in lung busting gulps of mild air allowing them to work even harder. Using a range of three gears they begin to outpace a number of the more sporty types. DI Clarke trails along some way behind. The ride leader having seen his charges off on their way tags on behind as the last man. It is not long before he passes Clarke and is soon up with the rear wheels of Cole and Markham and moves past them with ease.

"He's a showy prat," says Markham.

Taking a right turn at a cross roads brings the leading riders to the summit of their Sunday ride where cycles are laid on grass verges either side of the road, stiff legs and aching backs get some respite. A gate and a steep and winding well-trodden path invite a short walk to the top of Beacon Hill, a rugged rounded plateau with outcrops of jagged granite rock. Markham takes his sandwiches from a saddle bag and Cole unclips one of the panniers off the rear of his cycle: the two cyclists walk to the top of Beacon Hill and with no other takers they are able to talk freely.

"So, when's the drop?"

"Don't ask; just have the safety deposit boxes available."

"Ok, so it's pretty soon?"

"Maybe."

"How are you going to get out here?"

"Not sure as yet, I've got a couple of options. As long as I get my bearings today, all will be alright."

"It'll be tough on a bike," jokes Markham bringing a smile to Cole's face.

Both men look south east across a patchwork of wooded slopes and grassy fields towards Leicester and unseen over the horizon Cole's Fatherland. Each of them knows that they are set on a dangerous mission that may prove fatal.

Harry Cole looks south, back down the path and above the clump of trees standing between the hill top and the road; he then scans to the east and north seeing there are trees on the hill slopes. To the west the slopes are clear of trees but are strewn with loose rocks and the most likely drop zone for a special delivery.

"From which ever direction the plane comes the drop needs to be a perfect one". Cole is aware of booby traps and the limited time to collect.

"So why not drop into an open field?" asks Markham.

"No cover and parachutes can easily be tracked to the ground. It may be difficult here but better for me. Besides, I know that only the best pilots and navigators will be assigned for this type of mission, all will be right on the night."

"So, which way will they come then?"

"Maybe the east, clearing the trees and drop on the top of the hill and if the plane does overshoot, the rocky west slopes will be better than a chute stuck in a tree. Maybe they will come from the west to ensure a good sighting of the signal against the black backdrop of the trees, I'm only guessing. Whichever way they come, it'll be deathly quiet I will hear them coming from a long way off, I will be ready."

The men part to find a tree to relieve themselves against and whilst Markham spatters bark Harry Cole foregoes a call of nature and continues to check the lie of the land ready for his next visit to Beacon Hill.

Returning to the road the two men can see DI Clarke looking over their bikes.

"Nice bikes these, one with waterproof panniers and dyno lights, properly prepared ready for the blackout too. Perhaps I'll treat myself to an upgrade." A puffed red faced policeman rubs his palm over the Raleigh bike's badge catching his glove on a raised crack running across its heron's red neck.

"Not bad bikes at all, that one the Raleigh's mine," replies Cole.

"It was rescued off a bomb site and sold to me as scrap. Nasty Gerry bomber left it with a buckled wheel; still, I got it dirt cheap as scrap as the owner, poor sod, needed all the cash he could make."

"And the other, the Elswick, belongs to me," William Markham remarks haughtily.

"I suggest you may have to stick with what you have, yours is not a bad model at all."

"Thanks, I may have to as new bikes are a thing of the past till this mess with Germany is sorted out, Raleigh and other bike makers are tied up in munitions or other engineering work supporting the war effort."

The ride leader again points the way. There is some easy riding as the cyclists free-wheel downhill, slowly at first followed by the helter-skelter to the edge of Woodhouse Eaves where they brake hard taking a right turn at The Old Bull's Head public house. It's then a gentle ride into the village passing the red brick Methodist church, before a stiff uphill ride out of the village centre passing the granite and slate built St Paul's church with its grave yard split either side of the road.

The next objective for the cyclists is the Griffin Inn in Swithland. The serious uphill riding has been done by now and it's time to enjoy the ride back to Leicester.

Purposely lagging behind the main group Harry Cole stops for a breather at the right turn by The Old Bulls Head. He ponders his location and recalls from previous rides that should he go straight ahead he will reach Quorn and a railway station some one and a quarter miles away. There are no road signs to help as these have been removed by the Home Guard or local council so as not to direct any invading German parachutists. Behind him and last man DI Clarke catches up and screeches to a halt.

"Got a problem?"

"No, and thanks for asking, just got a bit of stitch, shouldn't have rushed my sandwiches."

The two cyclists turn right and head towards the centre of Woodhouse Eves. Harry Cole applies extra effort to his pedalling and pulls ahead, the less time he spends with DI Clarke or any constable, whether off duty or not the better for him.

Easing over the summit of the climb out of the village, just beyond St Paul's church, it's now all downhill or on the flat to the Griffin Inn. No invitations are required and chains accelerate as feet on pedals become a blur. Bitter and mild ales are soon being supped and thirsts slaked. There is a general sense among the group that they are on the home run even though there is a fair few miles and a few smaller hill climbs to go.

A short back tracking from the Griffin Inn and a left turn set the cyclists on their way to Leicester via the west side of Cropston and into Thurcaston. Here those of a mind sup even more ale at The Wheatsheaf public house. Drinkers and non-drinkers thereafter keep on the Thurcaston Road, heading toward Leicester. It's a long descent into Abbey Lane, Abbey Park Road and Belgrave Road back into Leicester.

Harry Cole and William Markham part company with the main group on Abbey Park Road and cut through Abbey Park coming out near St Margaret's Pasture. William Markham heads off up Lower Church Gate and Harry Cole turns right into Heanor Street and is soon at home.

A tired DI Clarke dismounts in Charles Street and pushes his bike the remainder of his way home going past his police station and heads up Swain Street, over the LMS Railway and into Highfields where he has rented rooms.

CHAPTER 3

MONDAY 14TH DECEMBER 1942

Major Krueger has travelled from Sachsenhausen Concentration Camp to Deelen airfield in Holland where the KG2 Battle Wing is stationed. He is keen to observe the preparations and briefing for the flight to England and the safe delivery of Kinder-B. During the seemingly endless eight hour journey his chauffeur driven car was subject to delays at checkpoints and by troop movement's criss-crossing his route. The delays did not last long, as soon as he produced his major's identity card his car was quickly waved on.

An aide is waiting at Deelen airfield's main gate and escorts Major Krueger to the commanding officer's office where he is respectfully greeted and re-freshed with coffee and biscuits. The two men talk in private with Krueger doing most of the talking, mainly about his aspirations for his project Kinder-B and its hoped for success in supporting the Fuehrer approved Bernhard. The coffee is followed by a glass of fine quality sherry reserved for special visitors.

Following the tête-à-tête the two men are joined by the pilot and the nav-igator selected for the mission. The two gunners who make up the four man aircrew are in the mess downing cups of coffee and catching up on week old newspapers. Such is the secret nature of the mission the fewer in the know, the better for all. As more sherry is sipped by the officers, the pilot and his navigator drink coffee.

Only the officers know exactly what is to be delivered to a hillside in Leicestershire, secrecy demands that the pilot and navigator need only know the time and place for the delivery of Kinder-B. The commanding officer struts around the room, halts his posturing, looks each of the air crew in the eye and speaks with passion.

"Gentlemen, the successful delivery of Kinder-B, to our brave agents in England is vital to overcoming the enemy on its own soil. This operation and another now headed by Major Krueger has been three years in the making and

19

its undoubted success will help bring victory for Germany. KG2 Battle Wing has been selected for this most special operation because, I believe, it has the best pilots and navigators in the whole of the Luftwaffe.

Pilot Officer Kappel, to locate the drop zone your skills at low-level flying will be tested to the full and your navigator's plotting and timing will need to be at their very best. As the English are fond of saying, you must find a needle in a haystack. Our fearless agents will be waiting for a special delivery where accuracy in flying, navigation and timing is vital."

Pausing and taking a sip of sherry to moisten his drying lips, the commanding officer turns with a long cane to point at a wall map of the British Isles and continues with his brief.

"Gentlemen, your plane will be prepared by the finest engineers and made ready for you to fly a mission within a mission. I repeat, it will be your flying and navigational skills that will be tested to the limit and you will be flying to my direct instructions."

Pausing again, he takes another sip of sherry before continuing.

"The main mission will be a raid out of Deelen flying north-west above the North Sea before turning south and crossing the coast here near Whitby. It will continue across the North Yorkshire Moors on its way to bomb, dare I say it, the beautiful city of York targeting its rail marshalling yards and junctions. The secondary target will be here, the docks at Hull.

However, gentlemen, your secondary destination is here, here at Beacon Hill in the quiet countryside of rural Leicestershire. You will take off with the squadron and call at York before leaving the main mission and continue south over Yorkshire, Nottinghamshire and on into Leicestershire. You are now descending for your tree top flight to the drop zone. The detailed flight plan will be worked out and agreed over the next day or so." The commanding officer pauses, allowing what he has said to sink in.

"Finally gentlemen, I must stress that on the approach to the drop zone you are required to fly as low and as slow as is practicable to ensure that your delivery is accurate and when the parachutes are deployed they spend the least possible time in the air. The drums and their contents have a limited lifespan, our agents on the ground have just thirty minutes to recover and secure the contents before they automatically self-destruct. A necessary precaution to ensure the contents never fall into the enemy's hands.

Your signal from the agents on the ground will be a flashing white light. Today is the 14th and you will fly on this coming Thursday, the night of the 17th. Any questions?"

"Sir," begins the pilot,

"You have been most complimentary about our flying abilities but may I be permitted to ask?"

"Go on, I did say any questions."

"Sir, why has K2 been given this honour instead of that other and secretive outfit, the Rowehl Group that is attached to the Abwehr, Germany's military intelligence department?"

"Suffice it to say that this mission is the most secretive and is in my command. Worry no more about it and remember to speak to no one about it, not even your raid leader to York, such is the necessary secrecy. Understood?"

The pilot and navigator have nothing more to ask knowing that for them the devil will be in the detail of the flight plan and with pursed lips gently nod their heads.

"Yes sir."

There are a few moments of collective reflection as four pairs of narrowed eyes gaze at the wall map focusing on the small dot, north of the City of Leicester that is Beacon Hill.

Major Krueger rises to his feet and looks towards the pilot and his navigator.

"Gentlemen, I wish you a safe journey and a safe return. The drop zone is in a difficult location for you, however it has been chosen as it is remote yet close enough to local populated areas where our agents can quickly regain cover by losing themselves in a nearby town. Be aware of the sudden changes in ground level, Beacon Hill is an old volcanic rock formation, not very high but high enough to be an obstruction and very hard if you fly into it. Good luck."

The two airmen salute their superiors and leave the room knowing that they, along with the squadron operations officer need time and space to plan their route from York to Beacon Hill and back to base at Deelen.

In an ante room to the airfield's main operations room, a room with map covered walls showing the latest information on the locations of British fighter squadrons and anti-aircraft gun emplacements, they set about planning a detailed flight plan; they now have just three days to get the detail right and the commanding officer's approval.

What they don't know is that Kinder-B has no other approval other than that of Major Krueger and his boss Walter Schellenberg. Nor do they know that their commanding officer has been persuaded that it is in his financial interest to lay on a slight detour for one of his bombers.

The commanding officer and Major Krueger take an evening meal in the officers' mess; there is no talk of babies or of special deliveries. The chat is of times before the war and what may lie ahead when Germany is victorious. The possibility of losing the war is never a consideration.

A staff car takes the two officers to a quiet corner of the air field and nudges close to a parked Dornier 217E fighter bomber.

"Major, this plane will deliver your Kinder-B. It's a little battered and bruised but in excellent flying order, as are all of my planes."

"Sir, do we really need a plane of this size and capacity?"

"Technically no, but as part of the subterfuge or any interception by the enemy, it will be seen as being on the bombing mission to York and as a diversion as it heads towards the cities of Nottingham, Derby and Leicester in lieu of the main mission's secondary target at Hull. In addition, it will retain some of its bombs after York and in the unlikely event that it is brought down it will be seen as an unfortunate lone bomber and no one will be any the wiser about Kinder-B and Beacon Hill."

"What of Kinder-B if the plane is intercepted or damaged and can't make it to Beacon Hill?"

"If the pilot cannot make the delivery at Beacon Hill and is in danger of being brought down the drums will still be parachuted and the built in security devices will take their course and self-destruct. Alternatively the plane with its special cargo activated to self-destruct will be ditched in the sea. If, for whatever reason, neither of these options is available the crew will still activate the devices inside the aircraft while they are still in the plane and still in flight."

"In flight, while they are still inside the plane? Surely that will mean certain death?"

"They are my crew and if they are unable to bail out they will obey my orders to the letter."

Major Krueger says no more as he fears his Kinder-B takes on the look of a possible suicide mission; something he was unprepared for and any such failure which could see him sent to the front line or even suffers a worse fate.

"Don't worry major; my men will fail neither me nor you."

With hands clasped behind their backs the two officers strut around and inspect the aircraft. Battered and bruised it may be but the German markings have been touched up or repainted making them as fresh and crisp in their detail as the day it left the factory.

The bomb bay doors are open and the delivery mechanisms await loading of their deadly cargo of bombs and Kinder-B's two valuable drums. Owing to British effective counter measures the clockwork mechanisms previously installed and used with radar guidance during the successful Coventry blitz two years ago have been modified to allow again a manual control cargo release.

A pensive Major Krueger tries to imagine the pilot and his crew flying first to York and then onto Beacon Hill to spot a white flashing light before giving Kinder-B its last second release: he thinks it is not going to be a walk in the park, their flying skills, as stressed by the commandant, will certainly be tested to the full.

Major Krueger is by now acutely aware that the efforts of his boss Walter Schellenberg to involve the KG2 Bomber Wing could see Kinder-B end in a fire ball in the air or crash on land or in the sea. Also, on the ground should there be any shortfall or overshoot of the drop zone and agents hampered in their recovery efforts the drums may well be destroyed by the petrol-magnesium security self-destruct devices.

"As I said major, don't worry." Krueger acknowledges the comforting remark with just a hint of a frown and gentle nod.

Major Krueger's car is refuelled ready for the six hundred kilometre journey back to Sachsenhausen. He declines the commanding officer's invitation for an overnight bed and some local entertainment preferring to keep his absence from Sachsenhausen to a minimum. He does ask if he may return on Thursday evening to follow the mission as it unfolds. His request is granted.

In the operations ante room several alternative detailed flight plans are considered and evaluated. These plans concern the detour from the main mission at York, its flight and line of approach to Beacon Hill and the waiting agents.

To confuse the British intelligence as to the true destinations of the main mission and its secondary targets disinformation messages will be broadcast. Should the Kinder-B detour toward Beacon Hill be detected and it not being a significant military target it would not enter British Intelligence concerns as it warns defences in Nottingham, Derby and Leicester. Loughborough would also receive a warning as would its close neighbour the listening centre at Beaumanor Hall.

Leaning across the table and giving full face to the navigator the squadron operations officer asks,

"Hans, this will be like your mother threading the eye of a needle in the dark, can we do it?"

"Can we do it? We have to and what's more we will."

Harry Cole works a normal Monday morning sorting scrap metal brought in on the previous Saturday by the usual bunch of rag and bone men. There are a few new faces amongst the general public as more and more of the poorer folk of Leicester do whatever they can to raise a little extra cash, particularly with it being close to Christmas.

Cole is expecting a delivery of a lorry load of wrought iron railings with an assortment of metal pots and pans collected by the City Council on behalf of the citizens of Leicester to support the City's war effort. Additional funding is needed to pay for the building of a new Spitfire to replace the Supermarine City of Leicester 1 that crashed on Stanhope Common, County Durham. The plane was returning from patrol duties over Seaham Harbour when it got into difficulties and crashed killing its Canadian pilot. Sorting scrap and waiting for a delivery he may be but Cole constantly thinks of how he intends to meet and collect his special delivery on Thursday night at eleven o'clock.

It's now twelve-thirty and the scrap yard gates are closed. Harry Cole and his two labourers break for lunch, any one arriving now will have to wait till one o'clock. In his shack of an office Harry Cole sits at what used to be a school ma'am's sloping desk with a mug of tea finalising, in his mind, his plan for his Thursday night out.

The drop zone at Beacon Hill is isolated, away from any main roads and will be quiet. These are plus factors but Harry Cole knows that if he uses his lorry in the still of the night it will be heard a country mile away. It is sure to be spotted as it grunts and grinds its way up Beacon Hill, drawing unwanted attention most likely from the Home Guard on patrol from Woodhouse Eves or local farmers. He has to collect and transport a hundred bundles of one thousand pounds in compressed five pound notes. Banknotes that will have some weight and require some space; he has a germ of an idea of what he will do as options and details whirr round in his head.

A clanging of opening corrugated iron gates brings the scrap yard alive, a council lorry with its railings and assorted scrap metal is unloaded, a tramp with a pram load of broken cast iron guttering and a dinted kettle is rewarded with a few pennies.

Leaving the scrap yard Harry Cole heads off to the Vestry Street slipper baths for a bath and spruce up before meeting William Markham in the Turkey Café opposite the Midland Bank. An hour later he enters the café and seeing Markham he calls out,

"Hello there, may I join you?"

"Seat's free," replies Markham, "Good ride out yesterday?"

"Just the job, got all I needed to know. Are my boxes ready?"

"Yes, you will have no bother."

"Ok, I'll be in the bank shortly."

The two men make to leave separately, the assistant chief cashier paying for his cup of tea and biscuits on his way out. A few minutes later the scrap merchant rubs away the crumbs of something purporting to be a slice of Victoria sponge before pulling on a cloth cap. He grabs hold of a battered leather briefcase, pays his bill and generously leaves a tanner tip.

Across the road William Markham has already entered the bank by the staff entrance in Bishop Street. Harry Cole pushes his bike over the tram lines and leans it against the railings that surround the bank and enters the main entrance angled on the corner of Granby Street and Bishop Street.

Inside the bank William Markham collects monies from the tellers' deep drawers. Paper packets of coins and bundles of banknotes in a velvet bag, closed with a draw cord, are taken to the rear office behind the main counter where the cash is recounted and sorted. Coins are re-bagged and notes are separated and bundled by denomination; five pound notes are in two hundred note wads and bound with a Midland Bank stamped magenta red paper band.

Every hour on the half hour the checked cash with notes again in velvet bags and coins now in much stronger cloth bags are loaded onto a dumb-waiter. It is a short journey to the basement where the cash is met by William Markham.

The velvet bags are picked up by the assistant chief cashier and carried into the main vault; the much heavier bags of coin are loaded onto a trolley and pulled along by a clerk. Coins are stacked on low metal open racking and the wads of notes are carefully stacked on shelves inside metal cabinets. All deposits into the vault are carefully entered into a large leather bound ledger. Whatever cash goes into or comes out of the vault is carefully monitored by the chief cashier or more often as not by his assistant, William Markham.

Markham completes the ledger entries and leaves the main vault. He ducks and passes through the main vault door, made out of four inches of solid steel. Next he passes through and locks behind him a steel grille gate. Immediately to his left is the dumb-waiter from the cash office above, opposite and to his right is a locked oak door leading to a spiral staircase going up to the same cash office.

Courteously Markham opens the stairs door and he dismisses the clerk back to the cash office. In front of him is another oak door, he checks through a spy hole to see who may be in the corridor before turning a heavy key. He goes through, locking the door behind him and as he turns he nods at a guard appearing at the far end of the corridor making his usual patrol: the guard is required to walk that part of the corridor and the stairs from the public foyer every fifteen minutes.

Twenty yards ahead of Markham is another steel grille gate, a further ten yards beyond that is the foot of stairs from the bank's main foyer at which and to the right is the safety box deposit vault. During opening hours the oak outer and the main vault doors are open with the intermediate steel grille gate remaining locked and only to be opened by Markham or an ever present safety deposit box attendant stationed between the grille gate and the outer oak door.

Glancing through the open vault's outer oak door and the grille gate William Markham catches sight of his cycling companion Harry Cole.

"Good afternoon Mr. Cole, are your new boxes sufficient for your needs?" Sat at a table and turning to peer from behind an alcove provided for customers' privacy, Harry Cole replies,

"Yes thanks, just the job for these bulky papers." He places a bundle of newspaper filled manila envelopes into each of two safety deposit boxes, presented to him earlier with lids open by the attendant. The open and empty boxes assured Cole and the attendant clerk that they were indeed empty and ready for his sole use.

Finished, Harry Cole closes the box lids and beckons the clerk to come forward. The clerk slots each box back into its allotted and snug safe place before closing the bronze doors and locking each with one unique customer's key and a bank master key. The two unique safety deposit box keys are handed back to Harry Cole for his safe keeping. The master key never leaves the clerk's key ring or the bank; it is locked in the bank's time locked key safe along with Markham's master vault keys at the end of the working day.

Passing the guard patrolling the corridor, Harry Cole is escorted back to the foot of stairs leading to the main foyer at ground level where he turns to the clerk and confirms his next appointment.

"Same time tomorrow, then?"

"Not a problem Mr. Cole, goodbye."

In the foyer and walking towards the main exit Cole is intercepted by Markham,

"Everything is to your satisfaction, Mr. Cole?"

"Excellent, will do nicely thanks." The men make eye contact and shake hands at which time Cole palms a safety deposit box key to Markham who quickly and carefully drops it into his coat pocket making sure he is not seen by anyone from within the bank. The scrap merchant cycles back to his yard while the assistant chief cashier loads a dumb waiter.

Sifting through a pile of twisted scrap cycles Cole salvages a saddle bag and fixes it to the seat of his Raleigh bike. He reckons that the saddle bag and the two rear mounted panniers will be sufficient to carry a hundred wads of five pound notes. The evening light is fading fast and as it is slack in the yard Cole allows his labourers to knock-off early.

"He calls this early, it's ten to five now and we go at five."

Exactly at five Cole draws the yard gates together, snaps a heavy padlock shut and gives it a sharp tug to make sure. He crosses the road before carrying his cycle down to the canal towpath and takes a steady ride home.

In the Midland Bank, William Markham supervises the locking up of the bank. Tellers' drawers have been emptied and the dumb-waiter has made its final descent to the basement. Bags of coins and bank notes are recorded in the ledger and locked away for the night. First the main vault door is closed and locked, next locked is the grille gate, followed by a check through the spy hole in the solid oak outer door; Markham goes through into the basement corridor and locking the door behind him.

At the far end of the corridor beyond the intermediate grille gate the safety deposit clerk attendant is dismissed and climbs the stairs passing a seated guard on the way. Markham, now alone, enters the safety deposit vault and locates a box and slots in Harry Cole's key followed by his own master key. In a matter of a few seconds he draws out a safety deposit box and drops in three empty velvet cash bags and a wad of Midland Bank magenta paper bands. Closing and locking the bronze door he quickly removes the two keys to his jacket pocket.

"Everything all right Mr. Markham?" calls an inquisitive guard appearing at the corridor door.

"Yes, just checking the boxes; I'm coming now." Startled but remaining composed Markham follows the same sequence as the main vault for closing and locking up the safety deposit vault. He calmly climbs the public staircase as the guard takes one last stroll along the corridor towards the intermediate grille gate, twisting and pulling door handles as he goes along, all are secure.

CHAPTER 4

TUESDAY 15TH DECEMBER 1942

Harry Cole arrives at the Midland Bank at his appointed time of two o'clock. He is greeted by a tense assistant chief cashier; a warm and sweaty security key is palmed back to Cole as the two men shake hands.

"Thank you Mr. Markham, all well with you?" asks Cole clutching the damp key in a tight fist.

"Yes, thank you."

"Sure?"

"Yes, really I am. Quiet day today, has been known to be busier. No market today makes a difference. I'll be there tonight, will you?" Cole has a quizzical look about him, before realising what Markham is referring to.

"Ah yes, of course it's the *Arses* monthly meet at the pub. Bit of a posh venue tonight being at the Grand Hotel. Yes I'm coming, we can chat later."

"See you later then, Miss Frobisher is on safety deposit duty today."

In the safety deposit box ante room Harry Cole sits at a table in one of two private alcoves set diagonally opposite each other allowing customers the maximum privacy. Cole is at the far end of the room almost unseen as two large boxes are placed at the side of his table by the petite Miss Frobisher who returns to sit at her station between the metal grille and the oak entrance door. Unseen, Cole retrieves the newspaper filled envelopes and transfers them along with three velvet money bags and a wad of paper bands into his tired looking leather briefcase.

"Miss Frobisher, I've finished."

Harry Cole is handed his two keys and heads back to his yard to check on the efforts of his labourers. Wagons should be full and ready for marshalling ready for the next scrap train to Sheffield, they are.

Apart from his recent extra visits to the bank Cole works to a routine that does not arouse suspicion. It's soon five o'clock and the yard gates are closed on time and locked for the night.

On his bike ride home Cole calls at Burberry's fish and chip shop in North Gate Street. A small piece of battered cod and two penn'th of chips are salted, doused with vinegar and wrapped in newspaper, all for nine pence. Stuffing the paper parcel inside his coat he hurries home to put the kettle on and eats his fish and chips straight out of their paper wrapping.

⬥

In the main operations room at Deelen airfield, Pilot Officer Kappel his navigator and the squadron operations officer have a proposal for a flight plan. A flight plan within a flight plan on a mission within a mission that Major Krueger hopes will result in guaranteeing the continuation of Bernhard and hopefully save him from the Russian front.

The commanding officer stares intently at the operations room's wall map as the brief begins. He is informed that all timings will relate to a parachute delivery at Beacon Hill at 11pm local time.

With an extended cane the route is outlined on the map. The Dornier bomber, call sign *Mutter*, will fly north by north-west with the rest of K2 Battle Wing over the North Sea before crossing the British coast line between Whitby and Middlesbrough. Flying over the North Yorkshire Moors they will continue on the squadron's set course for the bombing run over the primary target of York.

Leaving the skies above York the squadron will set on a course for its return to Deelen via the secondary target the docks at Hull, no bombs are to be brought back. However, having dropped part of its payload over York the detour mission bomber code name *Mutter* will part from the squadron and continue south to the east side of Nottingham and down to a height of 1500 feet.

Once clearing Nottingham *Mutter's* route will follow the lines of the Great Central Railway as it heads into Leicestershire. The aircraft will make a right turn before commencing a long circling turn to the left, gradually losing more height to 1000 feet and lower ready for the low level run towards Beacon Hill. The circling left turn continues until *Mutter* comes onto a south west course flying over Blackbrook Reservoir heading towards Rothley railway station on the Great Central Railway. Before reaching Rothley and to the left will be Swithland Reservoir and to the right another reservoir at Cropston: before passing between these reservoirs and directly ahead of *Mutter* and in line with the railway station is Beacon Hill. *Mutter* is now making its final approach to the drop zone.

The flashing ground signal will now be visible and the parachute drop can be executed. Once done *Mutter* will turn north-east, take the shortest route to The Wash and the relative safety of the North Sea and trail the main squadron back to base at Deelen.

The commanding officer rises to his feet, nods his approval to the squadron operations officer before turning to pilot and navigator.

"Gentlemen, given good weather, the rest is all down to you and your flying skills, I know I have said it before but not without just cause. Now, we again fly our planes with skilled pilots and navigators rather than depend on the X-Gerat or Y-Gerat Radio beams. Those are no longer of use to us, not since the British have been able to deploy effective counter measures preventing the Luftwaffe reaching the accuracies in guidance and target locating as achieved during the Coventry Blitz.

Finally, just be aware of enemy airfields and their defences as you make your run for The Wash and the North Sea."

This may be all the Commander has to say to the pilot and navigator but he has real concerns and keeps them to himself. He knows that in spite of all his trumpeting that K2 Battle Wing has the best aircrew, it is hollow praise since most are lacking experience and too many planes are still being lost in accidents, including some not even having engaged the enemy.

In the Grand Hotel's lounge bar, Leicester, the Ratae Convivial Cycling Club meeting is over and members sit around tables discussing anything and everything as pints of bitter or mild are downed. Harry Cole and William Markham nod an acknowledgement toward DI Clarke as he chats with the club's secretary and move away to find a quiet corner and settle on comfortable leather seats.

"You've had a good day today Harry."

"You could say we've both had a good day."

"So, when and how are you going to make the pick up?"

"When? It's the day after tomorrow, Thursday, late at night and as you know it's at Beacon Hill. Drink up, let's have another and I'll tell you the rest."

As William Markham strolls to the bar with empty glasses he is passed by DI Clarke. Harry Cole stands up as he is approached by the policeman.

"Hello again, didn't see you much after the last stop at the Wheatsheaf; did you get back ok with the stitch you had?"

"Yes thanks, and you?"

"Struggled on the last bit into town; finished up walking."

"It gets easier, I can assure you."

"Thanks, ah here's your drink, I'll leave you two to your chat. I'm just trying to mingle as a new face should do, see you again." DI Clarke acknowledges the beer carrying William Markham with a parting question.

"Know anyone with a decent bike for sale?" The two men exchange a friendly smile: Markham's is through gritted teeth as he shakes his head.

"What did he want?" asks Markham.

"Nothing in particular just socialising."

"The less we see of him the better. Now tell me what you have in mind for Thursday night."

Harry Cole describes how he intends to meet and collect the delivery of Kinder-B. Under the guise of taking a trip to Nottingham, nothing unusual in that, he will first cycle to the Central railway station, sometime after tea time. He will buy a ticket for Nottingham and as he sometimes does will take his cycle along with him.

The first stop for the train is Quorn and Woodhouse, usually shortened to Quorn located on the fringe of Charnwood Forest. The railway station and nearby village stand on the lower slopes of ancient volcanic lava flows where the landscape has been eroded and blunted by millions of seasons. Here, he will leave the train early and collect his cycle from the guard's van.

"What if you are challenged, after all you are buying a ticket for Nottingham?"

"Easy, I will just say I have forgotten something and need to get a train back to Leicester."

From Quorn station it is a continuous uphill ride, steady at first but soon becomes a stiff climb to reach Beacon Hill. At a gate and footpath leading to the summit, the same place where tea and sandwiches were taken during the previous weekend's club ride, Harry Cole will hide his cycle and climb the path that leads him through a small clump of trees to the edge of the plantation. He will make himself comfortable while waiting and listening for the aircraft and its special delivery.

Just before 11pm he will get ready the lamp to be used to signal to the approaching aircraft. He has stolen a railway guard's hand lamp from a shunter's cabin in the marshalling yard that serves his scrap yard. An oil burning wick is set behind a bulbous lens with a choice of red, green and white aspects that when lit can be seen over a mile away. The flashing white signal will be done by twisting the three pronged lens handle to close off the light and back again to make a flash.

"Why not just use a torch?"

"Household torch or even bike lamp won't be strong enough and a specialist military signaller difficult to get hold of or explain away if I am stopped. It's my choice; I have to improvise as best I can."

"But carrying a railway lamp in the middle of nowhere would seem odd, too?"

"Won't be a problem, it's already out there. Remember when I disappeared for a piss just before we came back down the hill last Sunday, just before we bumped into the policeman?"

"You mean you hid it while we were on the ride?"

"Yes, nice and cosy, safe and dry under a pile of rocks."

"Little wonder you kept your distance from the copper."

After the delivery has been collected there will be a cyclist riding at full tilt downhill to Quorn station to catch the 11.55 train back to Leicester. On arrival at Leicester Harry Cole will be just a few minutes away from his home. He is confident that his plan will work since he will be out and back in a few hours during which time his only contacts will be railway staff who will think nothing of a regular tripper who has changed his mind and changes trains at Quorn.

"What about the railway staff at Quorn, they don't know you?"

"Not a problem, they don't know of me and if asked, I'll tell them the same story of forgetfulness and whilst at Quorn I'll be taking the opportunity to spend a few hours with friends and family before catching the last train back to Leicester."

"It all sounds simple and I do think the simpler a plan is the better it is but can anything go wrong?"

"Nothing. All will be fine."

"But what if the delivery is late and you miss the train back?"

"Hmm... I will have a long night out and a long bike ride back in the dark."

Harry Cole goes on to explain why he believes the cycle and train are the best option. He doesn't want to use his lorry not just from it being noisy and can be heard a country mile away but moreover, in these petrol rationing times, it would be difficult to explain, if stopped, why he needs to be out in the middle of the night with a scrap lorry. Using the bike and train limits other people seeing or hearing him and the bike will be easy to hide as he lies in wait for the delivery. He admits he has some hard cycling to do but contents himself that it is pretty well all downhill back to Quorn station.

"I wish you well and look forward to seeing you in the bank on Friday?"

"You will, I'll be there, have no fear of that."

The cycle club meeting ends around ten o'clock and everyone makes their way home. Harry Cole saunters down Granby Street past the Midland Bank, continuing into Gallowtree Gate before passing the clock tower and heads off down Church Gate into Pasture Lane and takes in a half pint at the Heanor Boat public house.

On his way home under an overcast sky and the blackout being strictly adhered to Cole hears more people than he sees. He even bumps into a couple of strangers much the worse for drink.

"How can they afford it?" he thinks.

"No doubt some like 'em will be in the yard tomorrow with a bit of scrap."

———————◆———————

In Sachsenhausen, Major Krueger and his counterfeit team of inmates continue to perfect the white £5 and other English banknotes. Senior engravers and Krueger know that their part in the operation will soon come to an end as mass production is soon to commence following the acceptance of counterfeit notes as genuine by a Swiss bank. There is a general unease in Blocks 18 &19 amongst those skilled men rescued from certain and in some cases imminent death in the gas chambers or by other vile means. However, a lifeline thrown as the engravers are ordered by Krueger to concentrate more and more of their efforts on now forging the American 100 dollar bill. This means that there will still be a requirement for engravers, printers, checkers, counters and others already supporting Bernhard.

Those still marked for death will live a little longer and Major Krueger, for the time being, is still safe from the Russian front. Krueger orders the inmates to celebrate what they have achieved so far by organising a party and a table tennis game is presented to the counterfeiters as a reward.

At the Reichstag in Berlin, Adolf Hitler holds a private meeting with his inner circle. Those present includes the doubting Goebbels, the enthusiastic Himmler and Schellenberg's new boss Ernst Kaltenbrunner appointed after Reinhardt Heydrich died in Prague earlier in the year, mortally wounded by an assassin. Heir apparent to Hitler's reign Reich Marshall Goering, struggling to win the aerial battle against the Allies, is not present. The last item on the agenda is a discussion on the way forward for Bernhard.

Hitler knows he cannot afford to release enough planes for Bernhard to complete its original aim to deliver a snowstorm of counterfeit money across the British Isles. Almost every major city or conurbation needs to be targeted for it to be effective and the Luftwaffe is already struggling to supply the armies in the east. Hitler is reticent in backing any policy change before the end of the year and abruptly closes the agenda item without any meaningful discussion about Bernhard declaring, "That's enough for now."

He shuffles his papers together, closes the meeting and struts off to his private rooms leaving Bernhard superficially intact.

As the door closes behind Hitler, Himmler addresses those remaining.

"Gentlemen, before we disperse I have something to share with you."

Himmler empties the contents of an attaché case onto the table and a bundle of counterfeit money is heaped in the middle. The quality of the English notes is seen as Himmler, buoyed by their passing the closest inspection yet at a Swiss bank, fans out split wads of English counterfeit money across the whole of the table for all to examine.

Himmler talks of alternative schemes for Bernhard, including forging the100 US dollar bill, the purchase of strategic supplies and services and even the possibility of personal resettlement accounts being opened in South America. Goebbels is mollified, won over as Himmler passes him a wad of 200 white five pound notes again suggesting that there are viable alternatives to capitalise on the work done in Blocks 18 &19 in Sachsenhausen. He brags that his own organisation, is being squeezed of SS funding and he is already skimming the best of the counterfeits to pay for his own espionage activities in Europe and non-allied countries.

"Gentlemen, I stress that there are real opportunities here and they are not to be missed, I urge you to think about them, think about the future and the alternatives that Bernhard can offer."

CHAPTER 5

WEDNESDAY 16TH & THURSDAY 17TH DECEMBER 1942

It's the middle of the week and so far the mid-morning of a normal Wednesday. Harry Cole is at his scrap yard, it's a hum drum day for William Markham at the bank and DI Clarke has a number of enquiries to make.

In Cole's scrap yard, work stops for a tea break. Strong tea is sipped and fingers are warmed clasped around heavily stained enamel mugs. A shunting engine brings in empty wagons to load the scrap metals destined for the foundries at Sheffield. A peak capped shunter pins down a hand brake on the wagon next to the engine. With a wave he beckons the driver to ease the engine forward to slacken the coupling which he quickly releases with a hooked pole.

"Hey, Mr. Cole."

"Yes?"

"Had any break-ins lately?"

"No. Why?"

"Reckon we've had some kids in. Brand new hand lamp's gone missing. Kids break out the bull's eye glass lens and use it to start fires from the sun's rays, the little beggars."

"Oh, we're alright in here. Nothing appears to have gone missing."

Leaving the scrap men to get on and sort more and more metals the shunter with a cheery smile steps onto the engine and leaves to collect loaded wagons off an adjacent line. The loaded wagons travel across a weighbridge, weighed and moved to the marshalling yard.

It's not long before the yard stops work again, this time unexpectedly as a police car draws across the gates and a constable posted to prevent anyone entering or leaving the yard. Two more constables flank a plain clothed officer who without knocking enters Harry Cole's site office.

"Morning Mr. Cole, we meet again."

"Sooner than I would've thought Mr. Clarke. What's with all the cavalry, I take it's not a social call?"

"Well, it's nothing to do with the cycling club or the want of a new bike, that's for sure."

DI Clarke is investigating a number of thefts of jewellery, mostly gold rings and bracelets. During his enquiries he has been made aware by an informant, confirmed by colleagues in CID that Harry Cole deals in second hand jewellery, particularly items of gold, not always legitimately.

"Yes, I deal in gold and jewellery. All accounted for."

"All?"

"You can be certain it is. How can I help you?"

"Last Sunday while we were out riding with the club a number of gold rings and a diamond bracelet went missing in the Stoneygate area, anything similar been offered to you?"

"No nothing, no dealings for over a fortnight. Here, take a look at the books."

"Yes, yes, I know all about books."

"What are you insinuating?"

"Nothing, you can be sure of that. I'm new to the patch and just have to be open minded about anyone and everyone, more so at this time of year being especially wary of kings bearing gifts."

Harry Cole is taken aback at the inspector's innuendo that he doesn't always account for everything and that some dealers may have some police on their Christmas gift list.

"That's as may be but whatever you think I ain't a king from the east. My books are straight and I'm straight."

"Everything appears to be in order, but sometimes all is not what it seems and as I've said, I have to be open minded even it upsets people in the process. It's just routine and questions just have to be asked."

Harry Cole slams his books shut and looks DI Clarke straight in the eye.

"You'll have no need to worry about me."

"Well I'm sorry to have bothered you but everyone is treated the same, no offence intended. If you are offered anything, let me know."

Cole escorts the DI to the gate calling out,

"Come on you two buggers stop gawping and get back to work, get on with it."

"I see you use your bike for work as well as pleasure," remarks DI Clarke stopping and gesturing at Harry Cole's Raleigh cycle propped up against an oil drum.

"It's a case of needs must, petrol's rationed and what little I get is needed for the yard's lorry. At any rate I'm only a five minutes away from home along the tow path."

"Panniers and now a saddle bag as well, planning something special?"

Harry Cole's demeanour is now not of apparent indignation, it changes to being a little nervy and wonders if the inspector knows something about his Thursday night's clandestine outing to Beacon Hill. Cole relaxes a little and comforts himself thinking that it is impossible for the policeman to know anything at all, how on earth could he? He tries to make light of the situation.

"No, not really, just a bag I salvaged from another German air raid, you'd think they had better and more important targets than to go after bikes."

DI Clarke does not respond, tilts his trilby and swivels on his heels to leave.

With the police gone the labourers are once again chivvied to get on with some work, breaking and sorting scrap metals. Harry Cole returns to his office where straightaway he snatches up the phone and asks the operator for a Nottingham number.

"Vince, is that you?"

"Why, who wants him?"

"Listen, it's Harry from Leicester; I'll be over soon with some pieces I know you will be interested in."

"Ok, and remember to make it a Saturday or any day in the week, never on a Sunday it's my day off."

Harry Cole does have some recent acquisitions and the sooner he moves them on the better because, as DI Clarke suspects, not all transactions are accounted for and as Harry is wont to say, "Gold is gold."

———•———

In a villa, forcibly taken from a Jewish businessman and just a few miles from Sachsenhausen concentration camp, Major Krueger is entertaining his boss Walter Schellenberg, chief of the SS-foreign intelligence. The conversation is led by the invited guest. He informs Krueger that Bernhard has been the subject of a short discussion between Hitler, Goebbels, Himmler and Kaltenbrunner concerning its future. He makes a point that notably missing at the meeting was Goering or any representative from the Luftwaffe suggesting that the operation may be close to being wound up. However, since Hitler was reticent to make any instant changes and so, for the time being, Bernhard carries on.

Schellenberg and Krueger are still of the same opinion, agreeing that success with Kinder-B will advance the chances of Bernhard continuing as originally planned. However, there is no mention by Schellenberg of Himmler's suggestion about there being real alternatives to Bernhard's original aim or of himself and Himmler using counterfeit pounds to support their own organisations.

Krueger continues the discussion. He asserts that the success of Kinder-B will provide the tangible evidence for Himmler to persuade Goebbels and other dissenters that Bernhard must go forward. The snowstorm of counterfeit English money combined with a leaked revelation that counterfeit notes are already in existence within the banks will undoubtedly damage the British banking system. The impact would be far reaching as rapidly rising inflation combined with a worldwide loss of confidence will lead to the total mistrust of any English banknote of any denomination.

No matter how confident Krueger is about his proposal he is mindful that if there were to be any failure of Kinder-B and it is exposed it will probably accelerate the end of Bernhard and likely to see him either being posted to the Russian Front or receive an even worse fate. For the engravers and the rest of his counterfeit team, those already having been marked for death, will without any doubt be executed sooner rather than later as all evidence surrounding Kinder-B and Bernhard is erased.

The fact that the Luftwaffe was not included in the high level talks does not bode well for Bernhard as conceived and Major Krueger knows he has to come to terms with a dilemma. Should he propose the abandonment of Kinder-B and hope for at best an extension to his work at Sachsenhausen printing more pounds and continue perfecting plates for the US 100 dollar bill or continue with his plan and risk its outcome. He does not share his thoughts.

Schellenberg, on the other hand, is not as concerned for his own wellbeing as Krueger is for his. He believes his involvement in Kinder-B cannot be traced, after all he is the German spy leader and he manages any amount of secrecy on a daily basis determining who sees what and what is not to be seen by anyone or everyone; he feels he is in control of his situation.

In making the arrangements for the parachute drop at Beacon Hill, Schellenberg confirms he has bought the silence of the K2 Battle Wing's commanding officer and operations officer at Deelen. He has opened Swiss bank accounts in their names with skimmed off counterfeit money and is available to draw on.

Of the others involved Krueger confirms he is confident that his forced workers will utter nothing against him as they hope to extend their miserable lives on a day by day basis. They will continue to eke out their existence perfecting and printing fake British pounds and use their talents to go on and counterfeit the American 100 dollar bill.

Schellenberg's influence is far reaching and the two engineers who secured and booby trapped the Kinder-B drums have already been posted to the Russian front and will not return. The pilot and navigator of the Dornier bomber are in the control of the commanding officer who guarantees their silence by whatever means are necessary.

"Even the agents in England know nothing of me, you or of Kinder-B's set up. If any of them should be captured and tortured they do not have any information about us that will be of interest to the British and in any event will likely be summarily executed as spies. You see Krueger, we have no loose ends. We have nothing to worry about."

Schellenberg further boasts that he intends to continue to finance his own organization and at the same time line his own pockets by creaming off counterfeit British notes and American bills. He urges the tight lipped Krueger to have faith in his own project.

"We, the Fatherland, will win this filthy war. Krueger, you and I will survive it and make ourselves very rich in the process.

Once a week let me have all that you can produce and I will take a little here and a little there and arrange for deposits into our Swiss bank accounts. Now and again I'll change some for Swiss francs to use as ready money should circumstances ever change for the worse.

You must keep your nerve Krueger. It is in our joint interest to keep Bernhard alive and moving forward whatever it takes."

"But what if it goes wrong and we are caught out?" asks Krueger.

"Krueger my dear friend, you are skilled at getting your Jews and others to counterfeit British pounds to the highest levels of perfection that pass even the closest inspection. Your skills and my expertise in laundering the money through my agents in Italy and other countries, even allied countries, will ensure that we will not fail."

This answer does not fully satisfy Krueger's question but he does not press the point and as the men part he has the last word.

"Tomorrow I will be at Deelen, let's hope I get back here as planned."

What's more, he has a last thought about his dilemma, thinking it would be better to agree with Schellenberg, say nothing and see Kinder-B fly.

As normal as yesterday was, apart from Harry Cole being paid a visit by the local constabulary, today Thursday 17th December will be very much the opposite. A carefully worked out plan to fly to England £100,000 worth of counterfeit £5 pound notes and deliver them into the hands of an apparently respectable scrap metal merchant has been set in motion. At 11pm Cole will collect a double parachute drop on Beacon Hill.

Dressed early, Harry Cole clears the fire grate of cold ashes and sets a fire ready for his return after a day at his scrap yard. Straightening himself up, he stands in front of the mantel piece, his steely blue eyes gaze at the postcard with a picture of a granite hillside. Mumbling to himself,

"Yes it's Beacon Hill alright. *Mercury's* having one of his little jokes. All that effort to post and then decode three postcards and the final answer, location any way is right here, a picture of it right in front of me. But credit where credit is due, without the other two cards it is just any one of a thousand hillsides anywhere."

Skipping breakfast and outside his terraced house, Cole pockets his cap and wheels his bike into the empty street and cycles to work, a mild breeze blows back his thinning hair. At his yard at eight o'clock he soon has two keen labourers on his shoulder; he unlocks the heavy padlock on the makeshift corrugated gate.

First order of the day is for a cup of tea all-round, he puts the kettle on. The daily routine sets in as scrap is sorted, loaded, shunted and weighed ready for a trip to the Sheffield foundries and steel mills. Metal sorting is occasionally interrupted as horse carts, prams and homemade boxes on wheels bring a trickle of scrap into the muddy yard to be exchanged for a few coppers.

In his villa near Sachsenhausen Major Krueger looks at himself in a shaving mirror, thinking out loud,

"Get this Kinder-B wrong and I'm done for. Schellenberg is part of it but he has covered his tracks well and if it goes pear shaped the buck stops with me."

Having momentarily lost concentration he nicks himself with the cut throat razor and a trickle of blood runs down the side of his face, he dabs and presses a towel to stem the flow. He hopes that this is all the spilt blood he will see or hear about over the next twenty four hours or so. During that time, Kinder-B, a mission within a mission, will take off and return having hopefully completed a successful parachute drop of £100,000 of counterfeit British fivers.

Outside a military chauffeur and limousine patiently waits on the gravel driveway. Major Krueger, smart in his black uniform and highly polished boots acknowledges the driver's salute. Removing his cap he slides into the rear seat as the driver opens and sharply closes the door. Ready for the off, Krueger taps the efficient driver on the shoulder to gain his attention.

"Driver, it's a long way and there is no rush, let's be sure to get there in one piece. We'll take a short break at Hanover."

Ahead is an eight hour journey and Krueger reflects on the work he is doing at Sachsenhausen to support the war effort. He is in a privileged position and safe from any frontline combat but it is a different matter for those inmates who work for him. Krueger holds the sword of Damocles over his workers; he is in charge of their destiny which can be brought to finality with a nod of his head or the stroke of a pen. However, he is not a man without a conscience, a conscience that makes him often sleep with a restlessness that causes him to awaken still feeling tired.

Soon the journey takes Krueger out of the town where hedgerows and fields first appear then disappear into a blur as the car speeds along. Krueger nods and drops into a deep sleep, he starts to dream, his mind fills with a recent recurring dream.

In his dream world he is back in Blocks 18 and 19 at Sachsenhausen concentration camp. As always, he is being approached on all sides by seemingly well fed prisoners in civilian clothes with outstretched arms and inked black imploring hands, they are calling out to him but no voices are ever heard. Grubby fingers claw at his face, scratching and drawing blood. Behind the prisoners' hands and forlorn faces he can see rows of seated inmates with dusty and dirty hands rubbing and folding newly forged notes to artificially age the paper; some are even simulating bank tellers by using straight pins to hold a few together. Another row of men remove the pins and press the roughened notes flat into neat bundles before binding them with brown paper bands in wads of £1,000.

Outside the secure huts living skeletons in striped pyjama like uniforms hammer gnarled bony fists at the blacked out windows. Gun shots ring out and they disappear in a blinding white flash only to be replaced again and again by even more gaunt spectres doing the same.

Back inside hut 19, in a corner, a printing press spews out a fountain of white counterfeit £5 notes. Circling the press are grotesque uniformed dwarf caricatures of Himmler and Schellenberg stuffing their pockets to overflowing.

Suddenly the dream changes into a different nightmare as a door bursts open and a goggled pilot in a tattered flying suit rushes in carrying a drab and green painted drum draped in a parachute silk. There is an inferno as the drum explodes in his face.

Major Krueger wakes with a start and sweating calls out,

"Pull over driver, pull over."

Krueger hauls himself out of the car taking in gulps of fresh air and rubs away the beads of sweat with an increasingly wet handkerchief. The handkerchief is turning red as his shaving wound is open again. Stemming the blood, he composes himself, relieves himself in a ditch, straightens his uniform and returns to the car.

"Just felt a bit queasy, must be something I ate. Drive on."

Major Krueger is still three hours away from Deelen airfield where the aircrews for the raid on York are receiving a final briefing. The timings, the routes and the targets are described as the squadron operations officer outlines the main mission with an extended cane on a wall sized map.

The commanding officer enters the room, sits to one side of the gathering and one by one looks at each of the concentrated faces of his bomber crews. He knows, despite his often made assertions that his K2 Battle Wing has the best pilots and navigators within the Luftwaffe, this is not the case. Some of these men, mostly young in their early twenties, flying and fighting for their country, are not all as experienced and skilled as he would have liked to have them. He is genuinely concerned that one or more of the planes will not return but he has available trained aircrew and he has orders to fly all available airworthy planes on this raid; no one can be excused however inexperienced.

Searching among the faces, shrouded by the drifting plumes of cigarette smoke, the commanding officer picks out Pilot Officer Kappel and his navigator who have been selected to deliver Kinder-B. These men are two of the better ones he has flying for him, they look relaxed as they concentrate on the brief ready for what lies ahead. Eye contact is made between the commanding officer and the pilot and each acknowledges the other with a barely perceptible nod.

The briefing for the raid on York and the secondary target at Hull Docks ends with a report of the weather that can be expected.

"England has had an unseasonably wet and mild December so far, with changeable fronts from the Atlantic in the west bringing some heavy downpours of rain. Tonight will be no different, you can expect some low cloud cover and rain but there will be breaks with almost a full moon. Winds are generally west to south west. That's all, good luck."

The aircrews file out of the briefing room, some head for the canteen, some settle for a couple of hours shut-eye while others contemplate the planned raid as they write a letter to a girlfriend, their wife or their parents.

<hr />

In Leicester the mild weather has brought with it another rainy day and it is a sodden Harry Cole who has a few things to sort out before he locks up for the day. He cleans out an old lemonade bottle and fills it with lamp oil and pushes on the wire sprung and rubber sealed white porcelain stopper. The bottle of oil and a small pair of sharpened scissors are wrapped in a rag of an old tea towel and stashed in the reclaimed saddle bag of Harry Cole's bike, its two leather straps and buckles pulled together and closed tight.

Cole now pays some attention to his cycle; tyre pressures are checked and are ok but none the less he gives them extra two or three pumps of air. The brakes need no adjustment and the dyno operated front and rear lights are in order just needing a wipe over the blackout half-shrouded lenses. The cycle is ready for its night ride to Beacon Hill and all that Cole has to do now is to get home and ready himself for what could be a long night. It's now five o'clock as he leaves the yard; he has a train to catch at 6.49 and hurries along.

In the dimly lit kitchen at his terraced house Harry Cole rids himself of damp and dirty work clothes and stands naked at a low stone sink. He washes with a chunk of carbolic soap and a bowl of cold water, rubbing himself down with a frayed flannel before drying of with a clean towel. The slipper baths in Vestry Street would have been his preferred choice but time was against him. None the less, he manages to smarten himself up for his supposed train journey to Nottingham on one of his regular business trips or even to friends and family at Quorn should he ever be challenged.

Cole dresses deliberately in dark clothing. Different shades of black are found to cover him from head to toe, the only exception is a navy blue duffle coat.

"That will have to do, should be able to lose myself in the bushes."

On a two ringed gas hob, a pan of potatoes, an onion and half a carrot are on the boil. Cole does not light the set fire in the living room preferring to stay in the kitchen to have his meal of mashed vegetables which are bulked out with the crust end of a tin loaf. The food is soon eaten and the dirty pots left in the sink.

CHAPTER 6

THURSDAY 17TH DECEMBER
1942 CONTINUED

Major Krueger arrives at Deelen airfield. He is late. The K2 Battle Wing's mission to bomb York and Hull docks has already taken off with just four available bombers and are by now over the North Sea.

At one end of the operations room, on a raised platform, the commanding officer and Major Krueger stand behind the seated operations officer who is busy on a telephone. They peer over his shoulders down onto the rest of the room and a plotting table covered with a map of the western coast of Europe, the English Channel and the British Isles.

The York mission is represented by a green wooden block being pushed gradually along by plotters as bearings are radioed in, the four bombers are making steady and unhindered progress.

"Nothing we can do here, let's retire to my office for coffee."

Major Krueger nods in agreement and the two officers leave for the first of many coffees to be had during what is expected to be a long night.

———◆———

At Leicester Central railway station Harry Cole has missed his intended 6.49 evening train to Nottingham. Anxiously he checks his pocket watch against the station clock and glances across to a chalked up departure board, the usual finger pointing departure signs have been stored for the duration of the war. Fortunately, he only has to wait another five minutes and catches the waiting slow train to Nottingham. He stows his cycle in the guard's van and shows his tickets, one for himself and one for his cycle.

"Nottingham, eh? We'll there at 7.47."

Cole pockets his tickets and climbs aboard the adjacent third class carriage as the steam train is whistled away on its journey to Nottingham. The 6.54 is on time.

The engine driver skillfully regulates steam into the pistons allowing the engine, seemingly effortlessly, to turn the wheels and draw its rake of carriages out of the station. First it passes by the Leicester North signal box and next over a girder bridge crossing the canal.

Through an open window Harry Cole can just make out the back profiles of terraced houses in Heanor Street. Hooped railings or brick walls stand at the bottom of blue brick tiled yards that back onto the eerily black and still water of the canal. Leaving behind a snaking blue brick viaduct the train crosses over the River Soar and rumbles along glistening rails raised high on an embankment towards Abbey Sidings.

First stop in a few minutes will be Belgrave and Birstall, followed by Rothley, before arriving at Quorn and Woodhouse at 7.11: just ten minutes later than had Cole caught his intended train. Unfortunately he had now been seen by many more passengers who may remember him should his trail to Beacon Hill ever be investigated.

"I worry too much, I'll be ok."

As the engine, four carriages and a guard's van trundle to a halt at Quorn and Woodhouse station, Harry Cole is quickly off the train and at the guard's van door to collect his cycle.

"We're not at Nottingham yet sir," shouts the guard.

"I know, I know. Unfortunately I've left some important papers at the office and I need to get them, pointless journey otherwise. My fault, rushing to catch the train, Nottingham will just have to be another day I'm afraid."

Harry Cole lifts his cycle down onto the platform and not wanting to draw attention calmly walks towards the exit. He is stopped and asked for his tickets by a member of the station staff who clips them without even a check knowing that the sooner he can get the cyclist and a couple of weary travellers off on their way he too will be on his way, heading for home and a waiting meal.

Quorn and Woodhouse station, like many on the Great Central Railway, is built with an island platform with a central staircase leading to an exit on the road bridge above the station and tracks. At the top of the flight of stairs Harry Cole turns left, slips on a pair of cycle clips, pulls on his flat cap and wastes no time mounting his cycle. He quickly pedals away from the station and village leaving his co-travellers well behind making their way foot.

After a wet day the night is so far dry but low clouds hint at yet more rain to come. From the station the road gently rises and falls as it crosses the shallow contours of the land; Cole knows this is the easy part and it will be uphill for most of the way. Beacon Hill now begins to rise in the skyline in front of him.

He is soon in Woodhouse, a village noted for its stately building Beaumanor Hall, built nearly a hundred years ago in the Elizabethan style for the Herrick family. Now requisitioned by the War Office, it's an open secret that it has been transformed from an elegant residence into a Y-Station. The hall is a listening centre where radio operators of British Signals Intelligence monitor enemy signals and transmissions to and from Germany, German held territories and aircraft communications. All information is collated on red forms, prioritised and most of it forwarded to the X-Station at Bletchley Park for its legion of code breakers to decipher.

In the quiet of the night cycling at a steady pace with only the whirr of a dynamo on his rear wheel and the hum of rubber tyres on the road giving any hint of his presence, Cole approaches a guard's hut stationed at the entrance to Beaumanor Hall. Off the saddle and walking he lifts his cycle onto his shoulder and carries it quietly past the guard's hut, inside two army privates sip tea unaware of the closeness of an enemy agent. Twenty yards past and out of sight Cole remounts his cycle. He is soon taking a right fork at St Mary in the Elms church and heads off towards another village, Woodhouse Eves.

Cole's fitness is now to be tested as he begins to climb the steepening lower slopes of Charnwood Forest heading towards Beacon Hill. The pedalling becomes harder as the gradient begins to tell on his calves as he reaches and passes the next landmark The Old Bull's Head public house on the edge of Woodhouse Eves. From this point on, he is out of the comfort of the saddle as he relentlessly pumps harder and harder on the pedals, climbing the steepening gradients.

Passing a public house on his left and soon after a road to his right, locally known as Breakback Road, on the east side of Beacon Hill, Cole is now on his final and stiffest climb so far.

With the low cloud thickening and no moonlight it is now almost pitch-black with skyline and ground merging into a blur. Unaware of and marching downhill towards Cole is a two man Home Guard patrol. His slow going can be seen in the dynamo powered head lamp that barely raises a flicker. In the darkness and through drops of rain he is spotted.

"Halt, who goes there", shouts a Home Guard.

Some 20 yards ahead of Cole, a corporal assumes a bayonet thrusting stance, closely followed by another bayonet prodding part time soldier who between them block the road. He does not answer and jumping off his bike, spins it around, remounts and pedals as fast as he can back down the hill before screeching almost to a stop. Turning left into Breakback Road he quickly dismounts, lifts his bike over a five bar gate and takes refuge in a water filled field ditch, cowering behind a hawthorn hedge and below a leafless oak tree.

Bemused and unsure what to do now, the open mouthed Home Guard patrol begin to chase in vain after a fast disappearing stranger and get as far as the Breakback Road junction and give up the pursuit. A breathless private, a farm hand by day asks,

"What, what now, Corporal?"

"I dun'ow, we've lost him, he'll be well away by now, it's all downhill to the Bull's Head and beyond. Best catch our breath and carry on to the pub and report to the sergeant."

Just a few yards away Cole crouches low and holds his breath straining to hear what the two Home Guard soldiers are talking about. He hears nothing save the rhythmic crunch of boots on gravel as his two pursuers continue their downhill march intent on reporting their encounter to the sergeant.

Following his meet and retreat from the Home Guard and standing for about twenty minutes in a wet ditch till certain no one else was about Cole's resolve to continue his outing is being tested. He still has about a mile to go to reach the gated access to Beacon Hill. Recalling the damage inflicted on his home town of Cologne and gritting his teeth he urges himself on, remounts his cycle and pedals on.

It's becoming hard work and Cole has to take a short rest before walking and pushing his bike the last hundred yards or so searching the hedgerow for the gate and path leading to Beacon Hill.

It's now 8.15 pm and Cole reaches the gate and wastes no time getting off the road. He hastily props his cycle against a silver birch tree and takes the tea towel bundle with its bottle of lamp oil and scissors out of the saddle bag. The cycle is not secure and before long slides down the smooth bark of the tree and lies flat surrounded by bushes and out of sight of anyone likely to pass by on the road, Cole leaves it where it is.

Cole makes for the rocky outcrop to retrieve the stashed away railway guard's lamp. He'd hidden the lamp there four days earlier during his cycle club's Sunday ride out. In the dark he has at times to feel his way on all fours through the undergrowth of died back ferns and the loose rocks beneath his feet.

Under a weathered overhang of granite Cole separates a muddled pile of stones and pulls out a matt black guard's lamp with its bull's eye lens. Removing the oil burner he trims the wick to a clean edge and tops up the oil reservoir before returning it to the body of the lamp. Striking a match on a stone he lights the wick, adjusts it to a steady flame and closes the lamp's back cover. There is a strong white light emitted through the lens. He is careful not to draw attention by shrouding the lamp with his open duffle coat.

Satisfied all is in order the lamp is extinguished and with time to kill Cole settles himself as best he can among the rocky outcrop. A passing fox stops in its tracks, sniffs the air and checks out a stranger before quietly slinking away. The stranger constantly pulls out his pocket watch and checks the time.

High above the City of York two Luftwaffe Dornier bombers are busy unloading their deadly cargo of high explosives. Pilot Officer Kappel releases most of his plane's load of bombs, while keeping Kinder-B secure and ready for its parachute drop later at Beacon Hill.

Of the four bombers that set off to target York, two were lost out of formation just after the squadron crossed the coastline between Whitby and Middlesbrough crashing on the North Yorkshire Moors close to Hawnby and Pickering. A third plane is now in trouble and it is with a grimace and an air of sadness that the squadron leader sees yet another of his flight veer sharply right and downwards, quickly losing height. No escaping parachutes can be seen, he salutes the loss of even more of his comrades.

"Good men, too young much too young."

Clear of the searchlights and unseen by the squadron leader the third Dornier gradually regains height. Pilot Officer Kappel sets a course heading due south across the remainder of Yorkshire, over Nottinghamshire and into Leicestershire en route to complete its detour and deliver Kinder-B at Beacon Hill.

For the Luftwaffe it has proved to be a poor mission to York, leaving behind just a severely damaged school and two gas holders set on fire at an apparent cost of three lost aircraft. The squadron leader sets his remaining bomber an easterly course and heads for the North Sea and relative safety.

In the operations room at Deelen the commanding officer is passed a folded message by the operations officer: he reads the decoded message and a smile runs across his face as he hands it on to Major Krueger,

Mutter detached, on course, on time.

At the same time and back in England, two miles or so away from Beacon Hill and the patiently waiting but wet and wholly uncomfortable Harry Cole, there is a hive of activity in the radio monitoring room at Beaumanor Hall.

A coded message from a German aircraft operating in the north of England is intercepted, timed and recorded on a standard red form. The coded message is copied and added to a bundle of other messages collected from the airwaves. At first light and because the newly installed teleprinter is not working a motor cycle despatch rider will be summoned to take the messages to the British Intelligence's Headquarters at Bletchley Park.

On Beacon Hill Harry Cole checks his watch again, it's 10.45 and time to make a move. He breaks his cover and shuffles along the sheep trodden path that leads to the top of Beacon Hill. At the summit, below the low cloud and with no moonlight it is pitch-black as he lights the railway guard's lamp. He makes sure that the lens faces towards his duffle coat as he turns on the spot trying to hear and pinpoint the direction of an approaching aeroplane.

Pilot Officer Kappel skillfully flies his bomber with its precious cargo and edges to the east of Worksop before starting his descent over the suburbs of Nottingham. Kappel now follows the lines of the Great Central Railway from Ruddington heading south into Leicestershire before making a sweeping right turn towards the northern edge of the village of Shepshed. At a height of 1000 feet he starts to descend and fly even closer to the ground and opens the bomb bay doors. The plane turns steadily left and rounds the northern edge of Shepshed village and the pilot sets a course heading south-east towards Rothley railway station.

In the distance and to the left and right Kappel can make out the still and black tar like patches that are Swithland and Cropston Reservoirs that begin to glisten as rays of strong moonlight break through the weakening cloud and dance across the water. The clear sightings of the man-made lakes give assurance to Kappel that he is on course and Beacon Hill will shortly be directly below the plane.

At Beacon Hill with his feet firmly on the ground, Harry Cole hears the engines of the approaching plane and sensing its direction he turns with his signalling lamp in front of him. Alternately twisting the tap like lens handle to the right and back again he creates a strong white flashing light.

Flying below the clouds and the ground seemingly coming up too fast to meet the underside of his plane Kappel picks out the fast approaching signal. He holds his course and height steady as beads of sweat run off his forehead.

Two drab and green painted drums slip through the bomb bay doors and the parachutes are immediately deployed but are struggling to fully open. The parachutes descents are keenly watched by Harry Cole who has already extinguished his lamp. Also watching is a bewildered jaw dropping private from the Home Guard as he walks up the road from The Old Bull's Head. Pilot Officer Kappel throttles up the plane making a steep and rapid climb through the enveloping clouds and shouts for the bomb bay doors to be shut. The bomber flies east towards the North Sea.

A second coded message is transmitted to Deelen,
Kinder-B delivered.

One parachute finally billows out into a mushroom before being carried high above Cole's head and over the copse behind him landing in a ditch at the side of the road opposite the gate leading to the top of Beacon Hill. Cole concentrates his gaze on the second parachute as it still struggles to fully open. The camouflaged drum's descent is too fast and crashes into the granite scree strewn hillside. Scrambling over the scree Cole reaches the drum, it is scuffed and dented but otherwise intact.

Mindful of the back-up incendiary self-destruct device Cole wastes no time as he stands the drum on its end and by dialling 1809, his unique agent number, he is able to unlock the lid and starts to make the drum safe. Next he carefully unscrews the lid to stop the clockwork incendiary priming mechanism to the self-destruct device intended to destroy the drum and its contents. He pulls out a laden canvas sack and refits the lid which automatically restarts the incendiary detonating mechanism.

Quickly as he can he gathers in the parachute and wraps it around the drum and eases the bundle into a deep rift in the rocks.

Turning away with a sack and a railway lamp held to his chest Cole scrambles, sometimes crawls, across the loose scree to a firmer footing on the sheep path and makes his way back to the copse and his hidden cycle. Unbeknown to Cole the detonation mechanism had been damaged and the emptied drum and parachute wrapping are turned into an inferno ten minutes earlier than expected.

"Lucky me".

Close to Cole, as he is stuffs panniers and a saddle bag full with wads of counterfeit banknotes, the second drum is found by the gobsmacked Home Guard private. Not sure of what it is and not looking like anything he had been trained to recognise the private prods it gingerly at arm's length with his rifle muzzle. Without warning the drum erupts into a fireball as petrol saturates the wads of forged notes before being set alight by the exploding magnesium incendiary: the drum's contents are being incinerated. The soldier is blown off his feet and sprayed from head to toe with flaming petrol, burning magnesium and lumps of shrapnel as one half of Kinder-B self-destructs.

Cole winces as the soldier's screams pierce the now again still night air; he instantly recalls his time in the trenches at Messines Ridge. It is a memory of a comrade's painful squeals and his certain death.

Cole has no time for compassion and must act quickly, using his cycle pump he rakes out a shallow trench and buries the empty sack, the signal lamp and the cloth wrapped oil bottle; he slips the scissors into his coat pocket. Out of the copse and through the gate Cole walks his bike quietly and slowly past the writhing soldier who with his hands clamped tight over his seared face sees and hears nothing.

Cole mounts his bike and starts to free wheel down the steepening hill, his speed increases and is in full flight as he now pedals ever harder and harder, slicing through the dark and flashing through the intermittent rays of moonlight.

Further down the hill at Woodhouse Eves the Home Guard have been alerted by a farmer who has seen a low flying air craft and thinks he has heard one or two explosions. A corporal and a private are despatched and are trotting up the steep road to Beacon Hill and unwittingly towards the on rushing Cole.

Once again Cole is confronted, but this time he has no time to stop and clatters into the near breathless guards knocking them to the ground. Cole is slewed sideward and crashes heavily onto the gravelled road twisting his handlebars and a heron's red head breaks off the already cracked Raleigh badge. Dazed but first to react is a fitter Cole who is soon on his feet and wheels his bike away into the increasing gloom. More low cloud moves in and rain begins to fall again. Sat helpless with rifles askew on the road the two soldiers gather in their wits about them. The corporal is winded and is lost for words and the private is almost bursting a blood vessel.

"Two sodding bikes in one night. Just what the fuck's going on corp?"

"Jesus Christ," squeals the corporal as he leans onto an unseen jagged edged piece of metal that cuts deep into his palm and draws blood.

Safe and out of sight Cole catches his breath and twists his handlebars straight. Back on the saddle he cycles quietly and unnoticed past the nearby Bull's Head public house and St. Mary's church further down the hill.

The downhill helter-skelter eases to a gentler ride. Still pedalling and steering with one hand Cole feels for the saddle bag behind his seat with the other, it is still there. The two panniers are seen as he casts backward glances to the left and right: he knows at least one half of Kinder-B is safe. Now all he has to do is get by the guard's hut at the entrance to Beaumanor Hall and catch his train at Quorn station.

As he had done a few hours earlier Cole dismounts and lifts his cycle onto his shoulder: the extra weight of Kinder-B is hardly noticed by strong arms, back and leg muscles more used to lifting and lobbing heavy metal scrap into railway wagons. He need not have worried about another encounter as the hut is empty; the two guards have wandered off away from the road into an open field between their hut and the hall to look at the night sky, they have also been warned of low flying aircraft and bomb explosions. It starts to rain harder and the guards return to their hut, Cole is well past them by now.

It is a wet and dishevelled but unruffled Cole that carries his cycle down the stairs from the road onto the island platform at Quorn station. The last train of the day to Leicester arrives on time in a shroud of billowing steam and smoke. Cole's nose twitches as the railway's peculiar atmosphere is drawn into his nostrils.

Harry Cole boards the train and stands with his cycle with its stuffed bags in the guard's van.

"You can take a seat in a carriage sir; your bike will be safe with me,"

"No, no thanks, I'm dripping wet. I'll wait here, only going as far as Leicester; it's not far, let's keep the seats dry."

"As you wish sir," mumbles the guard as he clips two tickets, one for a dripping wet cyclist and one for his bicycle.

"Mmm… daren't leave my bike and its valuable cargo," mumbles Cole to himself.

"A cargo that is a germ of disease that will grow and fester into a virus that will bring down the pound destroying the British economy; my involvement is my way of helping to bring the certain victory for Germany and in particular some recompense for the bombing of my beloved Cologne."

Off the train in a jiffy at Leicester Central station and quickly down the stairs Cole stands in the subway beneath the platforms and peers through the cavernous and dark tunnel leading to the roadside exit, he'll soon be home. The enforced blackout and the shrouding low cloud and its rain will provide Cole a perfect cover.

Cole is out of the station cycling left into Great Central Street, a broad thoroughfare built, named after and paid for by Britain's last main line providing a new road link between St Nicholas Street and North Gate Street to serve Leicester's newest station built on a majestic blue brick viaduct.

Cole is once again struggling against the elements. Cycling at a stuttering pace he almost stalls and falls when a crosswind catches him as he rides into North Gate Street at its junction with Sanvey Gate. He cycles under the grey lattice steel bridge that carries the railway, turns right into the jitty that leads under its blue viaduct and past a blacksmith's workshop into Harding Street. He is barely a couple of minutes from being home. Pushing his bike into the kitchen he lets out a sigh of relief and locks the door.

Harry Cole has collected at least half of Kinder-B and wonders if the second drum has been completely destroyed.

Over the North Sea, Pilot Officer Kappel's navigator and gunners are getting increasingly anxious as he struggles to maintain height. The Dornier bomber has already lost power in one engine and fuel is dangerously low. Unknown to the pilot and crew a fuel line has been leaking since leaving Deelen.

"Bail out, bail out," screams Kappel. The navigator at first struggles to pull open the escape hatch before it finally gives and three silk mushrooms drift in silence toward the icy waters. Pilot Officer Kappel is concussed after being bounced around like a rubber ball. He is thrown onto his back before being thumped into the fuselage sides and roof as the plane twists and spirals out of control. The ill-fated bomber crashes headlong into the sea snapping off its wings and sinks within seconds taking its pilot to a watery grave.

The three airmen lucky enough to escape the doomed Dornier are now drifting helpless in the sea with little hope of being rescued. Hyperthermia soon sets in and each man gradually succumbs to an eternal sleep, adding to the statistics of those on both sides listed as missing and presumed killed in action.

At Deelen airfield the operations room falls silent and the commanding officer is stern faced as news filters through that just one plane returns from the raid on York. The squadron operations officer stands outside over a fire in an old oil drum and feeds it with all copies of Kinder-B's flight plan.

Major Krueger calls Walter Schellenberg and informs him of the successful delivery of Kinder-B. He sends for his chauffeur and leaves quietly for Sachsenhausen.

CHAPTER 7

FRIDAY 18TH DECEMBER 1942

etective Inspector Clarke is in his office early at Charles Street police station and has a visitor, another policeman. A DI from the Nottingham City Police who has had a tip-off concerning some gold items he has recovered from a jeweller in the Radford area of Nottingham.

"These items, five rings and a bracelet, match the descriptions of jewellery reported stolen on your patch and as I understand it, in the Stoneygate area of the city."

"Hmm… I agree they pretty well fit the descriptions. I just need to check with the owners. Can I give them back if an owner identifies any of them?"

"No, not just yet: we only have the buyer, at one end of the trail and not the fence or the thief, both suspected as working on your patch here in Leicester."

"Reasonable assumption but first things first a cup of tea then we'll pay a couple of visits."

At home in Heanor Street, following his secretive round trip to Beacon Hill, Harry Cole sharpens his senses washing with the usual carbolic soap and a bowl of cold water. He has had a restless night with just a couple of hours sleep.

Before retiring Cole had removed what he managed to collect of Kinder-B from the panniers and saddle bag and stacked £50,000 worth of forged five pound notes, all 50 wads, onto the living room table. Then, by lamp light he had neatly replaced the brown paper bands with the magenta red bands stamped Midland Bank provided by William Markham.

Forty wads, each being two hundred pressed £5 notes are stuffed into two of the three velvet money bags, also provided by Markham. The velvet bags are then packed into a small leather suitcase, taken upstairs and shoved under Cole's bed for what was left of the night. The remaining £10,000 is dropped into the third velvet bag and stashed in Cole's wall safe hidden behind the chimney breast's dummy flue cover.

Not all money skimmers are at home in the Fatherland. Cole regards the £10,000 as insurance available to him should things go pear shaped and he has to do a runner. That's his thinking at least till the switching of counterfeits for real monies is made at the bank, after which time he hopes to be a genuinely rich man.

Cole restricts breakfast to a cup of tea and sets off for his scrap yard cycling with one hand on the handlebars and one carrying a suitcase.

On the other side of town William Markham catches a maroon and cream liveried tram on London Road in Stoneygate. As the tram trundles on its way into the city centre Markham peers aimlessly out of the spotlessly clean and leather dried windows pondering on the day ahead, he has a usual nothing out of the ordinary day that may change dramatically dependent what news Harry Cole has for him about his previous night's work in Charnwood Forest.

"Was there a plane? Was there a delivery? Did he catch the train?" he repeatedly asks himself.

If the answer is yes to all three questions Markham will know he is in for a somewhat different day to the usual monotony of any Friday in the bank. He'll get the answers when he meets Cole later in the day as arranged at the Turkey Café.

Someone rings the tram bell signalling a stop and Markham alights at the corner of Bishop Street and Granby Street, he heads for the staff entrance where he is met by a number of early bird colleagues treading the pavement waiting for the trusted key holder.

It's 11.30 and the previous night's rain has cleared away and the sun is out. Harry Cole leaves the Vestry Street slipper baths having shaved, and bathed carrying a small leather suitcase, the contents of which may well help decide the outcome of the war. Though tired from his exertions and lack of sleep Cole has chosen to walk, rather than cycle, from his scrap yard across the town to the slipper baths before calling at the Midland Bank and then to a meeting with Markham in the Turkey Café.

The walk, the fresh air, a hot bath and the prospect of securing a vital advantage for the Fatherland ensures that any adrenalin Cole has left will keep him going. Upright and chest out he strides towards the clock tower before turning left into Gallowtree Gate and on into Granby Street. Standing outside the Midland Bank Harry Cole holds the small leather suitcase to his chest and strums his fingers on its hard leather and glances across to the Turkey Café and back to the imposing red brick façade of the bank thinking,

"It won't be long now. Deposit this lot in my new safety deposit boxes, safe and secure in the bowels of the bank then a cup of tea and chat with Markham about making the switch."

A few more paces and Cole is climbing the stone steps taking him into the bank's main foyer where William Markham shouts out a greeting.

"Good morning Mr. Cole." Cole acknowledges the welcome in silence by raising an open palm, trying not to draw any more unnecessary attention as Markham strides purposely towards him.

"Usual, Mr. Cole?" asks the assistant chief cashier and before Cole can muster a reply,

"You'll find Miss Frobisher on duty down stairs today, she'll look after you."

"Thanks, will I see you later?"

"Certainly will, as arranged." For the benefit of any one listening nearby Markham raises his voice a notch,

"We need to sort out the route for the next cycle run; it's our turn and we must keep the club secretary happy."

"Fine, let's say 12.30 then?"

"Fine by me and word has it that some form of chocolate cake is available."

"I'll look forward to that." Cole wonders what sort of quality the cake will be in these times of food shortages and make do and mend.

Five minutes later Cole, having secured two counterfeit laden velvet bags in the bank's safety deposit vault is back out on the street. He crosses directly to the Turkey Café where he takes a seat in a quiet corner away from the counter and other customers. Hardly settled he is pounced on,

"Good afternoon sir, will you be dining today? Would you like to order?" Cole pauses as the doorbell rings out as customers come and go.

"No, not a meal but a pot of tea for two and as rumour has it you have some, two slices of your chocolate cake please."

Behind the waitress stands the towering frame of William Markham and being something of a womaniser stands his ground and the waitress is forced to squeeze between him and adjacent table and chairs: Markham never misses an opportunity to flirt and the waitress knows him of old and brushes past him in a huff.

"Mr. Markham, have a seat; I've ordered for two." Markham pulls out a chair, gets comfortable as best he can with his long legs stretched either side of the round table and leans across to face Cole.

"Well, can I presume you have had a successful trip?"

"Not too bad, not too bad at all. However, half the delivery is lost."

"Lost?"

"The pilot did his best, thought at one stage he would crash and the drop itself was not entirely successful. I got one package but the other over shot the hill and went up in flames and that's not all."

"Not all, what do you mean, what are you trying to tell me?"

"I had a run-in with the Home Guard, twice!"

"Did they see you, will they recognise you?"

"I don't think so; at times it was pitch-black out there. Also, another one of them, poor sod, got too nosey with the other package and took it full in his face."

"Is he dead?"

"Don't know, but more likely as not. He was a mess."

"You said you got half the counterfeits, what about the rest?"

"You are not listening. As I said, the guard got too nosey and took the full force of the blast in his face. The package was detonated by the built in self-destruct device, incinerating and destroying the contents, all £50,000 of it."

The two men sup tea and nibble at a passable chocolate sponge cake as they discuss what they have achieved and what their next moves are.

Cole, so far, has done his bit since being contacted by *Mercury*, he has received and deciphered the place and time for delivery of Kinder-B and although only partly successful in collecting half of the counterfeit fivers he has managed, with Markham's help, to get £40,000 of them into Leicester and into safety deposit boxes at the Midland Bank. Cole tells Markham that he has stashed away the remaining £10,000 as insurance or at least until Markham has done his bit in switching counterfeits for the real stuff.

"When can you make the switch? How do you propose to do it?" Markham's voice rises in response.

"Exactly… exactly as we've already agreed."

"Are you sure it will work?"

"Of course I am," is an indignant Markham's sharp reply.

"I have the run of the bank, come and go as I please. After the manager and the chief cashier I'm next in seniority and have the vaults under my control."

"Ok, I've got the counterfeits in, now it's down to you. When do want to do it?"

"Monday… afternoon is best after the morning rush. Let's make it two o'clock, that'll keep us half an hour clear of the hourly run of cash deposits into the vault."

"No problem, I'll be there ready and waiting."

With the teapot empty and cake finished the men leave together before going their separate ways.

Back in the café Cole and Markham were not as alone as they thought. On the other side of the room and just out of sight but not earshot and hidden by an ornately decorated wooden screen sits a smartly dressed middle aged woman, it is Miss Frobisher from the bank. Miss Frobisher had heard parts of the sometimes excitable conversation between Cole and her colleague Mr. Markham. She tries to make sense of what she has heard,

"Counterfeits, switch, vaults. What on earth is going on?"

D I Clarke stands on platform 2 at Leicester London Road railway station as his Nottingham colleague hangs out of an open carriage door window.

"Thanks for your assistance, least now we have found some owners and the start of the trail. As agreed, I'll leave you to follow up the local enquiries."

"I will. Have a safe journey and stay in touch."

Returning to his office DI Clarke goes through his in-tray and thumbs through the sheets of tissue thin paper and singles out a typed report for Leicester & Leicestershire listing the significant or unusual police, military or ARP (air raid patrol) events during the previous twenty-four hours. There are just three items listed. First there is a beat bobby's report of a drunken brawl at the Eclipse Public House in Eastgates. Second there is a note of a collision between a tram and a motor vehicle in Humberstone Gate and last is a report from the Woodhouse Eves Home Guard of a cyclist or two failing to stop when challenged.

Clarke has no interest in the pub fracas as it is hardly worth a significant event rating and is one for the beat sergeant to follow through. Similarly the tram collision is one for the traffic superintendent to sort if there is a need. As for the cyclists avoiding the Home Guard, DI Clarke is at first somewhat amused and thinking aloud,

"If they can't stop a couple of cyclists God help us if we are ever invaded." However, Clarke's mocking smile drops away and changes to a rueful grin as he reads the Home Guard incident in full which ends,

Following the second cyclist incident a missing private was found, a little further up the road towards Beacon Hill, lying injured in the road. He was found to have sustained severe shrapnel and burn wounds to the body, face and hands: he later died

in hospital. It is thought that the private sustained his injuries after coming across what is believed to have been a new type of anti-personal or incendiary bomb: there had been several reports of low flying aircraft and bomb explosions in the Beacon Hill area.

"Poor sod; had it been last Sunday it could have been me and the cycling club involved." A chastened Clarke comforts himself at what is a stupid assumption...

"It was Beacon Hill, but at night time so we wouldn't have been there anyway. However, I wonder what was a plane doing there in the first place? There have been no bombing reports on industrial or civilian targets, maybe the pilot was lost or perhaps looking for Loughborough's nearby Wymeswold airfield or even more likely that listening centre at Beaumanor Hall? Anyway, it's not really one for me and perhaps best I leave it to the military."

Major Krueger has had an incident free return journey home to his villa where he showers and changes into civilian clothes, his usual form of dress when working in blocks 18 and 19 at Sachsenhausen concentration camp. He grabs a sandwich and returns there without further delay.

At the camp the counterfeit team, Krueger's hand-picked team relentlessly print, check, age, pin, unpin and bundle forged pounds ready for despatch to Berlin and beyond to the money launderers. The work is progressing at a pace producing notes of almost indistinguishable quality when compared to the real thing. Reports continue to trickle in that bank tellers in the UK and the rest of Europe are accepting the counterfeit notes as genuine. Krueger is in his office and takes a telephone call; it is his boss Walter Schellenberg.

"Congratulations Krueger, we've done it."

"Sir, I'm not sure."

"But the message came back, *Kinder-B delivered.*"

"I agree, up to that point we have succeeded but there is no confirmation that the drop was collected."

"Don't worry my friend it takes a little time to get confirmation. Relax and take the weekend off, we'll talk again soon."

It's a pensive Krueger that replaces the phone on its cradle and a diligent Krueger who knows he'd be better employed at work than taking time off.

"Bring me some coffee," he shouts at no one in particular.

Friday afternoon darkens into evening in Germany and England. Major

Krueger leaves Sachsenhausen concentration camp soon after despatching his weekly consignment of counterfeit currency packed into in reinforced wooden crates to Berlin. He will return on Saturday till mid-afternoon, at which time he can take time off, rest and wait for a call from Walter Schellenberg and hopefully some good news of Kinder-B.

———————•◆•———————

Cole locks up at the scrap yard and calls at the Freeman's Arms public house in Harding Street. He thinks it will be a long weekend of waiting before he can return to the Midland Bank and plant a virus of counterfeit fivers into the British banking system. A long weekend it may seem but downing the first of several pints he is smug in the knowledge not only that he may be at a turning point of the war but is on the brink of becoming a rich man. He will indeed be a very rich man when he collects a windfall of switched bona fide five pound notes.

DI Clarke is also about to have a drink: curiosity about cycles, planes and unexplained explosions have got the better of him and he has driven off his city patch into the county and out to The Old Bull's Head, Woodhouse Eves.

"Corporal, isn't it?"

"That's right sir. Woodhouse Eves detachment."

"Pint?"

In the Grand Hotel lounge William Markham catches up with Miss Frobisher and buys her a gin and tonic. Mary Frobisher, a fifty year old spinster with no close family is besotted with the lothario Markham, she craves his attention.

"Now my dear, how about that little chat you wanted to have?"

What follows are more questions than answers as Markham becomes concerned and evasive.

"Willy, I was in the Turkey Café at lunchtime. What are you up to with Mr. Cole?"

"Mary love, I don't know what on earth you are talking about?"

"*Counterfeits, vaults, switch*, need I say more?"

"Shush Mary love, we must be careful what we say out loud in public. Drink up and let's go to my place and I'll explain all."

Markham's place is a bachelor flat in a pile of red bricks known as Stoneygate Court, about a mile and a half out of town; the hand holding couple catches a tram. For the next two hours spent mostly in the bedroom with a bottle of whisky Markham spins a yarn of conspiracy and the shadowy work of government agents. As yarns go Markham's is a good one and here is a story teller intent on talking more fiction than fact.

Not able to discern fact from fiction is of no matter for the gullible, drunk and seduced Miss Frobisher who by now believes she is in a position of great trust. She is expected to assist her lover and a government agent. The supposed agent is Mr. Cole who is on a secret mission to seek out counterfeit government documents that need to be securely held in non-government locations until all conspirators are identified, arrested and brought to trial.

"That's right Mary, do that for me on Monday and you will be well rewarded."

CHAPTER 8

MONDAY 21ST DECEMBER 1942

At precisely one minute to two o'clock Assistant Chief Cashier William Markham with his ring of security keys slips out of the rear office and skips down a spiral staircase to the basement. He lets himself through an oak door, goes through a steel grille gate and enters the main vault. In front of him are rows of locked steel cabinets, some standing on steel racks. Looking about him he is making sure he is alone before unlocking and opening a grey painted cabinet. He calmly helps himself to forty wads of 200 white five pound notes, stuffing them into two velvet money bags.

Along the basement corridor in the safety deposit box vault at the stroke of two o'clock Harry Cole hands two keys to Miss Frobisher who with the bank's master key releases two safety deposit boxes. Two large metal containers are brought to Harry Cole who sits at a small table in an alcove affording him privacy. Miss Frobisher, instead of retreating to her desk as she would normally do when a customer is present, climbs the public stairs and engages the guard in a little office tittle-tattle. Harry Cole places two velvet bags on the table, a bead of sweat runs out of his hairline and down his temple; he smudges it away with a greying white handkerchief.

Just as the safety deposit boxes were being rested at Cole's side, William Markham leaves the main vault with the two velvet money bags each stuffed with £20,000 of used Bank of England white five pound notes. Markham has timed this part of the operation to occur when there are no others present in or near the vaults and with the guard being kept busy by Miss Frobisher he has a clear run along the connecting corridor to the safety deposit box vault. Calmly, Markham enters the vault and walks straight towards Cole, not a word is said between them as he drops one velvet bag into each of two now empty safety deposit boxes. Markham then scoops up two similar velvet bags containing the magenta ribbon bound wads of counterfeit fivers.

Remaining calm Markham quickly retraces his steps to the main vault and neatly stacks the counterfeit money in amongst neatly stacked wads of genuine used five pound notes.

The whole operation is over inside three minutes from the moment Cole had arrived and handed his two keys to Miss Frobisher to him calling her back announcing he had completed his business and ready to return his two boxes to their positions in the serried rows of security.

The distracted guard is none the wiser as Miss Frobisher excuses herself from his company and Markham having successfully planted the virus climbs the spiral staircase back to the rear office where bank staff, who have not missed him, are busy counting and bagging monies ready for his authority to load into the dumb waiter ready for his signal to start the 2.30 cash delivery to the main vault.

"Thank you Miss Frobisher, as always, you have been very helpful, you will be rewarded."

"Thank you Mr. Cole. Willy is such a dear; he has told me about your government work and the need for absolute secrecy. I'm glad to have been assistance and mums the word."

"Ehmm... that's right, government work. Goodbye for now and should I not see you again before Friday, have a good Christmas."

Cole walks slowly to the top of the stairs leading to the bank's main foyer nodding an acknowledgement to the guard as they pass. In the foyer Cole sees Markham standing behind the tellers' counter and making eye contact they allow themselves a hint of a smile at what they have just accomplished.

Outside the bank Cole collects his cycle and wastes no time returning to his scrap yard: a train of empty wagons is expected and needs to be loaded as quickly as possible ready for marshalling and despatch to feed insatiable furnaces.

Inside the bank, William Markham approaches Miss Frobisher,

"Mmm... Well done Mary. Can I treat you to a drink tonight to celebrate?"

"Sorry, I'm busy tonight Willy but I'm free on Thursday, Christmas Eve?"

"It's a date; I'll look forward to seeing you then."

Not far from the Midland Bank, not much more than a stone's throw, a burly sergeant at Charles Street police station escorts a prisoner to an interview room; waiting for the prisoner is DI Clarke. The room is simply furnished with a table and four chairs. The walls are a two tone green wash; dark green to chest level and light green to the white ceiling. Separating the greens is an inch wide band of even darker green gloss. The lighting is daylight streaming through a small barred window and a single electric bulb dangling from the centre of the ceiling.

"Hello Charlie, come in and take a seat." The prisoner eases onto a chair and pulls it forward to the table.

"G'd afternoon Mr. Clarke."

"Not too clever this time Charlie, caught in the act?"

Charlie is a career criminal, never had a proper job and always somehow avoided being called up. He has been interviewed many times before and is aware that this time the cards are stacked against him and a custodial sentence is certain to be coming his way.

"Just my luck, I'd have been clean away but for twisting my ankle jumping out of the kitchen window."

"Life's a bitch Charlie; you've had a good run."

"Look Mr. Clarke... can we cut a deal?"

"What's on offer Charlie?"

"Mr. Clarke, you know and I know I am a simple thief and small fry and what I eventually get out of a job is less than a quarter of its true value. There are bigger fish out there to be had, get what I mean?"

"Carry on."

"If I give you a name, a big name... say like a fence, will you put a word in for me?"

"You know the score Charlie, no promises. Now, just who are you trying to put in the picture?"

Charlie rests his elbows on the table and leans forward to give full face to DI Clarke and looks him squarely in the eyes before whispering a familiar name, adding,

"Don't forget Mr. Clarke, I've given you a big one, now you look after me?"

"As I said Charlie, no promises. So long as I am not chasing a hare I'll see what I can do, but for the time being all I'll be guaranteeing you is a Christmas dinner... in the nick: I'll be opposing bail. Take him away sergeant."

———•———

In the Finance Ministry building in Wilhelmstrasse, Berlin, Bernhard is again on the agenda at a meeting this time chaired by Heinrich Himmler. Attending are Joseph Goebbels, Ernst Kaltenbrunner and his charge Walter Schellenberg.

It's a meeting that's come too soon for Schellenberg as he still awaits confirmation of Kinder-B being collected at Beacon Hill. He had wanted to inform the meeting of the success of the daring plan led by Major Krueger, a plan aimed at winning over those with reservations, a plan that would put a virus of counterfeit money directly into the British banking system that would alongside Bernhard accelerate the expected downfall of the pound: Schellenberg mentions nothing of Kinder-B. Himmler nods at Schellenberg who opens with his progress report.

There is the very good news that English banknotes continue to be produced in large quantities. Production increases on a weekly basis now that additional printers have been transferred from the original factory used for Andreas. As instructed all notes continue to be forwarded to Berlin and are being used for the purchase of strategic supplies, a euphemism for armaments and payment of spying operations.

At this point Himmler, peering over his glasses, interjects and as he alternates between the pursing and wetting of his lips with a viperous tongue asks those present if they are content with the arrangements so far. This is a clear inference that he is well aware of the practice of the skimming of counterfeit banknotes: notes are being hoarded or banked for personal use and possibly to be used later as get out money to buy safe passage by those present. No one is unhappy, least of all Himmler who now has his own supply direct from Schellenberg.

Schellenberg completes his report stating that whilst the production of a counterfeit 100 American dollar plate is proving more difficult than originally anticipated, work is progressing in the right direction. Schellenberg still makes no mention of Kinder-B; this turns out to be a wise move.

Himmler makes it clear that Schellenberg has two straight forward objectives. First, he must make arrangements to continue with the success achieved so far with the outstanding quality of English pounds and to accelerate the quantities produced. He emphasises that there must be increased production of English pounds on a week by week basis. Second, Schellenberg must personally ensure that work on the counterfeiting the American 100 dollar bill must move forward without any more delay with all acceptable bills forwarded to Berlin.

The two objectives outlined by Himmler are little more than a repeat of Shellenberg's report of work in progress, he is not impressed.

Schellenberg quizzically looks across the table at his boss Kaltenbrunner, there is no mention of the way forward for Bernhard and its original aim to destabilise the British economy by littering the countryside with counterfeits dropped by the Luftwaffe. Raising an eyebrow Kaltenbrunner looks back at Schellenberg and says nothing. The meeting is closed.

Kaltenbrunner and Schellenberg return to the latter's office in the nearby Berkaer Strasse where over a cup of coffee Kaltenbrunner divulges what he has been made aware of. He explains that there has been a change in the aims of Bernhard and that the change has been personally authorised by the Fuehrer. Kaltenbrunner had been briefed by Himmler who had received notice of Bernhard's change of strategy during one of Hitler's rants that he receives on almost a daily basis.

Continuing in a measured tone Kaltenbrunner reiterates what was previously stated by Himmler that the counterfeits must continue to flow and with an increased rate of production. The quality of the British notes produced is so good they are now being laundered as the preferred cash payment for arms and espionage agents. This decision has somewhat been forced on Hitler since Goering's Luftwaffe is no longer able to supply any planes to support Bernhard. There aren't even enough planes to supply the Russian Front, a fact well known about for some time but only just finally accepted by Hitler who has now irrevocably changed the direction of Bernhard.

The irony of the situation is not missed by Schellenberg. Such is the quality of the notes produced by Krueger's team in Sachsenhausen means that the counterfeit English pounds are now the preferred cash chip as the Reichsmark loses favour on the international markets and not least amongst arms dealers selling to the highest bidder.

Kaltenbrunner places his empty coffee cup on the table and turns to Schellenberg, leans close to him and whispers in his ear,

"Walter, my friend, now is the time for you to shut down Kinder-B and concentrate on Bernhard."

Schellenberg's brow glistens with sweat, in a dry voice,

"But, sir."

"No more discussion. That is an order." Kaltenbrunner salutes and leaves.

Kaltenbrunner will provide no written order for Schellenberg to have evidence of or to show compliance with, he just has to make sure what he is told to do is done.

Many other orders are now routinely being given by word of mouth and becoming the norm particularly within the German high command where everyone is watching their own backs in fear of back stabbers and recriminations. Conscientious officers do try to obtain written confirmation of orders so that they can be presented as defence evidence if things should go wrong, their requests more often than not fall on deaf ears. The culture of oral orders has been set right from the top, by Hitler who is well used to issuing orders by mouth that can be readily refuted if it turns out to be the wrong decision or not in his best interest.

Schellenberg bites his lip at having been ordered to shut down Kinder-B. He knows that without any possibility of Luftwaffe support it is the correct decision. He also knows he will not receive a written order since Kaltenbrunner wants no criticism to come back on him, especially so since Kinder-B does not officially exist.

Schellenberg drafts a message to be coded and sent to the agent in England known only as *Mercury*,

Abort Kinder-B.

Schellenberg must now contact and speak with Krueger at Sachsenhausen Concentration Camp.

"Krueger, is that you?"

"Sir, yes, it's me."

"Krueger, Bernhard has a new direction."

"What do you mean?"

"No questions. First of all you must continue to accelerate the production of the English pounds; it goes without saying you must maintain their quality. Second, get the 100 dollar bill up and running as soon as possible."

"Sir, that's not a lot of difference, if any, to what is already being done, but what of the Luftwaffe and Bernard?"

"No questions over the phone Krueger. I will talk with you tomorrow, come to Berlin."

CHAPTER 9

TUESDAY 22ND DECEMBER 1942

It is 6.30am, still dark and the Grand Union Canal towpath is awash with puddles as heavy rain returns. Alongside the West Bridge coal wharf a boatman steps off his narrow boat and tugs on a tight fitting flat cloth cap. With rounded shoulders and hands in pockets he sets off at a steady gait heading for Harry Cole's scrap yard.

At the yard all is quiet, the boatman finding the corrugated gates shut and padlocked looks around for a possible way in. Near to a corner of the lot he manages to force apart two corrugated sheets sufficient enough allowing him to squeeze through. In the breaking dawn light he creeps and crawls his way through stacks of old cars and around piles of sorted miscellaneous metals.

Peering through the broken windows of an old bus he can see the outline of a ramshackle building, it is the remains of a once posh garden pavilion. Purchased as a pile of scrap timber following the Leicester blitz in 1940 the pavilion has been rebuilt and now serves as Cole's site office.

Picking up an iron bar the stranger easily springs the office door open which, under its own weight, swings slowly backwards squealing on its dry iron hinges. Startled rats scurry away chased by feral cats. Silence returns as the intruder finds the sloping school ma'am's desk that is now Cole's bureau. Wasting no time and by the flame of a cigarette lighter the boatman, using a six inch nail, scratches a message across the wooden slope. Such is the urgency of the situation there is no time for the niceties of leaving it in code,

Abort Kinder-B.

Holding his coat sleeve *Mercury* rubs his forearm hard across the dusty desk several times to tone down the freshly scratched message making it less conspicuous, anyone other than Cole would not give it a second look. He leaves the nail in the desk's pencil groove to draw attention to Cole that someone else had been at his desk.

Using the iron bar again, working it between the door edge and its jamb he springs the door back into the locked position. Cats are still chasing rats as corrugated sheets are pushed back into place leaving no sign of the intruder's visit.

Back at the coal wharf the boatman jumps aboard his narrow boat. The mooring rope is slack allowing the boat to rock on the water and the bow nudges against the coping stones separating canal and towpath. The rocking rubs away a little paint off the tail of a white lined blue letter *y*, it being the last letter of the boat's name, Mercury.

Harry Cole is still at home in Heanor Street when the narrow boat Mercury slips its mooring and sets off upstream towards Walnut Street and Gimson's timber yard. Cole has a thick head after the previous night's solitary drinking session in the Freeman's Arms; his early celebration is taking its toll. The only antidote he can muster is a cold wash, a cup of tea and an aspirin.

Paradoxically his pain is made worse by the immense buzz of satisfaction whirling around in his head after getting Kinder-B, almost half of it, into the Midland Bank's vaults.

Headache or not Cole still has some problems that he has to address before he can claim a complete success. Supping tea, the problems return to his banging forehead:

When to make the final switch of the remaining £10,000 of counterfeit fivers stashed in his chimney safe?

Cole reckons that this can now wait till after Christmas, although content that the virus has been planted there is still a possibility that the switch may be spotted, either inside the bank or outside in local businesses. The chimney money could be his insurance in the event he has to do a runner.

What to do with the £40,000 bona fide fivers laying in two safety deposit boxes in his account?

Cole prefers to leave the money where it is since there is no rush to move it, not least for the fact that there has been no message from *Mercury* as to what is to be done. Meantime, as his chimney safe is far too small, Cole decides he will make a safe hiding place at his yard ready for when he needs to shift the money from the bank.

How to deal with the excitable William Markham and his inquisitive lady friend Miss Frobisher?

As for the gullible Miss Frobisher it has already been agreed that she will be dealt with by the closet fascist Markham.

Markham is a different kettle of fish and once the final switch of counterfeits has been made he will have served his purpose as being the insider at the bank. Following the arranged disappearance of Miss Frobisher he too will have vanished leaving Cole holding the cash.

Cole is sure that should any of the counterfeits be spotted either at the bank or amongst its customers all suspicion will fall on the vanishing couple, Markham and his lady friend Miss Frobisher.

It's nearly eight o'clock and having just about settled his headache Harry Cole arrives at his yard. Standing astride his cycle he tosses his bunch of keys to one of his waiting labourers, the gates are swung open and the men are soon at work.

Nothing changes the yard's routine as old prams full of rags and pieces of metal are trundled in to exchange for a few extra coppers. Bedraggled poor souls leave with empty prams with just a few pennies in their pockets, not as much as they thought they would get but glad to accept that something is better than nothing. Cole's labourers sort the metal and rags into respective piles ready for loading.

Inside his site office, Cole drops his duffle coat across the sloping desk top unwittingly covering the scratched message from the boatman. He moves to an open grate and lights a fire of dry kindling and places a few lumps of coal collected off the railway sidings. Using a butcher's hook a billycan of water is hung onto an iron bar across the fire just above the licking flames. Cole has taken to the English liking for a cup of tea, often making a brew to share with his labourers.

In the yard Cole, with rolled up shirt sleeves lends a hand as another two wagons are shunted into the yard ready for loading.

"I'll be back this afternoon Mr. Cole for these two and the rest. Will they be ready?"

"No bother, the lads are on a Christmas bonus, everything is possible." Despite his headache returning Cole is still in high spirits and cockily calls out,

"Found your lamp yet?" he shouts, knowing full well that it is buried under the ferns on Beacon Hill.

"Not a chance."

"Not a chance of what?" enquires a voice behind Cole. Turning round Cole is unexpectedly confronted by DI Clarke.

"Oh it's you Mr. Clarke, shunter's lost a hand lamp, that's all and most probably the local kids have pinched it."

"Is that so?"

Cole changes the topic.

"So, Mr. Clarke what brings you here again, early too? No, wait let's go inside for a cup of tea, water should be boiling by now."

DI Clarke accepts the invitation and sits on a high stool with his back resting against the school ma'am's desk. Cole makes a brew in a brown enamelled tea pot; four stained mugs are lined up on top of a steel filing cabinet.

"Here lads, come and get it," the labourers need no second invitation.

"One for you, Mr. Clarke."

Cole flicks away a nail and stands a mug of tea at the top of the desk on the grooved narrow flat section of desk usually used for holding pencils and pens, not six inch nails. As he carefully drags off his coat, Cole's eyes are momentarily transfixed as he sees the scratched message *Abort Kinder-B*.

Cole acts quickly before DI Clarke turns to take his mug of tea.

"Sorry Mr. Clarke, this other one's yours, there's aspirin in that one, and I've got a bit of a headache."

"Ok that's fine." DI Clarke takes the second mug from Cole and again rests with his back leaning against the desk sipping tea.

"A bit more sociable than last time you called Mr. Clarke?"

"It may seem more sociable but I can assure you it's not, but the tea is welcome seeing as it's my first of the day."

"Well, enjoy it, but exactly why are you here this time?"

"Bought any gold lately? Sold any?" Cole rocks back on his heels.

"Ah, here we go again, shall I get the books out?"

"No, no need to see your books which I am sure will all be in order. Just thought I'd drop in and let you know that whoever is fencing here in Leicester will be in short supply and likewise stuck for a buyer as we have a tea-leaf in custody here in Leicester and the buyer is banged up in a Nottingham cell. Word is bound to get around and the middlemen, the fencers will go to ground for a while so be careful what you buy, who you buy from and continue to keep your books straight."

DI Clarke has purposely divulged information about a local thief and a Nottingham buyer in order to gauge Cole's reaction. He is not disappointed as he observes Cole's brow moisten with sweat and continually rubbing his palms together avoids making any eye contact.

"Guilty as hell," thinks DI Clarke and feels pretty confident that he has his quarry within his grasp and all he needs to do now is gather sufficient evidence to ensure a conviction.

What DI Clarke doesn't realise is that Cole was more nervous about the policeman seeing the message on the desk than any bother about a few pieces of jewellery or gold.

"Well I'd better be off now; will you be out with the cycling club on Boxing Day?"

"Not sure, could be otherwise engaged," is Cole's cagey reply. Clarke looks Cole in the eyes,

"May or may not see you then. Meantime just don't forget to be careful what you buy."

Stepping out of the office DI Clarke walks toward the open corrugated gates and stops. Taking an admiring look at Cole's Raleigh cycle he runs a hand across the handlebars, head stock and badge before bending to inspect the waterproof panniers.

Standing, framed in the open office door Cole mutters to himself.

"What the devil is he up to now?" He doesn't get a chance to ask anyone else as DI Clarke turns on his heels and is away to his car. Just as the police car speeds off across the Mill Lane canal bridge, the narrow boat Mercury passes underneath.

Harry Cole's headache gets worst as he is now flummoxed by the morning's events. A message he knows is from *Mercury*, hand delivered, not even in code and therefore must be urgent, followed by a visit from the police at a time when he is still suffering from the after effects of a quiet celebration thinking that all was going so well.

DI Clarke's visit is not Cole's main concern as he wonders why Kinder-B must be aborted, maybe the exploding second drum did not completely incinerate its contents and the counterfeit scam is exposed. Cole can only guess it is a problem close to him since he has no idea of the change of direction sanctioned by Hitler for the forged banknotes to be used to secure strategic supplies and services. Nor does he know of the Luftwaffe's inability to provide planes precipitating Hitler's forced decision.

It's not long before it dawns on Cole that he has a greater problem to deal with, speaking softly to himself and through gritted teeth.

"It's too bleeding late. Some of the money's in the bank already, I must call Markham and get it switched back." He calls the Midland Bank,

"Markham is that you?"

"Yes," Markham replies hesitantly, shocked at the sharpness of the callers tone.

"It's Harry Cole, we have to talk."

"Talk, what about?"

"Not now, later and somewhere quiet. Meet me in the lounge at the Grand Hotel."

"What time?"

"Make it eight o'clock tonight."

"I'll be there."

With the Nottingham City Police holding the buyer and the Leicester City Police holding the Stoneygate thief still on remand following his court appearance DI Clarke paces his office reviewing what little evidence there is against Harry Cole being a fence.

DI Clarke's ace in the pack is the tip-off from Charlie, the thief who fingered Cole as the fence he has had dealings with. Cole freely admits that he buys gold and jewellery and sells it on as part of his day to day business. DI Clarke knows that there is no likelihood of any discrepancies in the accounts at the scrap yard and he needs to find a link between Cole and the Nottingham buyer.

DI Clarke now considers Cole the man. Who is he, where is he from, who are his friends and what does he do outside of his business? Cole, on the face of it, appears to be a genuine businessman going about his normal activities dealing in scrap metal including well accounted for precious metals and jewellery.

DI Clarke pulls up a chair to his desk and from what he's learned about Cole from Charlie the thief, his CID colleagues and members of the Cycling Club he makes a list of what he knows about Cole and his background.

1. Sets up his own business after leaving a job as a foundry man, having earlier moved to Leicester from the Rugby area.

2. He has no known criminal record.

3. Owns and runs a business yet chooses to live alone in a poorer part of the town with no known family.

4. When not at work or home he can usually be found in the Freeman's Arms or Heanor Boat public houses.

5. No lady friend or any close friends other than members of the cycling club.

"Hmm…" thinks Clarke, "he does spend a lot of his time cycling, particularly with William Markham the Midland Bank's assistant chief cashier."

DI Clarke places the scribbled list into a manila folder and drops it into a drawer of a wooden filing cabinet and slams it shut.

"Nothing: well not enough, nowhere enough to charge him let alone make sure of a conviction."

DI Clarke's thoughts now wander back to his drive out to The Old Bull's

Head public house at Woodhouse Eaves. He recalls his chat with the Home Guard corporal who encountered one possibly two cyclists late at night five days ago before finding a private, close to Beacon Hill, mortally wounded with shrapnel and burn wounds.

The Corporal could give no real description of the cyclist, least not enough to identify him. He had remarked he'd a sense that the cyclist in the second collision had been hurt and appeared to be limping as he ran away, half lifting and half dragging his cycle. The cycle may have been damaged, probably a twisted front wheel fork that just needed straightening.

Injured or not, damaged bike or not it wasn't long before the corporal caught a glimpse of the cyclist flashing through the breaking shafts of moonlight heading downhill toward Woodhouse Eves.

The corporal had also cut his hand on a sharp piece of metal as he got back to his feet. He removed the jagged metal with his teeth and wrapped his bleeding palm with his handkerchief and pocketed the offending piece of metal. Twiddling the same bit of metal in his hand, DI Clarke had asked if he could keep it as he bought the corporal another pint of beer, it has something of a familiar look about it.

Other thoughts come into DI Clarke's mind. Could the cyclists, one or both of them, the dead private and the reports of low flying aircraft be connected in any way and why no other reports of bombings in the Loughborough area?

DI Clarke heads off to Beacon Hill where he has arranged to meet the corporal again. At the spot of the second encounter the corporal retells the story of his collision with an unknown cyclist. There is still a hint of a mark of blood, diluted by the rain, where the corporal had cut his hand.

In DI Clarke's car the two men ride uphill to where the private was found mortally wounded. The debris of what was thought to be a new type of exploding incendiary bomb has been carefully collected in by more Home Guards from nearby Loughborough, a hole in the side of the ditch and a missing section of hedgerow are all that remain. The dead private's spilt blood has been carefully and completely washed away by his comrades.

Opposite the damaged ditch are the gate and the sheep trodden track leading to the summit of Beacon Hill. Inexplicably, in DI Clarke's mind's eye pops up a vision of Cole and Markham claiming their cycles following a short break during the cycling club's recent Sunday ride out. DI Clarke thinks he has the beginnings of a crazy notion that as cycles and cyclists crop up, so do

Cole and Markham for it all to be just a coincidence, are they in any way linked to this incident?

Passing through the gate DI Clarke and the corporal are looking for the site of a farmer's reported sighting of a possible second explosion. Walking through the copse the corporal, a scoutmaster when not at work on a farm or doing his bit in the Home Guard, notices that the died back ferns have been scuffed about by someone walking or resting on them. Also noticed is a silver birch's bark has been snagged with a piece peeled back exposing the bare wood.

"Looks as though something or someone has been moving around in here and recent too, Mr. Clarke."

"I'll take your word for it, not much of a tracker myself," replies DI Clarke who heels out the disturbed fern pointed out to him and finds a piece of rag and then tugs on a metal handle to reveal a railway lamp and a lemonade bottle with lamp oil in it.

"Well, these certainly don't belong here, totally out of context with the surroundings that's for sure."

The two men take a steady walk to the summit where the passing seasons have taken their toll rounding old rocks and exposing other jagged monoliths and outcrops leaving the land only useful for sheep grazing. Now it is DI Clarke who notices something unusual, among some rocks he points out what appears to be soot and scorch marks. The corporal clambers across loose scree to the jagged rocks and rummages through the remains of what seems to be a small parachute, a pile of ashes and pieces of broken metal.

"Certainly a bit on the small size for a parachute landmine, could've been an incendiary device and confirms the farmer's report of two explosions. Corporal, you'll need to get your bomb disposal lads here who can check whether or not it is the same sort of bomb that killed your colleague."

Policeman and soldier make their way to The Old Bull's Head where they have another pint at DI Clarke's expense before they bid farewell. DI Clarke has other enquiries to make and his next stop is the guard's hut at the entrance to Beaumanor Hall in Woodhouse Village.

"Identification sir?" Clarke flashes his warrant card and the guard immediately stands to attention and salutes.

"It's alright private, no need for the ceremony but can I have a word?" asks Clarke getting out of his car.

"Certainly sir, what about?"

"Last Thursday night's low flying planes and bombs?"

"I heard about the Home Guard and farmer's reports and the private being killed but we saw nothing and heard nothing at all."

"See any cyclists?" The guard smiles in amusement.

"Cyclists at that time of night and with it the heavy rain and not fit to put a dog out? No, never saw a soul let alone a cyclist."

"Thanks, that's all."

Last stop before completing his trip to Charnwood Forest is the Great Central Railway's Quorn and Woodhouse station. DI Clarke enquires at the booking office if there were any passengers travelling late on the night of the 17th, the night of low flying aircraft and bomb explosions.

"Oh, yes!" recalls the clerk. "It was raining hard and there was one passenger with a bike who caught the last train to Leicester, the 11.55, five to midnight."

"What makes you so sure?"

"Hardly anyone ever catches the train from here at that time of night, usually just a few people dropping off after a night out in Nottingham or Loughborough. Plus, I don't often see campers' panniers on bikes at this time of year and I heard later that the man would not be separated from his bike preferring to stand with it in the guard's van."

"Do you know where he was going?"

"Leicester, he had a return ticket from Leicester to Nottingham, said he had to break his journey and return to Leicester."

It's a uniformed Major Krueger that stands at the heavy mahogany door to the Berlin office of Walter Schellenberg, Head of SS-foreign intelligence. Krueger recalls his first meeting with Schellenberg, unaware that he was to be given a new job resurrecting Andreas, producing counterfeit English pounds and American dollars. He felt as uneasy now as he did then.

Krueger further recalls a time, as a school boy, being called to the headmaster's study to be caned for eating sweets in the class room. This present call to the current headmaster's study could result in more serious consequences. Intimidated like many SS officers working in the often criminal and sadistic regime that is the SS it is an anxious Krueger who knocks on the door.

"Come in Krueger, take a seat, coffee?" Schellenberg's cordial invitation allays Krueger's initial fears as he holds himself composed and maintains eye contact with his boss.

"I'll come straight to the point Krueger. You will continue with your part in Bernhard. You must increase your output of English pounds and at the same time increase your efforts to make the plates for the American 100 dollar bill."

"Sir, you have already told me this, why bring me to Berlin?"

"Krueger, Bernhard does not now include littering the British mainland with counterfeits and before you ask, Kinder-B no longer exists either, nor for your sake has it ever existed. You have to cover your tracks and if you are ever questioned about it, it just never existed. I have done what I can, understood?" Krueger has no chance to answer as Schellenberg's rhetoric continues.

"The engineers who prepared the drums are at the Russian Front and will not survive the winter, the Deelen commander has been bought off as has his operations officer and the aircrew are missing presumed killed in action. All you have to do is to make sure there are no leaks out of Sachsenhausen. Do I make myself clear?"

The call to Schellenberg's office, as yet, does not seem fatal but it is still an uneasy Krueger that responds.

"Perfectly clear sir, but what of the money we've already dropped in England?"

"I have sent a message to *Mercury* to make contact with our agents in Leicester informing them that Kinder-B is to be aborted. It goes without saying that such a command requires all evidence of its existence is to be destroyed."

"Have they done it?"

"Probably, but I have not yet received confirmation."

Schellenberg is being careful with his words ensuring that, if there is any negative come back from Kinder-B, he will be in the clear and all responsibility will fall on Krueger and others' shoulders. Making a point of stressing Krueger's involvement and responsibilities, he continues,

"Your valiant and audacious enterprise to support Bernhard with your Kinder-B intended to plant a virus of counterfeit notes directly into the British banking system in advance of the Luftwaffe delivering Bernhard can only be held in the highest regard.

Since moving your operation to Sachsenhausen and employing the best engravers in Europe your work is of such a high standard, outstripping all expectations, it should come as no surprise that your pounds and dollars are being redirected elsewhere to benefit the Fatherland by buying strategic supplies and services."

Krueger now knows why he was called to Berlin and knows where he stands if Kinder-B is not aborted. He stands alone.

Krueger accepts that Hitler and his cohorts will now require a strong pound and not an inflation riddled pound on the foreign exchanges. Counterfeit British pounds are already being laundered to pay for the so called strategic supplies and services, spies and arms. He also accepts that Kinder-B has to be aborted and it is with trepidation that Krueger returns to Sachsenhausen hoping all the time that his once wished for counterfeit virus Kinder-B has been smothered out of existence.

Similarly it is an anxious Schellenberg who unfolds a hand delivered note and reads a decoded message from *Mercury*, it is short and to the point,

Abort command delivered - awaiting confirmation.

Schellenberg lights a cigarette and burns the message in an ash tray thinking,

"Krueger, we, no, you are on thin ice, just keep the counterfeits flowing and we'll be alright."

In Leicester, on the third day before Christmas the daily clamour and clanking in the scrap yard drags along. Harry Cole tries to maintain some sort of normality just to get through the day. He has a thick head, a lot on his mind and he has to find a way to deal with an unforeseen problem. There is no contingency plan in place to deal with *Mercury's* urgent message, *Abort Kinder-B.*

The day eventually comes to an end as the scrap yard closes promptly at five o'clock. With the gates shut and padlocked, Cole picks up his cycle and sets off across town to visit the Vestry Street slipper baths. He shaves before wallowing in a hot bath. His headache eases as he scrubs all over with carbolic soap and a stiff brush, water and suds soon turn grey A vigorous rub all over with a coarse towel soon gets him dry before resting a while on a stool. Refreshed with a much clearer head he thinks of his meeting later in the evening with Markham. How will he react to the abort command and can the money be switched back?

Cole dresses back into his work clothes and makes his way home to change for his appointment at the Grand Hotel. On the way, he calls at Burberry's fish and chip shop in North Gate Street for his tea.

In the Grand Hotel's lounge bar a grandfather clock strikes eight times. Cole, in a thread bare suit, collar and tie is on time and Markham is nowhere to be seen. Eight-thirty comes and goes, Cole stands at the bar buys another pint of bitter.

"Mine's a gin and tonic, please." William Markham, dapper in a sports jacket, cream shirt and cravat with brown trousers and polished brogues leans on the bar with an arm around Cole.

"Where in bleeding hell have you been?"

"Sorry about the delay old chap, had to work late at the bank making up some large money cash transfers. Leicester's local businesses are doing well out of supporting the war."

"Ok, never mind. Just listen to me, we've got a problem."

"A problem?"

Cole ushers Markham to a quiet corner and goes on to explain that all their efforts so far have been for nothing. Kinder-B has to be aborted with all evidence destroyed. Markham is aghast,

"But the counterfeit money is in the bank."

"We have to switch it back as soon as possible." Markham's expression changes from aghast to be a more thoughtful one.

"Hmm… well, that just can't be done."

"Why? Why not?"

"I've already shifted some of the counterfeit shit to other banks as part of the bank's policy to spread and even out cash stocks and even more will move tomorrow with the cash transfers to the local businesses as I've already mentioned. We have released a counterfeit virus that can't be stopped."

Cole is ashen as his jaw drops in disbelief at the swift progress Markham has achieved in spreading counterfeit money into the British banking system. Both men down their drinks and it is now a visibly excited Markham who calls to a waiter to bring another round. Shaking, the excited Markham stands, leans over the table and grabs Cole by the lapels and can hardly get his words out,

"You know… You know what this means, don't you?"

"What?"

"We've hit the jackpot: it's too late to abort what has been done and we now have forty grand kosher in the safety deposit boxes and still have another ten grand in forgeries. Christmas has come early."

Pushing Markham off his lapels Cole sips bitter ale before raging as best he can in suppressed tones.

"Sit down. You damn fool, don't you realise that we can't just ignore a command from Germany; do that and we are as good as signing our own death warrants."

Markham doesn't see it the same way as the patriotic Cole. He is convinced that they have been dealt a good hand and they are in a good position to pull off a profitable coup.

"Look, all we need to do is keep calm and tell Germany that we've done what they have ordered. It'll be your word, they will trust you and there's no way to check? Hold our nerve and we hold forty grand genuine and ten grand in duds."

"Are you certain we can't switch the money back?" Now it is an apoplectic flush faced Markham who bends Cole's ear in stifled tones,

"No, no, definitely not. Counterfeits have already left the bank and more will go out tomorrow. I've already told you that, are you not listening?"

A calmer, cool and collected Cole is not convinced by Markham's proposition. He knows that to do nothing will incur the wrath of the SS-foreign intelligence; at best he will be recalled and at worst executed by another compatriot agent probably here in Leicester. Alternatively, should ever any of the counterfeits be tracked back to him by the police, most likely through Markham, he will be tried by the British and hanged as a spy.

"Well are you game?" asks Markham.

"I'm not sure; I need to think this through. Give me a couple of days, there is more involved in this than you can imagine. Here, take this and buy yourself a drink, I'll be in touch." Cole tosses a half-crown onto the table, pulls on a flat cap and duffle coat. Markham is left alone and seething in the lounge bar.

Markham won't let it drop. He pockets the half-crown and catches up with Cole in the street.

"Ok a couple of days no more and what about Miss Frobisher?"

"She's your lady friend and for you to deal with, you know that. She's the weakest link, just let me know when you have sorted her out. Understood?"

"Right, yes I will."

Markham is less excited now, any thoughts of Christmas coming early are pushed to the back of his mind after being chillingly reminded by the calm, cautious and steely eyed Cole of what he has to do.

CHAPTER 10

WEDNESDAY 23RD & THURSDAY 24TH DECEMBER 1942

Harry Cole drops a small leather suitcase onto a grubby carpet next to his office bureau, inside is £40,000 taken from his two safety deposit boxes at the Midland Bank. He'd collected the money whilst William Markham was out of the bank assisting in cash deliveries. Including the £10,000 counterfeit money in his chimney breast safe Cole is a now a rich man but being rich is not his mission as he works as a sleeper agent for Germany. He works to orders and for the moment his only order is to *Abort Kinder-B*.

Unfortunately he and Markham have moved with remarkable speed in securing the transfer of £40,000 worth of counterfeits into the bank's main vault. Some of the cash has already been moved on by Markham to other banks and more into local businesses means that any switch back to recover the Sachsenhausen forgeries is impossible.

Cole had planned to leave the genuine money in the safety deposit boxes till after Christmas by which time he hoped he would have had orders on what is to be done. In collecting the cash it is out of the bank and in Cole's possession and control and means he does not need any more involvement of Markham or anyone else at the bank. In the scrap yard Cole has prepared a secure place to hold the cash.

The rebuilt garden pavilion now used as Cole's site office had been re-erected over a long forgotten manhole giving access to an inspection chamber of a disused storm drainage system. The drains existed before the building of the Great Central Railway and its sidings that now include Cole's scrap yard. The disused drain is bone dry and capped off at its outlet into the canal, the drain's other end is buried somewhere and some distance away under the railway tracks. The original water course has been diverted into a new system provided and paid for by the Great Central Railway Company as land was taken over for sidings and workshops.

Pulling the carpet to one side Cole lifts open a wooden trap door revealing, in the ground below, a padlocked steel manhole cover set into mortar bonded brickwork. Working quickly, Cole unlocks and lifts the cover. Picking up an oil lamp he lets himself into a short shaft to the inspection chamber and climbs down a dozen wrought iron foot holds. Standing on the chamber floor, slightly bent over, holding his lamp at arm's length he turns slowly and admires his handy work. He has bricked in the two three foot diameter culvert channels creating a closed chamber measuring six foot six inches square by six foot high.

Cole had found the old drain at the start of the war and had made use of it as an air raid shelter during the Leicester Blitz two years ago. He had been forewarned of the raid by *Mercury*. In one of the bricked in culvert openings Cole has installed a small wall safe. He unlocks the safe and small it may be but it's large enough to easily hold illegally bought in gold and jewellery and now includes forty £1,000 wads of English white fivers.

Closing and locking the chamber cover Cole thinks his vault is as secure as any English bank. He pulls back the carpet over the trap door and the work of the scrap yard carries on. It is a calm and content Cole who sorts amongst the scrap and pockets a short piece of lead water pipe.

Later, after work Harry Cole has another job to do, he needs to send a message back to Germany. During his six weeks training course prior to being despatched to the front line during WW1 he had been instructed that a rule of spy working is that all messages sent to agents must be answered or at least acknowledged. Failure to respond will be taken as a sign that the sleeper agent has been either exposed and heading for the gallows or is already dead. Cole needs to respond to the scratched message *Abort Kinder-B*.

Eager and with no time to cook a meal Cole makes do with a crust of bread and a pot of tea as he taps out a coded message on his Imperial typewriter. The message is for *Mercury* to collect and transmit to the SS-foreign intelligence, a message that will eventually land on Walter Schellenberg's desk as a folded note marked for his eyes only.

Cole feeds his Model B a blank sheet torn from one of his accounting books and typing with one finger, checking each coded letter as it is typed, keeps the message short.

Half package collected.

Virus planted and spreading.

Recovery impossible.

1809.

Cole carefully folds the message into a four inch square which is then rolled. He carefully feeds the roll of paper into a piece of lead pipe which is carefully eased into a rubber condom and sealed with a knot. The weighted and waterproofed message is dropped into Cole's jacket inside pocket. He is improvising as he was trained to do when preparing messages to be dropped off at secret collection points.

Preferring to leave his cycle in the back yard Cole sets off on foot, not heading to either of his usual locals he makes his way up Churchgate towards the clock tower in the centre of the town. Reaching the four dial faced landmark he turns left into Haymarket, crosses the road, passes by the tram depot's rear entrance and calls in at the White Horse pub in Belgrave Gate.

Cole has time for a couple of pints before coming back across the road to the Floral Hall cinema, next door to the Palace Theatre. He can catch the latest Pathe News showing General Sir Claude Auchinleck, Commander in Chief Middle East, inspecting paratroopers training in Egypt. The following feature film is *The Foreman Went to France* starring Tommy Trinder and Gordon Jackson.

Half way through the Pathe News with everyone's eyes fixed on the silver screen watching paratroopers jump out of Bristol Bombay aircraft Cole slides out of his seat on the end of a row close to an exit and quietly leaves the auditorium.

Striding quickly along a gas lit corridor towards the main entrance Cole nips into the gents' toilet and enters a cubicle, closing and locking the door behind him. Standing on the wooden toilet seat with his left hand lifts the cover to the cast iron cistern, with his right hand he feels for his inside pocket and brings out the water proofed weighted message and drops it gently into the cold water. He knows that before the feature film has finished the message will have been collected. *Mercury* will later transmit the coded message to Germany.

To keep a low profile and to maintain his cover *Mercury* works his narrow boat of the same name along the Grand Union Canal between the Gimson's timber yard on the Old River Soar, the coal yard at West Bridge in Leicester and the rural areas either side of the neighbouring town of Loughborough. He buys and sells what he can to maintain his pretence as a self-employed boatman.

By plying his wares along the canal he is able to move about generally unnoticed as his boat is just one amongst many. What's more, working the canal allows him plenty of opportunities for quiet moorings where he can set up his radio transmitter-receiver.

Mercury's practice is to set up his radio equipment at 10pm and again at 3am each night for just fifteen minutes during which time he monitors incoming messages, whenever he transmits he keeps his time on air as short as possible. Keeping on the move and transmitting from different locations for short spells ensures that his transmitter is difficult to locate by the British intelligence services.

Occasionally as well as transmitting other agents' messages he will send his own short reports on anything war related. Any information on the damage caused by bombing raids, the effect on the industries and morale will help his masters assess what life is like in England and how effective their campaigns are.

Information passed on from other agents working in Leicester or just passing through is collected at one of two regular drop-off points. One is in the gents' toilet at the Floral Hall cinema and the other is in toilets at the Pavilion Café in Abbey Park, both within easy reach of the canal.

Whenever *Mercury* needs to travel further afield to collect or deliver messages he does this by purposely using public transport, buses or trains, to be one of a crowd and less likely to draw attention to himself.

In Berlin, Walter Schellenberg leaves a brothel and returns to his office. He had left an order that he must be informed at once of any messages received from *Mercury*. With the decoded message, unfolded and lying on the desk in front of him, Schellenberg considers each line in turn while sipping a glass of sherry.

Half package collected.

At best the other half has been destroyed by the petrol and magnesium incendiary, at worst the counterfeits are in the enemy's hands.

Virus planted and spreading.

Here, he thinks of how well the handpicked agents have worked to complete what they can of their mission.

Recovery impossible.

This is the worse news Schellenberg had feared. Being unaware of the change of policy for Bernhard the agents have been good at their job, too good and it's too late to completely abort and erase Kinder-B to ease Schellenberg's concerns.

Following a few minutes quiet contemplation Schellenberg is convinced that were any counterfeits traced back to the Kinder-B parachute drop the Bank of England is unlikely to advertise the fact. Also, the possibility of more forgeries finding their way into the system would be denied as the bank maintains its dogmatic belief that it just could not be done and avoiding a run on the banks.

1809.

Here is an agent known only by a number who for years has put his life at risk, a man destined for honour, alive or dead.

Before returning to the brothel Schellenberg burns the message and scribbles out his last order to *Mercury*.

Clean up Kinder-B.

In Leicester it is three-fifteen in the morning of Christmas Eve. Harry Cole has long since succumbed to sleep after downing half a bottle of whisky in his own company. Moored somewhere on the Grand Union canal the patient *Mercury* deciphers a message and knows what he has to do.

At his villa near Sachsenhausen Major Krueger is having another restless night and wakes sweating profusely.

He has had another dream. This time it is not the clawing ink stained grubby fingers of the forlorn faced prisoners at the concentration camp that have disturbed him. Another surreal scene plays though his mind. In front of the Reichstag a pink stork with Luftwaffe markings delivers a baby's nappy overloaded with counterfeit English five pound notes hanging from its beak.

As the bird circles in the air more dwarf caricature figures appear, this time it's Hitler and Goering armed with machine guns trying to shoot the stork down. Snapping at their heels are the SS uniformed hunting dogs with faces contorted to be like those of Himmler, Goebbels, Kaltenbrunner and Schellenberg drooling in anticipation. The dogs wait impatiently to be commanded to fetch the shot down quarry. The air is filled with floating white five pound notes.

Krueger wakes, checks the time, it is five thirty and he drags himself off the sweated sheets and gets ready for work.

Christmas Eve in Leicester follows a pattern repeated elsewhere in war time Britain. Celebrations are muted with little or no luxuries available for presents; churches are doing well with increased congregations and cinemas showing newsreels are always full.

Most children have to make do with a homemade toy, perhaps a knitted doll made from unpicked woollen scraps or a whip and top fashioned out of bits of scrap wood and a leather bootlace. Some children in Heanor Street and Harding Street are in luck as Lottie at the corner shop, in spite of the sugar rationing, has managed to make and save a few sweets for mams and grand-parents to buy if they can afford it. Parents who can't afford sweets are quietly given some anyway.

At Charles Street police station DI Clarke, along with his colleagues in CID share a bottle of whisky provided by the chief constable who wishes them a good Christmas and thanks them for the year's work. DI Clarke feels a tap on his shoulder and turns, it's his chief inspector.

"Wallace can I have a word?"

"Certainly sir."

"My office, in five minutes.'

The chief inspector's office is spotlessly clean with more than a hint of that increasingly rare commodity, furniture polish. The room is light and airy with white washed walls dotted with framed photographs of rows of seated and standing policemen, certificates of exams passed and notable commendations earned. DI Clarke's senior officer sits behind a rosewood desk inlaid with a green leather mat for writing paper to rest on; Clarke is invited to take a seat.

DI Clarke is asked to bring his boss up to date on cases he is working on; in particular what is the position with the burglaries and theft of jewellery in the Stoneygate area. Clarke informs that with the assistance of the Nottingham City's CID and the arrest of a jeweller there for receiving and having one of the thieves, maybe the only one involved, in Leicester Gaol the evidence suggests that convictions at court are likely early in the New Year.

"But what of the fence, the middleman, I've read somewhere you have someone in mind?"

"There is a man, but as yet there is insufficient evidence to make an arrest stick."

"You're new here Wallace, you are beginning to make your mark and with luck I will have a new detective sergeant on the strength in the New Year, I would like him to team up with you. Keep up the good work."

"Thank you, sir."

"But so much for burglaries and thieving, what are you doing going off our patch and interviewing military personnel, the Home Guard at Woodhouse Eves and the army at Beaumanor Hall?"

"Not sure at the moment. Not too sure at all. Just a hunch I'm working on."

"Hmm… right, let's not waste too much time on hunches and be certain not to upset the military too much. We'll speak again after Christmas. By the way what are you doing for Christmas?"

"I've drawn the short straw, rather I've volunteered to cover the office for Christmas and New Year, and so it means canteen dinners for me."

Christmas Eve it may be but it is a full day's work at the Midland Bank with the public counters closing at three-thirty. With all cash and cheques accounted for and locked away in the vaults by four-thirty the bank manager gathers all the staff into the main public area. Standing beneath the cathedral-like ceiling he wishes them a merry Christmas and invites them to a tot of whisky or sherry before breaking for the holiday.

Last to leave the secured premises are Miss Frobisher and William Markham.

"See you later Willy?"

"But of course Mary my dear, I'll meet you in the Bell Hotel lounge bar at eight."

Later that evening at around ten, Mary Frobisher and William Markham leave the Bell Hotel in Humberstone Gate. Crossing the road at the clock tower into Eastgates and the start of the High Street where a tram stands waiting to depart.

"Let's carry on walking Mary, do us good, some fresh air."

Markham puts his arm around Mary's shoulders drawing her close to him as they walk along the High Street heading for the West End and Mary's home. She is drunk and Markham in spite of his appearance is not so drunk having been watering his whisky while ensuring Mary Frobisher had several gins, each mixed with less and less tonic.

The diminutive Miss Frobisher lives alone in modest accommodation, a terraced house west of the city centre in Kate Street, a side street off King Richard's Road. She invites Markham to stay the night, he accepts with a wink and a knowing smile as he walks her home.

During their drinks at the Bell Hotel Markham had led the intimate chat intent on finding out how much Mary Frobisher knew about his involvement with Harry Cole and his so called secret government work and if she had discussed it with anyone else. In between her hiccups and fits of alcohol induced laughter she tells Markham his secret is safe with her while at the same time pressing him for her promised reward.

"Later Mary, I'll give it to you later."

The innuendo is not lost on Mary Frobisher as she wistfully looks into his eyes and moistens her lips provocatively in anticipation. The walk to Mary's home takes them to the end of the High Street towards St. Nicholas Square and down Applegate Street before crossing the canal at West Bridge.

"Mary love, will you hang on a minute I need to have a pee?" Before Mary can answer, Markham is down the stone steps onto the towpath and into the darkness below the road and rail bridges that cross the canal providing a shadowy canopy.

After waiting for what seemed like an age, during which time she was twice propositioned as a prostitute it's an anxious Mary Frobisher that descends into the pitch-black in search of her Willy.

"Willy, where are you? Are you alright?"

Without a sound or a word being said Markham is suddenly behind her and with a house brick strikes her a bone crunching blow across the top of her head. Mary Frobisher, fast losing consciousness and with blood beginning to trickle across her face, half turns to see her assailant before crumpling to the ground clawing at Markham's coat as she desperately tries to make sense of it all. Markham bends to steady himself and gently drops the brick out of one hand into the black water of the canal while his other hand hangs on to the listless Mary slumped in a heap against his legs.

Grim faced, Markham lifts and shoulders the rag doll of a body, picks up her handbag and keeping to the towpath strides purposely away from the scene of the crime. He is making for the old coal wharf next to some railway sidings of the West Bridge Branch.

Still on the towpath he strips Mary Frobisher of all her clothing and jewellery, stuff that may help someone to identify her. He wraps her clothes and shoes into her overcoat and pockets her jewellery. Next, he carefully lines up her marble white body alongside the rounded edge of the tow path and gently rolls her over into the canal making hardly a splash.

To his horror the icy cold water shocks Mary out of her unconsciousness and raising a hand she struggles to wave and call for help. Her gasping, choking call is in vain as she slips silently below the water and the slow current takes her into the deeper middle of the canal: a few bubbles come to the surface as the disturbed water settles.

Murderer Markham furtively looks about and checks to see if anyone is around. He sees no one and hears nothing as he climbs over a wooden post and rail fence into the coal yard and heads for the loco shed. An engine stands quiet with its fire box raked level allowing hot ashes cool, dying embers still glow. Through the open fire box Markham throws in Mary Frobisher's coat, clothes and shoes, one item at a time, making sure each one catches fire. Last to go in is a pair of black French knickers that he caresses against his cheek muttering,

"Sorry Mary, I really am."

CHAPTER 11

1ST WEEK IN JANUARY 1943

Christmas and New Year have come and gone and life in wartime Leicester carries on as best it can. It is a Sunday; the last day of what in peacetime would be called the festive season and is the last day before the first full week of trading in 1943, banks and businesses are ready. Policemen are kept busy with a few drunks and misdemeanours and families continue to make do and mend in times of rationing food and general supplies.

Today is the last chance for a few weeks for the Ratae Convivial Cycle Club members to meet and cycle as a group: club cycle rides are suspended in January and February as winter sets in. The club members, as usual, gather at the clock tower for a half day ride called *The Parks*, riding a clockwise route around the west side of the city taking in Victoria, Braunstone, Western and Abbey Parks.

Among the club members are Harry Cole, William Markham and Wallace Clarke. Being just a half day outing the cyclists are keen and soon eat up the miles through Victoria and around Braunstone parks heading for their one and only stop. Not a pub or inn this time but a call at the tram terminus at the gates to Western Park on Hinckley Road for a toilet break and a short rest.

Markham shares a flask of tea with Cole. Markham has been unusually quiet throughout the ride and it's Cole who opens up the conversation.

"You're quiet today, have you done it?"

"You're right I am and yes I have, Mary Frobisher will never be a threat to us, ever." Markham holds his hand out to Cole and palms over a gold bracelet and a pair of matching ear rings.

"Here, how much for this little lot? No, on second thoughts wait, take them and pay me later and mind you give me a fair price."

"What's this?"

"It's a Christmas present from Mary," says Markham with a suppressed giggling laugh.

Cole drops the jewellery in his jacket inside pocket. Now it's Markham that leads the conversation,

"Have you heard anything more?"

"No, I haven't and that's got to be a worry."

"No, no. No news is good news as I see it. We are going to be rich. Filthy rich, fifty grand richer, what do you say to that?"

Cole takes a few moments to collect his thoughts and finishes his by now cold cup of tea.

"Aye and we could be the richest men in the cemetery. We still do nothing for the time being, we leave the money, the real stuff and the counterfeits where it is." Cole makes no mention of the cash he has removed from the bank safety deposit boxes to a safe in his makeshift air raid shelter under his office.

The cyclists enter Abbey Park opposite the main tram depot and complete their Sunday morning ride at the band stand. Club members bid farewell and disperse. Other than a courtesy nod or two, nothing has been said between DI Clarke and Cole or Markham during the whole of the morning's ride.

The next day, Monday, DI Clarke shakes hands with a newcomer, Detective Sergeant James Wilson.

"Will it be James or is it Jim?"

"Jim is fine by me; it's only my dear old mother who calls me James."

The policemen barely finish exchanging pleasantries before DI Clarke turns away and pulls out a manila file from a steel cabinet handing it to his new detective sergeant.

"Here, take a look at this, digest it and later we'll pay a few visits."

A knock at the door and the rattle of a trolley means it's time for a cup of tea. DI Clarke makes a point that this is not the normal service and the canteen will have to do after DS Wilson's first day.

"Two teas please, this is our new starter Detective Sergeant Jim Wilson, we have to look after him." DS Wilson smiles and is appreciative of DI Clarke's intention to make him feel at home.

At the Midland Bank a member of staff has not turned up for work: Mary Frobisher is missing, it was to be her first day back after taking Christmas and New Year leave, however there is no immediate concern. Assistant Chief Cashier William Markham makes some overtly supposedly well intended enquiries amongst the bank's staff but no one can shed any light on her absence. Markham delegates another to attend to the safety deposit vault duties.

The monotony at the Midland Bank is soon to be severely disrupted. First a lorry is parked at an angle to the kerb at the bank's rear wrought iron gated entrance in Every Street blocking the gate and road. The lorry with its bonnet up and the driver nowhere to be seen ensures a traffic jam starts to build back to Horsefair Street. At the same time a second lorry cuts in and damages the front offside wing of a saloon car, belonging to Corah's, a local Manufacturer, parked outside the bank's staff entrance around the corner in Bishop Street. Another traffic jam builds and there is an altercation between the two drivers.

During the distracting row, three masked and armed men, one with a gun, attack two plain clothed security guards as they step out of the staff entrance. One guard is struck across the temple and falls to the pavement cracking his head on the edge of a granite kerb, the other guard carrying a briefcase chained to his wrist has a gun barrel pushed hard into his cheek and is manhandled past Corah's saloon into the back of another car parked in front of the lorry. The assailants' car driver revs the engine hard and speeds off turning right before racing along Granby Street into London Road and out of town. Shocked passers-by rush to attend the injured guard, others run into the bank to raise the alarm and call the police.

Less than two minutes after the attack a man is pushed out of the back of a speeding car as it passes a tram terminus on the edge of the city near the race course.

DS Wilson's introduction to his new post quickly changes from one of smiling tea drinking pleasantries to one of being thrown into action as he and DI Clarke don't wait for a car and run the short distance from the police station to the Midland Bank to start their investigation.

In Bishop Street DI Clarke orders his new sergeant to organise the first at the scene beat constables till a senior uniformed officer arrives to take charge of traffic and crowd control. With uniforms soon in control DI Clarke and DS Wilson are now free to interview witnesses and establish exactly what has happened.

Bishop Street is quickly cordoned off as are the two abandoned lorries and Corah's saloon car. Constables call out for any witnesses to come forward and give their names and addresses for interview later. Vague descriptions of the attackers and their getaway car are quickly circulated to police patrol cars while other beat constables are eventually informed by phone as they report in or by word of mouth as officers meet in the street.

Inside the bank, the injured guard and Corah's driver sip on a cup of tea. The guard is unable to offer DI Clarke any real information; he cannot recall a thing since stepping out of the staff entrance into the street and struck across the side of his head with an iron bar. The iron bar was abandoned near to him as he laid semi-conscious and bleeding on the pavement. The Corah's driver can say that he'd counted three attackers in the street and saw another in a waiting car. The lorry driver he had a row with ran off towards the clock tower. There is no information on the driver who abandoned his lorry in Every Street at the bank's rear entrance. The injured guard is taken to hospital where he meets up with his colleague and Corah's driver is allowed to go home. DS Wilson will take their written statements later.

The bank manager steps forward and asks if there is anything he can help with.

"Can we go somewhere quiet?" asks DI Clarke.

"My office?"

"That will be fine, thanks."

During the interview the bank manager describes the events up to the moment of the attack, now clearly identified as an armed robbery involving a large sum of cash. For more precise details the assistant chief cashier is summoned. Entering the manager's office with its polished wood floor, plush furnishings and oak panelled walls William Markham checks his stride as he recognises the seated DI Clarke.

"What a coincidence, cycling together yesterday and now this incident today."

Markham supplies details of what monies have been stolen. It was a collection being made by Corah's, one of Leicester's leading manufacturers supporting the war. He hesitates before continuing and takes a breath,

"It was three thousand pounds in fivers. Three £1,000 wads, straight out of the vault."

"Do you have any serial numbers?"

"Unfortunately not, they were all used notes. We only keep a numbers register of new notes coming in and new notes going out, sorry."

DI Clarke asks the manager and his cashier to describe again today's routine collection, including giving names of all of those involved, in particular anyone who would know of the detailed arrangements, and of anyone not at work today.

DI Clarke and DS Wilson know they are in for a long day collecting statements but what they don't know is what Markham does. He knows that the Kinder-B's virus has now spread not just amongst customers, businesses and other banks but now also into the criminal fraternity.

"Thank you sir, we'll be in touch." The detective inspector and bank manager shake hands.

Leaving the bank DI Clarke and DS Wilson bump into Harry Cole climbing the stone steps at the bank's main entrance.

"Not you as well? Soon be enough here for a cycle club meeting."

"And a good morning to you too, Inspector Clarke what on earth are you going on about?"

"Just seen your friend Markham inside the bank; they've had a bit of bother this morning. I'll leave it to him to tell you all about it."

In the streets around the bank traffic begins to flow again as the obstructing lorries are removed allowing cars, vans and aging horse drawn traps to carry on their way.

"Come on Jim let's drop in here before we get back to the mad house." The two policemen cross the road to the Turkey Café which is busier than usual as some onlookers take a warming cup of tea since there is nothing more to see. Pouring from a fresh pot of tea, DS Wilson remarks,

"Sir, clean as a whistle that job. They were well prepared, slick and likely well informed."

"You could be right."

A steady walk back to the police station refreshes the policemen's senses. DI Clarke sets up an incident room; three black boards on easels are wheeled in and stood against a blank wall. Tables are arranged for statement and information sorting and two telephone desks connected to a direct line.

"Now all we need is for the information to flow in" says DI Clarke as DS Wilson organises two officers, showing them how he needs information and statements collated and indexed.

The week drags by as information barely trickles in and progress at identifying the armed gang is proving difficult, there is no information other than a few vague descriptions. DI Clarke and DS Wilson are of the same opinion that the gang have either gone to ground and hiding till the heat is off or is an outfit from out of town that have already made good their getaway. It's now late Friday afternoon, four days after the robbery. DI Clarke and new assistant DS Wilson are in the incident room alone as other officers are dismissed.

"We don't have a lot to go on Jim and I'm going to have to scale down the incident room. Are we missing something?"

"Definitely are and with not a lot to act on. We've just the vague descriptions of three attackers, one car driver and one of the two lorry drivers. The descriptions will fit half the men in Leicester."

"You're right and with the getaway car, stolen the day before, found burned out behind the football ground in Filbert Street and the two abandoned lorries sold at auction to that accountant of a scrap merchant Cole a couple of weeks ago, means we sure haven't got a lot to go on."

What little information they have has taken up space on just one of the three black boards. This lack of any information to act on, with witness statements concentrated around those few minutes it took to bundle a guard and his bag containing £3,000 into a car means the investigation is stalling.

DS Wilson is called to another office to take a phone call allowing DI Clarke to pay some attention to other cases he is dealing with; he picks up a new piece of chalk and starts to write. The second black board is headed *Stoneygate* and just three short lines are scribbled out:-

Charlie the burglar - in custody.

Nottingham Jeweller - in custody.

Cole-fence?

The third board is headed *Beacon Hill*, technically not yet a case but somewhat intriguing for Clarke, and has a chalked list including:-

Low flying aircraft.

Two explosions.

One dead Home Guard private.

One injured corporal.

One or two cyclists and panniers.

Staring at the boards in turn DI Clarke, not for the first time, sees in his mind's eye the faces of Cole and Markham popping up reminding him of his notion that they may well, in some as yet unexplained way, be connected with the Beacon Hill incident.

Cole also now figures in the Stoneygate burglaries as the probable fence and in this week's armed robbery as the man buying in two lorries for scrap before selling them on to someone connected with the heist.

Markham has a link as being the assistant chief cashier at the Midland Bank and lives in Stoneygate where the burglaries took place.

"Maybe all just a bunch of coincidences, I don't know." Lost in his own thoughts DI Clarke is politely nudged back into reality by DS Wilson as he returns.

"Sir, got something on your mind?"

"Oh, nothing Jim, just a crazy notion I have, I'll tell you about it some other time."

"Hmm… well, if you say so sir." DS Wilson is somewhat perplexed, and then he comes back to why he was called away.

"Sir, your friend Charlie wants a word with you."

"What about?"

"He's up for his burglary charge on Monday and he's asking about the deal you made with him?"

"No deals made and no promises given."

"He's saying he has more to offer."

"Has he? He'll have to wait till tomorrow; I've done for today and I'm off next door to the Spread Eagle for a jar. Coming?"

"Thanks, I will."

Also calling it a day is Harry Cole who closes the scrap yard gates and locks himself in as his two hardworking labourers leave for home. He returns to his office and makes a phone call.

"Vince, is that you?"

"Yes."

"I understand that someone in Nottingham has been arrested and probably with some of the stuff I sold you?"

"Yes, a jeweller in Radford. Don't worry; it can't be traced back to me let alone you. I used a courier brought in from Sheffield to make my drop-offs, a nobody who can't be traced: I don't use the same man twice."

"Ok I'll be over tomorrow, usual place Victoria Hotel lounge bar, 3.30?"

"No problem, I'll be there, what have you got for me?"

"Nice heavy gold bracelet and matching ear rings with a few bits more."

Before leaving the scrap yard Cole can't resist climbing down into his air raid shelter. He opens his newly installed safe and runs his hand over, caressing, forty wads of white fivers, used notes specially selected by William Markham. It is a satisfied Cole that locks the chamber hatch and pulls the carpet back over the wooden trap door thinking about Markham's assumption that no news is good news. He is now warming to the fact that he is for the moment very much in the running to become a very rich man.

Cycling home along the tow path Cole approaches a flotilla of narrow boats; they are empty and sit high in the water having unloaded their cargoes and now heading up stream to reload with coal at the West Bridge Wharf or timber at Gimson's Yard further upstream. He catches sight of their names gaudily painted on the bows. Reading them out loud as he passes by,

"Mars, Neptune."

"No, it can't be can it?"

He breaks into a sweat fretfully thinking that the last boat may somehow be *Mercury* his contact for messages. He need not have worried as it turns out to be Jupiter.

"I'm getting paranoid."

As Cole approaches North Lock heading for Burberry's fish and chip shop another narrow boat rises between the lock gates with a man stood on its stern end resting against the tiller. The two men make eye contact and Cole's look is a quizzical one, not knowing the boatman who stares back at him intently.

The moment soon passes and Cole is on the canal bridge, turning right following the smell of fried fish. The narrow boat's bow breasts through the lock gates as the canal and lock waters level out. Easing to the side of the canal the stranger moors his boat as two excited school boys run by with one chasing the other shouting,

"Look, look there's another planet on the water. We've got Mars, Neptune, and Jupiter and now we've spotted Mercury."

The excited boys stop briefly to admire the narrow boat then on a nearby factory wall one of the boys neatly chalks up Mercury, adding it to their list of planets they've so far seen.

"Let's see if we can find some more planets?"

Inside the narrow boat's small cabin and deep in his own thoughts *Mercury* dunks a crust of bread into a can of beef broth while in Heanor Street a contented Harry Cole finishes his fish and chips and makes a pot of tea. In his Stoneygate Court flat a nervous William Markham drinks himself into a drunken stupor and passes out on the kitchen floor. At the Spread Eagle pub, DI Clarke and DS Wilson part in good humour arranging to meet at nine o'clock tomorrow, Saturday morning, at Leicester's Gaol on Welford Road.

CHAPTER 12

SATURDAY 9ᵀᴴ JANUARY 1943

Nine o'clock on a Saturday morning is much the same as for any other day of the week in Leicester Gaol. Woken before seven the prisoners have long slopped out, washed and had breakfast by the time DI Clarke and his sergeant Jim Wilson are let into an interview room. Waiting for them is Charlie the Stoneygate burglar, held on remand over Christmas and New Year waiting for his court appearance on Monday next. In another attempt to try and limit the sentence he is sure to receive, he has let it be known that he has more information to trade with.

"Charlie, I told you no deals and no promises, what have you got for me now?"

"I've already given you a name, a big name, have you got him?"

"Just fingering someone is not enough, you know that."

"Look… If you want more just follow him to Nottingham, usually on a Saturday afternoon but sometimes he goes on a Thursday evening."

"I can't waste time tailing a man who may have a legitimate reason to visit Nottingham." DI Clarke is hanging out for more information, he is not disappointed,

"Maybe you're right but who would go all the way to Nottingham, only to catch the very next train back?" DI Clarke is intrigued by Charlie's tit bit of information.

"As I said before Charlie, I'll see what I can do but no promises. We're off."

"Wait, wait Mr. Clarke, I've more."

"More of what?"

"A little bird tells me armed robbers have gone to ground and a certain police investigation is going nowhere?" DI Clarke's and DS Wilson's ears prick up at hearing armed robbers; it can only mean Charlie knows something about the well-executed robbery outside the Midland Bank five days ago.

"What have you got?"

"What's in it for me?"

"As I keep saying no promises but I'll see what I can do, you have my word on that." Charlie whispers an address.

"You'd better be right Charlie."

Back at Charles Street police station DI Clarke is in discussion with the detective chief superintendent and requests authorisation to issue hand guns to himself, DS Wilson, four other CID officers and to summon two marksmen with their rifles.

The address given by Charlie is a semi-detached house on Evington Road inside the city's eastern limits where plain clothes CID officers are already observing the house from an unmarked car. From the front bedroom of a house almost opposite, more policemen peer through net curtains while the owner is busy making a pot of tea.

The house owner, an elderly widow, living alone is happy to have two pair of size nine boots for company and for her own safety is confined to the back of the house. In the kitchen DI Clarke chats with the owner and is able to glean more information about the watched house. It has been vacant for a while and thought to be waiting a new let. It is similar to the house being used as an observation post having the same internal layout with a bathroom and three bedrooms upstairs, two on the front and one on the back. Downstairs there is a lounge to the front, a back dining room and a small kitchen with the toilet outside. The front door lets into a hallway with stairs to the right with two doors on the left and one straight ahead into the kitchen.

What is not known is how many, if any, of the gang are holed up in the house. The widow has seen no cars arriving or leaving but she has occasionally seen a light go on in the kitchen just before the blackout curtains are drawn.

DI Clarke keeps the house under close observation, the curtains are drawn on the front and nothing stirs for the rest of the morning and it's not until about five o'clock in the afternoon that there is the first sign of any movement. The kitchen door opens and a man slips across to the outside lavatory, returning a few minutes later. The kitchen light is switched on and the curtains are drawn ready for the blackout, timed at around five twenty.

DI Clarke decides the waiting is over and intends to storm the house, he is confident that the man is alone and likely keeping to the kitchen, limiting his moves and reducing the chances of being seen. Clarke makes certain that his team will be at minimum risk. First he makes sure that one of the marksmen still has a clear line of sight, in spite of the failing light, to the front of the house covering the two bedroom and lounge bay windows. The same marksman also has a clear shot at the front door that is set back in a recess behind a brick arch. A second marksman has a clear shot at the kitchen door on the side of the house.

DS Wilson, with his rain coat collar turned up walks briskly by the house's front garden gate and path leading to the front door. As soon as he is obscured by the front fence and chest high privet hedge he ducks, turns, lifts the gate latch and enters the garden, crouching as low as possible he scampers sideways, crab like, to the side of the house. He flattens himself against the wall with his handgun ready.

At the back of the house two armed officers have been climbing fences from two doors away and provide more back up for DS Wilson as they watch from the bottom of the garden behind a timber trellis screening the garden's compost heap.

DI Clarke now crosses the road and calmly walks through the open gate heading for the front door; his back is covered by two officers at the ready behind the fence and a watching marksman across the road. Noted for his no nonsense approach when dealing with criminals who choose to use guns to break the law DI Clarke announces his presence at the front door by straight away drawing his gun from its holster, strapped to his left side under his arm, and with two rapid fire shots shoots out the door lock. He shoulders the door and is in the hallway heading for the kitchen. The two covering officers are in behind him and up the stairs checking for any suspects.

The man in the kitchen is startled by the commotion and grabs a gun off the kitchen table but never gets to his feet as DS Wilson, on hearing Clarke's shots, kicks in the unlocked kitchen door and shoots the man in the right shoulder as he levels his gun at the sergeant.

Clarke is through the hallway and kitchen door just in time to see the gunman drop to the floor.

"You ok Jim?"

"Flimsy latch on the door, a better one could have meant a different result. I'm fine thanks."

Despite his injury and screaming in pain the gunman is restrained with handcuffs behind his back, arrested and hauled away to a waiting car.

From the state of the kitchen and lounge it looks as if the man was alone living rough with a few meagre supplies and dossing on the settee. The house is thoroughly searched and a courier's bag containing £3,000 is found stashed in a cupboard underneath the stairs.

The house is made secure and two uniformed officers are posted and who, not wanting to be surprised by any of the gang returning, make their presence obvious by taking it in turns to parade up and down between the house and front gate crunching their heavy boots on the garden path.

With guns back under lock and key and all rounds accounted for DI Clarke pours out two shots of Scotch whisky.

"Good result sir, Charlie came up trumps."

"Aye a good start Jim, but we've still got five of the buggers to catch."

DS Wilson empties the courier's bag onto his boss's desk and three £1,000 Midland Bank's magenta banded wads of white fivers slide out. DS Wilson picks up one of the wads in his left hand and strums one end of the tight 200 fivers with his right thumb. The notes have a firm and clean new feel about them but have a general appearance that includes tears, creases and pin holes, the sort of things you would normally expect with the condition of well circulated used notes. DS Wilson points out this inconsistency to DI Clarke who feels the firmness of the wad and crispness of the notes.

DS Wilson snaps the paper band and fans the notes out on the table. This time his jaw drops and he is stuck for words as he sees a stream of sequential numbers. He pulls out about fifty notes; they all show the apparent signs of being in general circulation and some even have tellers' pen marks suggesting they have been counted as part of other wads.

"Sir, look at this."

"What am I looking at?"

"Supposedly old and used notes but these don't feel old yet they have the characteristics of the wear and tear of used notes but they just don't feel used, being quite the opposite they are clean and crisp and what's more there's a whole wad of them and to top that these fifty or so have sequential numbers, one note follows another."

"So, what are you suggesting?"

"Sir, if these were new notes and fresh out of the bank their numbers may well follow one another, but what are the chances of these fifty or so fivers having been in circulation as shown by the supposedly used condition ever coming back together again in a consecutively numbered wad? Unlikely I say. Very unlikely, something very peculiar is going on here. It could be an attempt at disguising forgeries?"

DI Clarke is impressed with his new DS's observations.

"If these are forgeries and whether intentional or not it seems as though someone has made an almighty cock-up in the attempt to disguise them, the look and feel of the paper has not been aged as good as the rest of the wad. Maybe just carelessness or sabotage by a member of the counterfeiting team, we may never know. Say nothing to anyone, bag the money, log it in at the front desk as evidence and get it locked away out of sight."

The adrenalin fuelled stake-out and capture of one of the gang of armed robbers is not the only police activity organised by DI Clarke. Based on information received from Charlie, the Stoneygate burglar turned grass, the detective inspector has arranged for Harry Cole to be watched and if the occasion arises, tail him from his house in Heanor Street to Nottingham.

With the scrap yard closing at one o'clock Harry Cole is soon home. Having washed and changed he grabs a duffle coat and leaves his house on foot. A car passes him in Heanor Street, careers left round the corner into Craven Street then sharp right into Harding Street. Parking outside Lottie's shop and looking through the wing mirror a plain clothes police officer, one of several taken out of the uniformed ranks to support DI Clarke's two simultaneous operations, sees Cole shrug his shoulders and tug on a flat cap. Cole passes the unmarked car keeping his head down in a freshening breeze; he is unaware of the driver and heads for the end of the street and through the jitty into North Gate Street.

Once through the jitty another officer follows Cole on foot and catches up with him at the junction with Sanvey Gate. The tail, thinking he may have been spotted, deliberately turns left into Sanvey gate and walks away. Cole carries on and crosses the road by the Central Hotel taking a right fork into Central Street and towards the station. Waiting outside Leicester Central railway station is another officer who, having seen Cole approaching, reads a timetable before following him into the booking hall.

Cole buys a return ticket to Nottingham. Waiting on the platform is another plain clothes officer, not one of DI Clarke's men but one from the Nottingham City Police sent as support to DI Clarke's operation. The usually careful Cole has a lot on his mind and although he catches glimpses of others in the street and on the platform, he is unaware of the keen interest being taken in him.

The 2.43 to Nottingham departs on time and Cole has the journey time to order his thoughts and decide what he has to do now that it seems to him he has been abandoned by the Fatherland. *Mercury* has been quiet, too quiet, giving Cole his cause for concern.

Cole has in his possession £50,000 worth of fivers, £40,000 of it genuine, being the net result of the aborted Kinder-B and he has had no instruction what to do with it. The others who know of it are *Mercury*, William Markham and possibly the missing Mary Frobisher. Cole has to make himself secure and free from possible exposure and capture.

Mercury is not, as yet, seen as a threat and William Markham has assured Cole that Mary Frobisher will never be a threat to either of them He has to accept that he has killed her leaving just the two of them as heirs apparent to a fortune. However, for Markham there is no future as a rich man, Cole knows he has to deal with him leaving just himself holding the profitable aborted Kinder-B.

The train calls at Loughborough, Cole checks his inside pocket and fingers a smooth leather pouch. His mind wanders back to Markham; he knows he has to deal with him as soon he can. Questions will be asked by the police about the missing Mary Frobisher and it's certain her involvement with Markham will come to light and the excitable closet fascist cannot be relied on to keep his mouth shut. Leaving Loughborough Cole stares aimlessly out of the window working out what needs to be done while in the next compartment a policeman can see his reflection in the corridor window and keeps watch.

By the time the train arrives at Nottingham Victoria Station, Cole has decided how to deal with Markham and to deal with him sooner rather than later. Passing through the ticket barrier one plain clothes police officer gives a knowing look to another and their quarry is tailed out of the station.

Cole heads straight to the adjacent Victoria Hotel and meets a man in the lounge bar who sits at a table in a quiet corner ready with two pints of local brew, Shipstone's bitter ale. As the men sip beer Cole passes, under the table, a leather pouch to Vince who now needs to pay a visit to the gents' toilet. Returning a few minutes later asking,

"How much for this nice little lot?"

"Forty, no less. You know it's good stuff."

A few minutes later Cole leaves the hotel forty pound better off and heads to catch the next train back to Leicester.

Cole has now been dropped by his police tail. The Nottingham City Police now follow his buyer Vince to his house where he is allowed to settle for just a few minutes. Vince's house is raided and he is arrested on suspicion of receiving stolen property, Cole's journey back to Leicester is uneventful.

The police now have Charlie the burglar turned grass and Vince the Nottingham buyer in custody and Harry Cole, the Leicester fence, is almost in their grasp. The CID officers in Nottingham and Leicester celebrate, early doors, with a well-earned pint at their respective watering holes, for DI Clarke and DS Wilson in the usual Spread Eagle and for their Nottingham colleagues it's a short walk to the Clinton Arms in Shakespeare Street.

For William Markham this Saturday is proving to be one he wished he could have skipped. He has seen again what he had for dinner and tea the day before and is physically weak from retching at the toilet bowl for the best part of the night. The brain splitting pain means his only moves for the whole of the day have been a struggle between his bedroom and the bathroom.

During one of his rare restful slumbers he is woken as a persistent doorbell rings on and on. Half asleep and bleary eyed he pulls on a paisley patterned silk dressing gown.

"I'm coming; I'm coming, stop the ringing please, please." Harry Cole eases back on his whitening thumb.

"Oh, you're in then?"

"You're a surprise, come in." Markham shows Cole into the lounge, a plush well-furnished room.

"I'll just take a minute to freshen up, help yourself to a drink." Cole eyes the open drinks cabinet selects a bottle and pours Scotch into two cut glass tumblers and sinks into a soft arm chair. He thinks of how well paid bank staff must be to afford such luxuries and of how soon he will be able to live the life of the well to do. Markham reappears at the door.

"Sorry about that, not been too well today, just needed to wash and clear the eyes. What brings you to this side of town?"

Cole fabricates a story telling Markham that he has had more instructions from Germany and expects even more tomorrow, Sunday. He wants Markham to meet him at his scrap yard where they will be alone and can talk freely.

"But we can talk here?"

"We can, but I've been instructed to reward all those that have been in-volved so far and that includes you. I'm talking about money, a lot of money." Cole's bait is almost taken as Markham butts in and tries to clarify the situation.

"But the money's in the bank, you only have the counterfeit stuff."

"Not any more, I've moved it to the yard."

Markham's sore head relents at the thought of receiving a windfall. Cole knows the bait has been taken as Markham asks,

"How much?"

"Enough, you'll be more than satisfied and no need to worry about double crossing anyone."

Cole now has Markham in his pocket as greed and the thought of easy money take hold, making him as gullible as the unfortunate Mary Frobisher.

"What time shall I come?"

"Let's say about two o'clock, I will have had the latest message from Germany by then."

"Not a problem, I'll cycle over. Let's have another drink."

"Not for me thanks."

Cole leaves to catch a tram while Markham celebrates what he thinks is his due reward for his part in a German plan to damage or even destroy the British economy

The narrow boat Mercury slips its mooring at North Lock. *Mercury* heads upstream to a quieter part of the canal between West Bridge and the spur for the Old River Soar and Gimson's timber yard. The boat is tied to an iron spike hammered into the bank on the opposite side to the towpath. Cole will not be troubled by passers-by.

The loan boatman sets up his radio receiver-transmitter, clips an aerial to the helm, connects its battery power pack and dons his earphones ready to listen for any secret messages sent by the SS-foreign intelligence. He has heard nothing since receiving his last command *Clean up Kinder-B.*

During his allotted times of 15 minutes at 10pm and 3am next morning he hears nothing but ear twitching crackles of static interference. The aerial is dismantled and the radio equipment is packed neatly into a water tight suitcase and stowed away. The suitcase is hidden behind a decorated wood panel alongside Cole's bunk bed at the back of the cramped cabin.

Mercury is well used to hearing nothing, sometimes for many weeks at a time but he keeps to his daily listening routine ready for whatever is asked of him. Settled down for the night, sitting on his bunk bed, he turns his attention to another hidey hole and pulls out a revolver and by the light of an oil lamp takes great care in cleaning it, keeping it loaded and ready for use.

CHAPTER 13

SUNDAY 10ᵀᴴ JANUARY 1943

Harry Cole, as usual, whether at work or on a day off, is up at six o'clock and it being a Sunday he has a proper breakfast. In Cole's house anything more than a cup of tea and a crust of bread is considered proper. His tea is brewing and today's proper breakfast is the luxury of a fried egg and a rasher of bacon with two rounds of toast.

Sunday is ordinarily a quiet day off for Cole but today is planned to be somewhat different. As soon as he has cleared the pots away, washed and left them to drain he is on his way to the scrap yard dressed not in his Sunday best but in his work clothes ready for a morning's hard graft before his two o'clock meeting with William Markham.

It's only seven o'clock and Cole has already locked himself inside the yard, he does not want to be disturbed. The yard is quiet and the frosted ground crunches under Cole's boots as he passes a rake of partly loaded railway wagons before stepping into the one time pavilion that is now his office.

Once inside he lights a lamp and closes the door. Also ready for a day's work are Cole's tools and materials standing sentinel like either side of the fireplace. On the one side are sledge and lump hammers with a variety of chisels; on the other are bags of sand, cement, a can of water and a trowel. Standing near to the school ma'am's desk is a neatly stacked pile of blue bricks.

Cole is soon in his air raid shelter and sets about his task and is sweating profusely, it's proving to be hard work in a confined space. He knocks out the new brickwork he had laid to block off the incoming end of the culvert and a pile of bricks, half bricks, pieces of mortar and dust is cleared away. He makes sure that all trace of his morning's work is out of the chamber and dumped around the yard well before Markham's arrival. To finish off Cole covers the chamber floor with an old tarpaulin sheet.

In his flat at Stoneygate Court William Markham has also started his breakfast with a Sunday treat, a pot of black coffee. The coffee cost him an arm and a leg in an under the counter purchase. For something to eat he had managed to acquire two eggs which he boiled for exactly three minutes and like a child he delighted in theatrically dunking buttered toast soldiers into salted runny yolks.

Unlike Cole, Markham plans to have a quiet and easy morning before taking lunch at the Grand Hotel intended to be a private celebration in his own company before taking delivery of his anticipated cash windfall.

After six days, six long days during which he had started a new job, familiarised himself with his boss's workload, assisted in investigating an armed robbery including taking a lead role in capturing of one of the gang, DS Wilson is glad for a day off. He has moved from Huddersfield with his wife, twelve year old son George and his mother in law to a new home on Uppingham Road where he is busy white washing the kitchen walls. Mrs. Wilson continues to do what she has done since moving in a week ago by cleaning again each room in turn and moving the furniture around till each table, chair or cabinet is placed just so and to her liking. Mr. Wilson does not interfere knowing that his wife is running out of combinations and will need to settle for one layout sooner rather than later.

Mother-in-law and son are in the front room and out of the way when there is a sharp rap at the front door, son George is soon on his feet to see who's about.

"Morning lad is your dad in?"

"Dad, it's for you, uniformed plod."

"Don't be cheeky George, show a little more respect. Morning Constable, what brings you here?"

"DI Clarke sends his compliments sir, can you come straight away? There is a body in the canal near to North Mills, not far from North Lock."

"Right, give me couple of minutes to clean up and I'll be right with you."

Fifteen minutes later, DS Wilson is pulling back an ambulance blanket covering the naked body of a woman, nearby a police surgeon packs his bag.

"Good morning, you are?"

"DS Wilson sir, what's the story here?"

"Post-mortem tomorrow but I can say for certain she's had a heavy blow to the back of the head with a blunt instrument, enough to probably kill her before going into the water but the post-mortem will give us the full picture. I reckon she's 45-50 and about four foot ten, maybe five foot tall and in the water for at least two weeks, perhaps three, we'll know more tomorrow."

DS Wilson turns to see DI Clarke approaching.

"Good work Jim, thought I'd let you lead on this one, no pun intended but dropped you in at the deep end as it were."

"Thank you sir, least it got me away from the decorating."

"While you were being fetched I called at the office and pulled the missing persons files. We may get an early result; just five local women went missing in the past twelve months."

DI Clarke reads out loud the last name on the list, the most recent female to have gone missing,

"Mary Frobisher."

"Sir isn't she…?"

"Yes, our missing clerk from the Midland Bank, missing on the day of the robbery. A lady gone AWOL and no one could tell us why. We probably know now."

As the dead woman's body is carried away to the waiting ambulance DI Clarke stands on the tow path and looks about him. The canal flows silently by behind him and factory walls with barred windows stand tall in front of him.

"Looks as though we've had some star gazers around here," he points at a neatly chalked up list of planets.

"Just kids sir, saw them writing the same list back there at the North Lock, names of narrow boats apparently."

In the surrounding area police enquiries are made house to house in a half mile radius to start with, closed businesses and factories nearby or any dependent on the canal will have a visit the next day. Additionally, boat to boat checks are made up stream as far as West Bridge.

In the North Bridge Inn next to the locks a boatman joins a crowded public bar and orders a pint.

"What's the bother Landlord?"

"Haven't you heard? Woman's naked body has just been dragged out of the canal, just above the locks between here and Hitchcock's Weir."

The boatman finishes his drink and leaves. He takes his boat downstream through Limekiln Lock and heads for quieter moorings out of the city at Rothley. *Mercury* has decided to lie low for the time being.

Lunch over; it is a well fed and slightly tipsy William Markham who collects his bike and cycles up Belvoir Street towards Welford Place and crosses the top end of Welford Road into Newarke Street. He heads down Newarke Street into an historical part of the city noted for its buildings.

After passing through the fifteenth century Magazine archway into The

Newarke, the remains of a Medieval Castle Motte and the later Castle Hall dating back to the 11th and 12th centuries are just off to his right, behind the old Trinity Hospital. Before long he crosses a stone bridge over the canal and turns left into Western Boulevard, Harry Cole's scrap yard is just a minute away.

The corrugated gates are unlocked and slightly ajar, Markham can hear a hammering on the inside, Cole is breaking up an old piano. Cole catches sight of his visitor,

"Come in my friend, come in, sorry about the mess, it comes with the job."

"Where there's muck there's money eh?" replies Markham who is ushered in and the gates locked again.

"I'm not late am I, you did say two o'clock?"

"You're spot on, right on time; I like that in a man. Leave your bike alongside mine. I'll clean up and we can have our little chat?"

Inside the site office, Markham takes what is the only clean seat available, the high stool next to the school ma'am's writing desk. Cole rubs most of the muck off his work worn hands with a dry cloth and washes in an enamel bowl with hot water taken from the billycan simmering over the dying embers of the open fire.

"So you've moved the money out of the bank, I didn't know?"

"Yes that's right, I did ask for you but you were apparently busy."

"What have you heard from Germany?"

"It's good news, good news for us any way, the operation has been abandoned and I am to destroy the counterfeits."

"But we can't, not all of them. You know that."

"I do and so does Germany."

"So what are you going to do?"

"Don't worry, the genuine stuff is ours. Most of it any way, thirty thousand between us two and ten thousand moved on to support other agents and as for the counterfeits I will burn them as instructed."

Markham has a gleam in his eye as the windfall is confirmed and is getting closer. However, he is still greedy for more.

"It's a shame about the duds; we could exchange them as we've already done. Who would be any the wiser?"

Cole has a thoughtful look about him and wanting to keep Markham in his pocket, continues the conversation,

"Maybe, maybe we could at that. Let's have a drink."

"But where's my money?"

"All in good time, it is safe where it is and going nowhere. Here take this." Cole passes Markham a good measure of whiskey.

"Mmm it's Irish and a nice one at that, thanks." For nearly an hour Cole plies Markham with even more whiskey and has less and less for himself.

"Now, do you want to see where your money is, see how safe it has been since leaving your bank?"

"Ok, let me see it."

From his perch a swaying Markham sees Cole pull the office carpet to one side and pull open a wooden trap door. He sees a key turned in a heavy duty padlock and a steel hatch is pulled back and propped open revealing a black void below.

"What is it?"

"It's my air raid shelter, an old inspection chamber in a disused drainage system and is as dry as a bone. I converted it to a shelter at the start of the war, let's go down."

"Where?"

"In there, if you want to see your money."

"But it's pitch-black."

Cole lights an oil lamp and climbs down into the darkness, the polished brass handle on the safe glints as it catches the flickering light.

"Come on, come down and see for yourself, it's a bit of a squeeze but we'll fit in. It'll be worth it."

Now drunk and with fluttering white five pound notes further confusing his thoughts Markham makes slow and unsteady progress as he climbs down the footholds that he grabs hold of with a vice like grip till he is sure his feet feel a firm footing. The two men squeeze together and juggle body positions till both are facing the same way, looking at the neatly bricked in safe.

"Look, what do you think?"

"If the money's still in there it don't matter what I think, come on let's have a look."

"Here, hang on to this," Cole passes Markham the lamp and feigns to look for the safe key in his overalls.

"Shit! I've left the key in my coat pocket. Wait here, I'll fetch it."

Before the unsteady Markham has time to react, Cole is out of the chamber and he is left alone looking at the safe and the carefully laid and pointed brickwork forming a solid plug to the one time culvert. He slowly turns round to see the gaping eerie black hole that once let water into the chamber on its way to be discharged into the canal.

After a couple of minutes that seem like a lot more Markham's mood changes from being in a state of happy delirium to one of unease, he bites his nails becoming more and more agitated and anxious that he is alone and that there is no sign Cole returning.

"Harry, Harry Cole where are you, are you up there?"

The air is filled with a deathly silence and remains so as Markham calls and calls again, there is still no answer. With the lamp in one hand Markham struggles to climb the foot holds on his way out to see what has happened to Cole.

Markham's balding pate pops through the wooden floor level of the office where from behind he is despatched into oblivion as Cole crashes a lump hammer into his skull. Markham purges his last breath, loses his grip and falls back into the black void like a sack of potatoes; the oil lamp follows him down, bounces off his chest and bursts into flames. Cole grabs a damp towel and is in the chamber in a flash to smother the fire. Choking on a mixture of smoke and dust Cole climbs out of the black void back into the office, opens the door and gulps in fresh air.

The air in the office and chamber clears and Cole locks the door and lights another oil lamp ready to deal with Markham's body. Down in the chamber with the lamp hanging from a foot hold, he checks the body, Markham remains dead. Cole strips Markham removing every bit of clothing including two rings which he forces off his fingers. He straightens the tall man as best he can and then grabs hold of a scaffold board, resting on three greased steel tubes he had earlier placed inside the re-opened culvert. He pulls it out to lie alongside the body and supports it on loose bricks. Markham's body is with great effort gradually eased onto the board and made secure by wrapping round bands of the newly available sticky duck-tape: it's proving to be harder work than Cole imagined when first planning how to deal with Markham. The corpse with its stiff board under it should now be easier to manoeuvre than had it been left limp.

Cole lifts, drags and inches the body and board up and onto the first steel tube ledged just inside and across the mouth of the culvert. It takes another twenty energy sapping minutes for Cole to lift, pull or push the board and its body level onto the second and third tubes. Lying on his back Cole puts his boots on Markham's shoulders and makes a final push to slide the corpse into the black hole for what he is confident will be its final resting place.

Cole takes a short breather before moving new bricks and mortar into the chamber and again seals up the culvert face taking just as much care to make it as neat and tidy a job as he had already done once before. The chamber is cleared of all tools, unused materials along with Markham's clothes including a scorched towel and a dusty, blood spattered tarpaulin.

By now it's five o'clock and Cole still isn't finished grafting. In the open yard he starts a fire in an old oil drum and feeds in Markham's clothes. The clothes are followed by the bloodied and cut up tarpaulin and scorched towel. Suddenly Cole is stopped in what he is doing by a loud urgent banging on the gate.

"Who's in there?" booms out a policeman. Cole drops the last of the tarpaulin pieces into the fire and he cautiously approaches the gate.

"Harry Cole, who wants to know?"

Through the gap in the slack gates Cole recognises the policeman as one of the usual beat bobbies that patrol the canal tow path.

"Busy today, Harry? Know anything about a body?" Cole stands stunned and rooted to the spot; his worry is short lived.

"We've fished a body of a woman out of the canal earlier. Heard of anyone gone missing?" It's a relieved Cole that shakes his head.

"No. No one. I'll let you know if I hear anything."

With the policeman gone and in the gathering gloom Cole completes his day's work in the yard. First with a pair of industrial bolt croppers he cuts Markham's bicycle into bits beyond recognition, next he lobs the jig saw pieces of bike into three separate wagons destined to leave for Sheffield the next day. Finally, the ashes of Markham's clothes, towel and tarpaulin are thoroughly mixed together and following an ease in temperature are spread around and trampled into the muddy yard.

CHAPTER 14

MONDAY 11TH JANUARY 1943

DI Wallace Clarke and DS Jim Wilson meet early at the office to review their case load. Top priority is given to the £3,000 armed robbery, next is the woman's body in the canal and last is the suspicions that surround Harry Cole fencing stolen jewellery, notably items of gold.

DI Clarke continues to lead on the robbery and Harry Cole while DS Wilson is pleased to cut his teeth as a new detective sergeant by investigating the suspicious death of a woman that has the look of it being a murder.

The captured armed robber has been charged and expected to be remanded in custody after appearing at the Magistrates Court, in the meantime he has been moved to the hospital wing of Leicester Gaol.

The oddity of the recovered five pound notes feeling new compared to their look of being used and being consecutively numbered is something that DI Clarke believes will be of significant interest to the grandees of the Bank of England.

Harry Cole will have to be put aside and wait for a day or two and although DS Wilson is expecting an early identification of the body in the canal, finding her killer may take a little longer. Splitting their resource DI Clarke leaves to catch a train at Leicester's London Road station and DS Wilson sets off to visit the police mortuary.

An express steam train leaves platform 3 for London St Pancras; DI Clarke makes himself comfortable in a reserved first class compartment. Travelling with him is a young detective constable, invalided out of the army after losing an eye during basic training: the fitness requirements for joining the police have been relaxed allowing him to be employed.

DI Clarke indicates to the DC to pull down the blinds to add to the compartment's privacy. The DC with a leather attaché case handcuffed to his wrist is standing in as DI Clarke's bag man in place of DS Wilson who has other enquiries to make.

DI Clarke reads his notes and reports from an ever thickening file on Harry Cole, a scrap metal merchant and a suspected fence, who also happens to be a fellow member of the Ratae Convivial Cycling Club. The young DC settles into the deep pile cushions and is soundly asleep by the time the train passes through Kibworth station; DI Clarke does not disturb him.

Left behind in Leicester DS Wilson arrives at the police mortuary to get the results of a post-mortem examination on a woman's body recovered from the canal. The police surgeon's examination confirms sex, height at four foot eleven, aged approximately 45-55. There are signs that she had been drinking and was dead in the water for at least two weeks possibly three: the cause of death was a single blow to the back of the head fracturing the skull and internal bleeding. There was a little canal water in her lungs suggesting the woman had succumbed to the head injury as she was dumped into the canal.

Examination around the wound revealed minute traces of reddish coloured fired clay embedded in the cracked skull, most probably from a house brick. There were no signs of any other wounds or bruising as would be expected if there had been a struggle, she was most probably attacked from behind. Other than well-manicured fingers and a good set of teeth there are no other clues as to what sort of woman she was but possibly a woman of substance or more likely someone from the middle classes at least as shown by her delicate hands. There are no calluses, corns, lumps or hard skin, indicative of being in manual work. Finally, there were no signs of sexual assault.

The police surgeon does have something of interest to offer DS Wilson. After death, rigor mortis had set in and held tight in the woman's right fist was a brown leather button, the sort that may be found on a sports jacket, a man's or a woman's. Whether it belonged to the dead woman or her assailant's is for DS Wilson to find out. DS Wilson reckons that the 2-3 weeks the body was in the water points towards it being that of the missing bank clerk Mary Frobisher.

DS Wilson leaves the mortuary and goes to an address in Kate Street in the West End area of the city to interview Mary Frobisher's next door neighbour, the named and so called informant on the missing person report.

"Saw her on Christmas Eve me duck and never again. After a week I thought I'd better tell the police."

"I understand you have a key to Miss Frobisher's house?"

"Yes, I straightened up after the last lot of police came; they said nothing seemed suspicious and said I could carry on and tidy round."

"You've held a spare key for long?"

"Since ten year ago when she moved in with her mam, I use to help 'em do a bit of shopping and cleaning. She lived alone for the last seven years after her mam died, Miss Frobisher told me to hang onto the key. I clean for her once a week, for a couple of bob."

"Are you aware of anything missing?"

"Not sure if anything is missing but her jewellery box was open and a thick gold bracelet of hearts had gone, she showed it me once along with matching earrings. She may have them with her."

"I understand there were no relations or friends?"

"No family that I'm aware of, as for friends there were the girls at the bank. There was a man, not a regular. I passed him a few times at the front door as he called for her, tall fellow and smart too; not from round here."

"Not from around here, how do you know?"

"Creases in his trousers sharp enough to cut a loaf of bread, too much shiny leather on his shoes and wearing smart clothes that anyone round here could only afford to look at in a shop window let alone buy. No, he ain't from round here, a real smart gent."

"Name?"

The neighbour shakes her head,

"Sorry me duck, but he must have been six foot or more."

DS Wilson allows the helpful neighbour to lock up but asks for the key, since he is now investigating a murdered woman and a missing woman, most probably one in the same, the house is not to be entered without a police presence.

The detective sergeant's next call is across the town in Granby Street at the Midland Bank and an appointment with the bank's manager.

"Last time I saw her was on Christmas Eve, but I told you that last week after the robbery."

"Just routine checks sir, that's all and nothing to worry about. What I don't know is if she had any friends at the bank, a gentleman friend perhaps?"

"What are you driving at?" DS Wilson does not mince his words,

"Sir, I believe there is a strong possibility that Mary Frobisher is dead and I'm trying to piece together her last moments alive. I have questions to ask and answers to find." The manager is visibly shaken by DS Wilson's revelation.

"Possibly dead? Oh my God there was some office tittle-tattle about Miss Frobisher and my Assistant Chief Cashier William Markham. You're not suggesting..."

"Sir, I suggest nothing. I would like a word with Mr. Markham."

"You can't."

"Can't? Why?"

"He's not in today, and I don't know why."

Alarm bells are ringing and DS Wilson wastes no time in getting to Stoneygate Court, ahead of him are two uniformed officers waiting for instructions. Markham's flat is found on the top floor, DS Wilson rings the bell for a third time and still gets no answer. He orders a burly constable to shoulder the door in; the lock soon gives way to a fifteen stoner.

Inside there is no sign of William Markham, the bachelor's flat is somewhat untidy and has plenty of signs of being lived in, pots and pans fill the kitchen sink, dirty washing trails between bathroom and bedroom. The bedroom is tidier with the bed made and the lounge, with settee cushions freshly puffed up looks to have been tidied too.

DS Wilson checks cupboards, a wardrobe and a tallboy. Clothes are available with no obvious signs of empty drawers, coat hangers or hooks suggesting Markham had packed a bag and is either temporarily away or done a runner. In the wardrobe DS Wilson checks for coats, he has plenty to look at and he is not disappointed. He orders an immediate guard on the broken-in door and calls for a scene of crime specialist to attend.

In Threadneedle Street at the Bank of England DI Clarke and his DC are met by a doorman in a maroon uniform trimmed in heavy gold braid and a matching top hat. The doorman escorts the policemen to a small side office where they introduce themselves to one of the bank's inspectors; the bank inspector's job is not only to count wads of banknotes but also take random samples and check their authenticity.

The inspector would check the serial number, date and location of issue, the paper quality, and look for any signs of misprint or discoloration of inks used. He would also look for specific misprints or faults in the note lettering and the picture of Britannia known as detectable flaws which have been purposely introduced by the bank during the printing process: such misprints and faults are known security marks. Security marks, such as a misplaced dot over the letter i in the Chief Cashier K O Peppiatt's signature or missing secret dots on Britannia's hand or a broken line in the Britannia medallion shading are known only to the bank itself. The security marks are intended to fool a counterfeiter who may unwittingly correct them as being genuine printing mistakes.

The DC hands the attaché case to DI Clarke who takes out three envelopes and places them on the table. From each envelope he takes five white £5 banknotes and fans them out. All fifteen notes are in used condition, having the look of being through a number of hands and transactions showing signs of general wear and tear. Some notes are creased where they have been folded in a wallet or pocket, some have pin holes where they have been collected together and some have tellers own penned notation or numbering.

"Sir, I have some suspicion that these notes may not be genuine. They were recovered following an armed robbery a week ago."

The inspector who constantly repositions his spectacles along the length of his nose and with an air of aloofness makes a cursory check of all fifteen notes.

"Mmm… at first glance they look quite genuine, numbering, lettering, tellers' marks and feel of paper etc. To be absolutely sure I will need to consult the bank's registers and with my colleagues in the Note Issue Office who have a more detailed knowledge available concerning any note's production and its genuineness."

"As you wish, but I must remind you that I require all of them back, even those you may suspect or find to be forgeries, normal banking rules don't apply here, they are evidence in a serious crime."

"Not a problem, may I be permitted to ask why three separate envelopes, is that significant?"

"They are samples taken from three separate £1,000 wads of notes recovered after the incident I referred to."

"Why do you think they, or some of them may be forgeries as you put it, the usual term would be counterfeit?"

DI Clarke, like a magician pulling the rabbit out of a top hat, produces a fourth envelope and fans out another five used but apparently sound £5 notes on the table.

"Well, let's say I have a gut feeling, a hunch say, particularly as I am certain these five notes will be of even more interest. Have a look and tell me what you think."

"Why do you think these will be of even more interest?"

"Used notes, found together as a group, taken from a wad of used notes and are sequentially numbered being preceded by the same alpha numeric code and all issued from London bearing the same issue date. What are the chances of that occurring?"

The Inspector takes hold of the notes and gives them a feel and carefully looks at each one in turn, looking more carefully than he had the other fifteen fivers. DI Clarke senses a moment of worry as the inspector first frowns then continually adjusts his spectacles to get a better focus.

"You can see my point, can't you?"

"Well, hmm... I still need to check with the Note Issue Office. Wait here I'll go upstairs, meanwhile make yourselves comfortable and I'll arrange for some tea and biscuits."

An hour passes, two cups of tea each are downed by the DI and his DC and who now only have the crumbs of four digestives to pick at. DI Clarke is becoming a little impatient and as he catches hold of the brass door knob, the door opens sharply inwards on him. The bank's inspector has returned with a senior manager from the Note Issue Office.

"Oops! Excuse me gents, I was coming to see if we had been forgotten."

The four envelopes with fivers are placed back on the table and the Bank of England officials sit opposite the two policemen from Leicester. After more polite introductions it's the manager from the Note Issue Office who leads the discussion.

"DI Clarke, this envelope contains five genuine five pound notes; that is the good news. The bad news is that these next two envelopes contain a selection of randomly numbered notes that have all the apparent hallmarks as being genuine, well used bearing the usual marks of wear and tear and even tellers marks and pin holes, but are in fact very good forgeries."

"How can you tell they are forgeries or should that be counterfeits?"

"That is for us to know and nobody else," is the snooty reply.

"And what of the last set of fivers in the fourth envelope, those sequentially numbered notes?"

"Again, these have, on the face of it, all the characteristics of being genuine but are in fact counterfeits and before you ask, their coming back together as a set, we are certain, is down to pure chance or spotted by a keen eyed teller gathering them in and pinning them together. Have a look, see how the pin holes line up, they have most probably spent their time together as a job lot passing through hands in the same transactions, probably as part of dealings amongst cash preferring businesses or even amongst members in your criminal fraternity?"

DI Clarke summarises the situation as he sees it.

"Thank you and so, as it stands, you say I have samples that are genuine in one envelope and the samples in the other three that are all counterfeit?"

"Yes that is correct," is a stiff upper lipped reply.

"Does that not worry you?"

"All counterfeits are of a concern but of the millions of notes we issue, your counterfeits are but a very small drop in the ocean."

DI Clarke, with many years of experience in interviewing criminals, senses that the Note Issue Office's manager is more concerned than he lets on as he twiddles his thumbs and avoids any eye contact, preferring to stare upwards into empty space.

"Normally we would confiscate any counterfeits but we respect your request but in turn we expect that after any use for evidence is completed the counterfeits must be surrendered here for destruction."

DI Clarke feels he is being fobbed off and certainly not impressed by the staff at the Bank of England with their general attitude and tone of voice that he considers is bordering on arrogance beyond belief. He is not finished and grasping five fivers he probes again.

"What of these five consecutively numbered £5 notes, and in appearance apparently well used notes, do you seriously believe that they have been regrouped by a teller or even less likely by pure chance or that they may not ever have been separated despite their patently obvious well-travelled appearance?"

"That's what we say."

"Not worried by, and you haven't mentioned it, but it was apparent to me that you felt the somewhat firmer paper than you would expect a used note to be?"

"No not really, concerned but no, not worried at all." The manager's twiddling thumbs accelerate.

"Not worried about the possibility of the mass production of counterfeit notes, each with their own unique number?"

"That's just not possible. On the one hand our method of ciphering and sequencing numbering is unique, and on the other hand the production runs are limited and often varied say a hundred thousand here or two hundred thousand there and issued from various locations. Our mass production processes just cannot be emulated."

What DI Clarke is not told is that counterfeit notes of denominations from five to fifty pounds have already appeared in Tangiers, Switzerland and even London. Furthermore, The Bank of England's senior managers, though they wouldn't admit to it, are worried at the improving quality of the counterfeits beginning to come to light. What DI Clarke doesn't need telling is that The Bank of England dogmatically believes that its notes cannot be counterfeited to any total value that would affect the stability of the pound.

DI Clarke thanks the bank's officers for their time and considerations; he gathers in the four envelopes and delivers a parting shot across the bows.

"Gentlemen, I think you should be concerned, even alarmed at the possibility of counterfeit notes flooding into the country."

"Inspector, I cannot agree with your view," is the manager's terse response.

"Well, it seems I have random counterfeit samples from two separate wads that are likely to prove to be all forgeries, making it likely I have £2,000 in fake fivers. If that's not bad enough the five sequentially numbered used notes on crisper or newer paper than their general condition would normally exhibit are just the first 5 of a total 100 similar five pound notes from the same robbery that are also sequentially numbered."

The manager from the Note Issue Office is stunned at the revelation. His jaw drops and his face drains of colour and ashen as DI Clarke ends with a final shot, this time below the water line.

"What's more, all of these notes and the rest to a total of £3,000 were robbed from security guards just a few minutes after they had been withdrawn from the Midland Bank in Leicester. It is one thing to recognise and confiscate the odd counterfeit coming over the counter but is another ball game for a bank to issue fakes, counterfeits as you say, in large numbers. I do really think you should be alarmed."

As DI Clarke and his DC board a train at St Pancras station, alarm bells are ringing around the sumptuous wood panelled corridors and offices at The Bank of England. Chief Cashier K O Peppiatt is briefed on a meeting called by a provincial police officer and about the particular evidence he holds suggesting that the Bank of England's safeguards against counterfeits have been severely breached. There is a possibility that forged banknotes by the hundreds, if not thousands, are being circulated into the public domain by at least one named major bank.

It's eight o'clock and a black night on the LMS railway between St. Pancras and Sheffield where a train bound for Leicester steams through Wellingborough station approaching the 67 mile post and will soon pass it going under a red brick bridge bearing the same number, 67. With still 32 miles to travel DI Clarke is chatting with his detective constable advising him on the prospects of working in CID and alluding several times to the fact that it is easier on the feet but usually more dangerous as it involves working against organised criminal gangs, who are often armed.

As the train passes the 67 mile post, a man walking his dog on bridge 67 above are enveloped in steam and smoke, some of which enters the first class compartment causing noses to twitch.

In Leicester at the Vestry Street slipper baths there is also steam in the air as Harry Cole slinks back into the deep bath water, enjoys the all-round warmth and closes his eyes. Suddenly he is grabbed by the throat. Startled, his eyes pop wide open, he is confronted by a man holding his index finger to his lips indicating to Cole that he should remain quiet and stay calm.

"Don't worry 1809; we need to talk, understood?" Cole nods and the man's hand on his throat is relaxed and moves to his shoulder holding him down in the bath water with just his head showing.

"Who are you?"

"1809 you know me as *Mercury*."

"What do you want?"

"Not now but we need to talk about Kinder-B. Be sure to be at home Friday night at nine o'clock." With that the intruder splashes soapy water into Cole's eyes and is gone.

CHAPTER 15

TUESDAY 12TH JANUARY 1943

DS Jim Wilson's preliminary report about a woman's body pulled from the canal is almost complete and he briefs DI Clarke on his investigation so far; he is sure it is the body of the missing Midland Bank clerk Mary Frobisher. Two people, the bank's manager and her helpful neighbour have seen photographs of the body's bloated and marble like features and are both almost certain that it is Frobisher. Manager and neighbour have agreed to view the body to confirm their view.

Samples of hair taken from a brush on a dressing table in Mary Frobisher's bedroom match the colour and texture of the corpse's hair, also the dead woman's red nail polish matches a half empty bottle found on the same table.

There was some canal water in the stomach and lungs but not enough to cause drowning and the post-mortem confirms death as a result of a single bone crushing blow to the head, most probably by a house brick from behind. She had not been sexually assaulted and there is no doubt it is murder.

Details of the woman and the circumstances of her death will be released to the local press later in the day to see if anyone will come forward and provide any information on the dead woman's last known movements.

Any murder has three common elements with any other, a motive, a method and opportunity. Motive may have been robbery as Miss Frobisher is known to have had a heavy gold bracelet and matching earrings, none of which were on the body, or any jewellery for that matter.

DS Wilson now has the method with a probable weapon in mind, a blunt instrument and most likely a house brick used in a single blow to the back of the head. The house brick has not been found even though a thorough search along the length of the canal from Freeman's Meadow Lock to the North Lock and Limekiln Lock downstream found plenty of bricks, none carried any evidence of blood: he reasonably reckons the brick is probably somewhere in the canal.

Why the dead woman was anywhere near the canal still needs to be understood but the quiet of the tow path and canal, particularly at night, present an ideal opportunity and location for a murder and easy disposal of a body.

As for the murderer DS Wilson has been given a strong lead. From the dead woman's rigor mortised fist and its vice like grip the police surgeon, who had to break a couple of fingers, prised out a leather button, a button that matches others on a sports jacket in William Markham's wardrobe; a jacket that has a button missing.

Markham is DS Wilson's prime suspect and is wanted for questioning but he is nowhere to be found and has not been seen since leaving the restaurant at the Granby Hotel, two days ago, where he left in good humour and apparently looking forward to a rewarding Sunday afternoon cycle ride.

Information on the suspected murderer has been circulated to all police forces around the country and by releasing the details to the local press it is hoped that a number of local memories will be jogged.

"Well done Jim."

"Thank you, sir."

"It's a waiting game now, we need a break. You do know Markham was pally with Harry Cole, the scrap merchant, and like me a member of the *Arses* cycling club. What's more there is another possible connection, gold. Harry Cole is suspected of fencing jewellery, gold in particular. Frobisher's gold bracelet and earrings, her friend Markham and Cole the fence may yet prove a worthy line of investigation, maybe?"

"Setting aside your known cycling connection sir, I've already had a word with Cole who is adamant he hasn't seen Markham since we bumped into him on the day of the robbery, that's his story and is sticking by it."

The office door swings open and a moustachioed portly figure fills the framed space, it is the detective chief superintendent, DI Clarke's boss, sent as an errand boy by the chief constable.

"Sir, sir" is the double barrelled acknowledgement of the senior officer's presence.

"Wallace, you'd better come with me, now."

In his office the immaculately uniformed chief constable is flanked by his secretary and a man wearing a smart grey suit, collar with tie and highly polished black Oxford styled shoes.

"DI Clarke, this is Detective Chief Inspector Johnson from Special Branch. He has something to tell us."

The Special Branch officer is in Leicester as a direct result of DI Clarke's visit to The Bank of England the day before. He and senior managers from The Bank of England's Note Issue Office and the Midland Bank's head office have travelled to Leicester on the first available morning train. The Special Branch officer is seeking the co-operation of the Leicester City Police on a matter of national importance. DI Clarke, for the time being and possibly even forever is requested to pigeon hole any reference to counterfeit five pound notes during his investigations into the £3,000 armed robbery. DI Clarke purses a wry smile.

"Dirty tricks war?"

"You could be right. At this moment the Bank of England has a delegation of accountants at your Midland Bank checking on all of its five pound notes and when that's done they will look at the ten, twenty and fifty pound notes."

"You really do think that someone, I guess Hitler and his cohorts, is capable of mass producing counterfeit Bank of England banknotes, don't you?"

"Let's say we've, MI5 in particular, had an inkling for some time of that possibility in spite of the bank's intransigent view that such a prospect is simply not possible."

Without rhyme or reason DI Clarke sees again the faces of Harry Cole and William Markham pop into his mind's eye as he asks,

"Have you any idea how the counterfeit money is getting into the country?"

"No. But most likely landed by submarine onto a lonely beach or by air and parachuted in. We maybe a small island but we can't patrol everywhere all of the time, opportunities are plenty. Getting the money here is one thing, getting it into the banks in large numbers is another matter."

The chief constable assures the Special Branch officer that Leicester City Police will co-operate in any way it can.

"We will do whatever is necessary and co-operate provided we are not required to bend or break the law. Only those present in this office plus DS Wilson, the sharp eyed sergeant who got us into this, know about this situation and I give you my assurance that the armed robbery investigation will be treated as though nothing is amiss with any of the banknotes recovered."

The meeting over the Special Branch officer next intends calling in at the listening centre at Beaumanor Hall and invites DI Clarke to join him, by inviting the DI he is sure of getting a lift. Clarke accepts the invitation and calls for a pool car.

As DI Clarke and DCI Johnson set off to the Y-Group listening centre stationed at Beaumanor Hall DS Wilson takes the opportunity of a lull in the Mary Frobisher investigation to bring himself up to date on the file on Harry Cole.

He soon builds up a picture of a scrap merchant who appears to be an honest one dealing in the buying, sorting and selling on scrap metals, with his business doing well with the war industries ravenous appetite for metal, all metals.

Usual among the prized metals for scrap merchants are copper, tin and the heavy metals bronze and lead. More especially prized by Cole is gold, a metal that he buys and sells legitimately; he has accounts to prove it. Recently on the strength of a tip-off from a grass trying to get a reduced sentence and Cole being tailed by the Nottingham City Police to meet a known buyer of stolen jewellery in a bar at the Victoria Hotel in Nottingham means he is seriously suspected of fencing stolen gold and jewellery.

Shortly after Cole had caught the train back to Leicester the man he met in The Victoria Hotel, who is well known to the Nottingham City Police, was followed and his house raided. The man had proved co-operative and being caught red handed he thought he would be better placed by accepting a fair cop with an improved chance of leniency at court by talking freely about his dealings, in particular those with Harry Cole.

The Nottingham City Police will be sending a copy of the man's statement along with a list of gold items he had bought off Cole, among the items being listed is a heavy gold bracelet consisting of a band of linked hearts and matching earrings.

Another report includes a statement by Cole on how he bought and sold the two lorries used in the £3,000 Corah's armed robbery. Cole states he bought them speculatively at auction fully expecting to get his money back plus a small profit as he broke them up for spares and scrap. However, he was made an offer he just couldn't refuse. The lorries were collected on the day of the robbery by two men Cole had never seen before nor could he give anything more than vague descriptions.

DS Wilson's mental picture of Harry Cole focusses sharply to one of a man who fronts a genuine business with criminal undertones but the problem so far has been the lack of hard evidence against him. He feels that with the evidence now coming to hand it won't be too long before DI Clarke moves to make an arrest.

"Morning sir, still looking for a cyclist?" is the cheeky welcome from the guard at the main gate to Beaumanor Hall.

"Cheery as ever private, obviously you know me and this is DCI Johnson a Special Branch colleague who has an urgent appointment at the hall."

"Straight on sir, you will meet another check point but I'll phone ahead and get you waved through."

Policemen Johnson and Clarke are met by a bespectacled civilian in a dirty brown hounds toothed tweed jacket, cream coloured shirt and a red paisley cravat with worn brown trousers and well-trodden brogues.

"Boffin," thinks Clarke. Alongside the dishevelled boffin is a neatly uniformed army captain from The Royal Corps of Signals seconded to British Signals Intelligence, SIGINT.

DI Clarke's visit to The Bank of England and his revelations about large sums of counterfeit five pound notes had got the Old Lady of Threadneedle Street rattled. Rattled enough for its Chief Cashier K O Peppiatt to contact and have a word with the bank's Governor Sir Montagu Norman who in turn called the Chancellor of the Exchequer Sir Kingsley Wood to raise the bank's concerns. Wood wasted no time in calling on Winston Churchill.

DCI Johnson had been briefed personally by Prime Minister Churchill. Wasting no time Johnson had urgently requested the British Intelligence Service at Bletchley Park to search and see if it or Beaumanor Hall had any information that may give a hint to enemy activity of either agents or parcels being parachuted into the Midlands area. Since Johnson's request had been routed via MI5 and personally endorsed by the Prime Minister additional SIGINT staff had worked through the night checking records.

The extra night shift at Bletchley Park had paid dividends. Code breakers identified at least one message forwarded to them by Beaumanor Hall and Beaumanor had another still in its possession. When both are put together the result may prove to be of significant interest to DCI Johnson.

Across a table the boffin lays out the two messages as they had originally been monitored, they are meaningless gobbledygook to Johnson and Clarke. Next he lays out the decoded versions,

Mutter detached, on course, on time.

Kinder-B delivered.

DCI Johnson is becoming impatient and wants to know the boffin's thinking,

"Why do you think these are significant?"

"Gentlemen take a closer look. Separately they are simple and complete messages in their own right. Together, from the same source, maybe the same plane, we have a longer single meaningful message when translated.

Mother detached, on course, on time. Baby-B delivered.

"You said maybe from the same plane, were they?"

"We believe so; they were monitored on the 17th December. The first came in as two Dorniers bombed York. One plane left heading for the North Sea and the other we temporarily lost contact with as it lost height and probably crashed. A wrong assumption as it happens as it later appeared North-West of here heading straight for us as its likely secondary target. We had a similar raid a couple of years ago, almost to the date." The boffin takes a sip of water and continues,

"The second message was picked up as the Dornier was almost on top of us before climbing steeply heading towards the East coast and The Wash leaving the hall unscathed."

DI Clarke has a question,

"I thought your station monitored messages and not plane movements, how can you be sure about the plane's route?" The boffin responds with a sharp reply,

"We don't just monitor messages you know. We also monitor enemy flight paths and do direction finding. Soon we will be able to identify individual transmitters." Pompously adding,

"But you didn't hear that last bit."

DI Clarke is a little embarrassed at his ignorance but at least he has an answer that gives him the confidence to ask another without fear of further awkwardness.

"You said December 17th; do you think the wounding of a Home Guard private on the same night could be in some way connected with the messages meaning that Kinder-B or Baby-B was part of a delivery that ultimately killed him?" DI Clarke appears to have touched on a nerve as the up to now silent captain interjects,

"Not an unreasonable proposition, you seem well informed?" Having been on the receiving end of one embarrassing put down, DI Clarke sees an opportunity to recover some ground.

"Well, contrary to popular belief that most coppers in the sticks act as country bumpkins. Some of us actually do know what our jobs are. Some of us actually did read the Significant Incident Report for that day and it is surprising what a couple of pints will do to loosen tongues."

"What do you mean?"

"Having read the report I made a few local enquiries out here, at Quorn railway station, at nearby Woodhouse Eves and Beacon Hill including a call to the Loughborough Home Guard's commanding officer."

"And?"

"There were at least two explosions that night which appeared to be hybrid incendiary devices, one Home Guard private fatally wounded and apparently no further investigations made other than a post-mortem."

"You are quite right. The incendiary devices were new to us, not the usual stick or burst and scatter type and certainly not landmines as some thought, much too small by a long chalk. What you don't know inspector is that further inquiries were actually made and the findings were circulated on a need to know basis."

"And the police were not on the mailing list?"

"Err… Hmm… that's correct. But since you are here at the request of the Prime Minister I feel it is in order to safely say that we believe it was a failed attempt to lay sophisticated target flares on Beaumanor Hall prior to it being bombed. If the incendiary flares had been on target the Luftwaffe could have made a better attack on the hall than it did during the already mentioned raid two years ago when only a nearby farmer's field was blown up."

"Is that what you really think was happening on that night?"

"No reason to doubt it, two misplaced parachute flares and the unfortunate private HG 888 in the wrong place at the wrong time."

Now it is DCI Johnson, with a somewhat puzzled expression that enters the discussion.

"HG 888, I thought the Home Guard, like the regular army mostly had six or seven digit service numbers?"

"You're quite right. It was just that when this unfortunate man was first treated in hospital a piece of paper was found trapped between his hand and cheek as he instinctively held his face after the blast and on the paper was a series of numbers, the last three of which transferred and dyed into his skin. The attending doctor scrawled 888 in place of a name on the patient's notes pending a proper identification."

"Do you still have the piece of paper?"

"All of the man's effects, uniform etc. other than personal items, including any bomb debris on or about him will have been stored."

The meeting close, the boffin and captain are thanked and DCI Johnson and DI Clarke start their drive back to Leicester.

"Inspector, do you think that the counterfeits are this so called Kinder-B or Baby-B and delivered on the 17th?"

"Possibly, but a closer look at the 888 piece of paper is a must."

"I'll arrange for the captain to bring it to you personally, will that do?" DI Clarke answers with a broad grin,

"That'll do nicely."

The Bank of England's team, assisted by the Midland Bank's head office managers, has completed their accounting in Granby Street, Leicester. They have identified and confiscated £22,000 pounds worth of counterfeit fivers, another £2,000 will also go back to London for further examination. Such is the quality of the counterfeit banknotes there is a grudging admiration of the forgers work amongst the Bank of England staff.

The results of the inspection are soon passing along the polished corridors at the Bank of England followed by a series of communications escalated between Chief Cashier K O Peppiatt and its Governor Sir Montague Norman up to Sir Kingsley Wood, the government's Chancellor of the Exchequer and Winston Churchill in his capacity as First Lord of the Treasury.

The Bank of England accepts that there are a number of counterfeit notes in the British banking system and it stands resolute on its view that the economy is not at risk. However, the bank stops the production and issue of new notes of ten pounds and above: no real explanation for this decision is ever given. Thus it appears that the Old Lady is alarmed as perceptively suggested it should be by DI Clarke but the bank fearing it would trigger a run on the country's banks admits nothing publicly.

In his scrap yard Harry Cole sees another three wagons shunted towards the weighbridge and calls time for a mid-day break and a mug of tea. His two labourers eat bread and cheese next to a brazier keeping warm while Cole heads for his office and sips tea at his school ma'am's desk.

Cole is a little worried at the prospect of *Mercury* paying him a visit later in the week. Worried because he knows it is not usual to make face to face contact with a radio operator, so it must be of a serious and urgent nature. Confident he has tied up any loose ends Cole never the less makes arrangements for his own safety.

On his office desk he rubs an arm across *Mercury's* message *Abort Kinder B* to freshen it up and uses his penknife to score out the letters *HG*, using a capital G rather than the usual lower case letter *g*. *Hg* being the symbol for the chemical element Mercury. He encloses the message and added initials in a circle and talks softly to himself,

"Postcards, scratched messages, messages left in toilet cisterns are a little impersonal, let's hope Friday's meeting is a little more civilised."

Civilised he hopes it may be but Cole has been taught to be on his guard at all times and trust no one, particularly someone he has only ever met in a bath house. He prepares to defend himself, he unlocks the bottom drawer of an old plan chest and takes out a sawn-off shot gun, snaps open the barrel and spends his lunch break cleaning the weapon.

CHAPTER 16

WEDNESDAY 13TH JANUARY 1943

DS Wilson's press release has paid off, a smartly dressed woman, about Mary Frobisher's age and hair colouring was seen leaving the Bell Hotel in Humberstone Gate arm in arm with a well-dressed man.

The informant particularly remembers her as he was struck by the height difference between the couple, the man over six foot and towering over the woman a mere slip of a thing at something under five feet. The woman was reported as being drunk requiring all the assistance of the gent to stop her keeling over.

A second informant, a man, who did not want to give his name phoned in to say he first saw a couple of similar description to the one described in the press release crossing the canal at West Bridge. A few minutes later he saw the woman standing alone by the canal steps and had propositioned her thinking she was a prostitute touting for business.

Both informants gave sighting times as between ten and ten-thirty on Christmas Eve. This additional information fits in with the dead woman being in the water for 2-3 weeks and being seen with a man over six foot tall is regarded as significant as it points towards the missing womaniser William Markham as her escort and probable murderer.

"Looks more and more like he's your man Jim, any news on him?"

"Not a thing, it's as though he has disappeared off the face of the earth."

"Perhaps another press release concentrating on William Markham and his last known movements in Belvoir Street after leaving the Grand Hotel may jog even more memories, just where did he go on that bike ride?"

"Maybe sir, but there's something else we have to consider."

"What's that?"

"Mary Frobisher may have been killed by someone else, or if it was Markham he may have had an accomplice."

"Interesting and not impossible, tell me more."

"This came in this morning's post, a photograph of the jewellery alleged to have been sold by your man Harry Cole on his last trip to Nottingham."

The photograph is of a laid out unbuckled bracelet of eight inter linked gold hearts and matching earrings, the jewellery fits the description given by Mary Frobisher's helpful neighbour.

"Well I did tell you that Markham was pally with Cole. So now we have a likely connection between all three of them and there may yet be another if we can link Markham or Cole to Frobisher's murder. How Cole got hold of the bracelet is key to finding the killer."

"Shall I bring Cole in?"

DI Clarke knows his sergeant is champing at the bit but he allows a moment's pause, collecting his thoughts, before answering.

"No, not just yet. I believe our Mr. Cole is an even bigger fish to be caught than a simple fence or even a suspected murderer."

"What, you don't think he's involved in the armed robbery? Do you?"

"No, least not directly, let me explain."

DI Clarke concentrates his thoughts about Harry Cole. First he deals with the evidence about him being a fence as fingered by Charlie the Stoneygate burglar. Any evidence there is, is mainly a burglar's word against Cole's.

It is true that Cole deals in gold and occasionally travels to Nottingham to sell it on and he keeps accounts which in themselves don't mean he is not fencing stolen gold. However, the gold bracelet of hearts and earrings are a different matter altogether, so far there is nothing to suggest how they came into Cole's possession. Did he acquire the pieces legitimately or not still needs to be asked; the answer may show at best he is no more than a fence and at worst he is involved in a brutal murder.

"So why don't we just bring him in and ask?"

"Patience Jim, let me finish then I'll tell what's to be done."

DI Clarke collects a bundle of notes, swivels on his chair, stands and starts to pace around his office. He talks of a scenario that borders on the unbelievable but if proved to be right then Harry Cole, whether he is a fence, a murderer or neither, is certain to have an appointment with the hangman.

Choosing his words carefully, prompting himself with his extensive hand written notes, making sure he differentiates between what is fact and what is an idea, a theory or a supposition Clarke paints a picture that implicates a man serving his country in what he believes is a just and fair cause. Doing a job that will have disastrous repercussions for the United Kingdom and doing this work at the leading edge of the war with Germany.

Constantly checking his notes DI Clarke lists his information about Harry Cole that he believes implicates him in a much murkier world of foreign agents' intent on undermining the British economy.

1. An enemy aircraft releases two parachutes with what were believed to be hybrid incendiary devices at Beacon Hill. Both devices ultimately explode; one device mortally wounds a Home Guard private covering him with bomb debris including shrapnel and bits of paper.

It is a fact that the wounded private had a piece of a £5 note with a serial number that was one of the next hundred notes sequentially printed to those picked out by DS Wilson and later confirmed as counterfeit.

It's a fact that considerably less bomb debris was found at the site of the second explosion. Was something taken from the container before it self-destructed?

It is also a fact that Cole and Markham had spent some time together on Beacon Hill just four days before the night of 17th December. Could they have been checking the lie of the land or hiding signalling equipment, maybe the railway guard's lamp found at the site and almost certain to have been the one stolen from a railway hut near to Cole's scrap yard?

2. Before and after the parachuted incendiary explosions a Home Guard corporal and a private tangled with a cyclist near Woodhouse Eves on the steep road up towards Beacon Hill.

In the second incident the corporal and private are bowled over by a cyclist pedalling hell for leather downhill and away from Beacon Hill. The corporal cuts his hand on a sharp piece of metal; it is part of a heron's red head as found on a Raleigh bike's badge.

It's a fact that Cole has a Raleigh bike and its badge was cracked on the 13th December, the day of the Ratae Cycling Club's ride out to Beacon Hill as felt by DI Clarke snagging his glove on it.

It is a fact that DI Clarke has since seen the bike again and the badge is now broken with a piece missing.

It is a fact that Cole has a limp; the corporal thought the cyclist had injured himself in the collision or was it that the cyclist already had a limp?

3. A cyclist caught the last train out of Quorn station to Leicester and wouldn't be separated from his cycle, a cycle noted as having panniers and unusual for the time of year, there not being many casual cyclists or campers about in winter.

It's a fact that Cole's cycle has water proof panniers and had recently fitted a saddle bag. Were the panniers and saddle bag used for carrying something away from Beacon Hill?

4. Cole banks at the Midland Bank where William Markham is the assistant chief cashier and who, according to the manager, has a free run of the premises including the vaults as a trusted key holder.

It's a fact that Mary Frobisher worked with Markham and is known to have had some sort of relationship with him. What if Cole had made a collection at Beacon Hill and somehow with the help of Markham and possibly Frobisher deposited counterfeit notes, probably thousands of pounds face value, into the bank's vaults?

DS Wilson sits flabbergasted at what he is hearing. DI Clarke raises his eyebrows with a questioning look and asks,

"What do you think of it so far Jim?"

"Not sure I'm taking all this in. Can we adjourn to the canteen, teas are on me, I need to digest what you are telling me, is that alright?"

"Fine by me."

The canteen is empty allowing Clarke and Wilson to continue to talk freely. DI Clarke asks his sergeant what he thinks is going on.

"Sir, from what you say Cole, subject to a couple of checks, is an enemy agent. An agent who has received a barrow load of counterfeit money delivered as part of a parachute drop, then somehow gets it into a bank, why?"

"A barrow load of money deposited into a bank? I estimate at least somewhere between eighty and one hundred thousand pounds, based on what the panniers and saddle bag could carry assuming none was stashed into coat pockets."

"That's a lot of money."

"Yes and if you think about it Jim, if it ever got out that the banks were dealing in counterfeit money to the point of dishing out counterfeit wads of thousands of pounds what would be the result?

It would cause a run on the banks, confidence in the banks would disappear and the effects would be felt not just here but likewise around the world. It would be catastrophic for the war effort as falling confidence will soon lead to a falling pound on the financial markets and no credit means no armaments, no ships, no fuel and no food, you name it. Moreover, ordinary people like you and me, just like businesses will want to know that the pound in our pockets is genuine and if it's not the result would be chaos."

"Enemy agents, counterfeit money, failing banks, this is heavy stuff sir."

"No doubt about that."

"Can you be certain?"

"I'm pretty sure and with a few more checks to come I'm certain that there are too many connections between Cole, Markham and Frobisher for it all to be a just a coincidence."

DS Wilson returns to his earlier question.

"The armed robbery, you said Cole was involved in it but not directly?"

"That's right, his only part in the robbery is that he genuinely buys and sells the two lorries used by the gang.

I believe that the finding of the counterfeits after the robbery exposed the scam earlier than what may have been planned and is a stroke of good luck for us and bad luck on his part which may yet prove fatal. It's that stroke of good luck combined with the numbers found on the face of the unfortunate private at Beacon Hill and cyclists popping up here there and everywhere that got me wondering if there was more to Cole and Markham than was first thought."

"Always do with a bit of luck, eh sir?"

"Aye, and but for the robbery the dodge may well have succeeded with all its repercussions."

"What was The Bank of England's reaction?"

"It maintains its intransigent view that its banknotes cannot be equalled, let alone be mass produced as individual sequentially numbered notes.

However, I believe that the Old Lady is deeply worried at what you've helped to uncover. A certain Special Branch birdie tells me that the grandees have stopped printing and issuing any more new notes of £10 value and above. The only official reason being given on a need to know basis is that it's getting ready to impose controls on the international use of sterling once the war is ended.

Those at the bank are worried alright and nervous about the repercussions should this whole episode ever be exposed."

"So when do we bring Cole in for questioning?"

"No rush, we know where he is and at any rate others are interested in him now."

"Special Branch?"

"Yes and they're working for MI5 on this one. They hope to catch more than Cole and Markham, too late for Frobisher but certainly they will be hoping to take Cole's handler, reckoned to be a radio operator passing information to and fro between here and Germany, based in or close to Leicester."

"What's the general plan then?"

"For the unfortunate Mary Frobisher you can tidy up your findings and put your report to one side but without closing the file just yet. For William Markham we keep on looking. As for Harry Cole I have another meeting with Special Branch either tomorrow or Thursday to look at Cole and others who may be involved. The meeting will give us the nod as to when we bring him in. As I've said before it's a waiting game as MI5 look to widen the net."

"Softly, softly approach?"

"That's right and what we know, what I've put to you stays between us for the time being, not a word to anyone." DI Clarke anticipates Wilson's next question.

"Before you ask, you are in on the meeting with Special Branch."

"Thank you sir, my feet haven't touched the ground since I started here and glad of it, not least as I've said before it's kept me off the decorating. I did tell the Missus that we ought to wait for the better weather."

On the other side of town and in his office Harry Cole is busy with a meeting, a meeting with himself. He puts his concern about his Friday rendezvous with *Mercury* to the back of his mind as he sets about checking and rechecking his contacts with William Markham and Mary Frobisher. He senses it won't be too long before he is paid yet another visit by DI Clarke, not least since he has already had a visit from his colleague DS Wilson.

Cole also checks and rechecks his accounts, particularly his gold transactions notably those involving his trips to Nottingham. Like a bolt out of the blue it dawns on him that other than his visits to the bank the only other thing connecting him to Frobisher is her gold bracelet and earrings, the jewellery he bought from Markham who joked it was a present from her.

"A present, more likely a poisoned chalice?"

Cole has been assured by Vince, his contact for buying stolen gold or jewellery, that nothing could ever be traced back to him. None the less it's a worry that gnaws away at his gut as he chews on his bottom lip. He decides he will try and buy the bracelet and earrings back to melt the gold down or lose it where it will never be found, probably in the canal. He rings a Nottingham number, there is no reply: he tries again and again but still no answer. Often when alone, Cole thinks aloud, rather he talks to himself as if there was someone else in the room with him.

"Maybe he's out, I'll try again later. I worry too much."

Down in his air raid shelter, now used as a vault for cash and a macabre tomb, Cole checks his safe; once again he fondles and caresses forty wads of white fivers, genuine banknotes, a windfall, a £40,000 fortune.

Holding a couple of wads in each hand, he turns to look and admire his brickwork behind which lies the decaying body of William Markham. Patriotism now takes second place to self-preservation as he talks to Markham's corpse through the pointed brickwork,

"No Markham, unlike you I won't be too greedy. I'll show *Mercury* the counterfeit shit then abort it by burning it in front of him. As for this little lot he knows nothing and without him knowing, at a time soon that suits me, I'll cut and run, disappear and start again. Start a new life somewhere else because it's going to be rough ride around here with you missing and your lady friend dead in the water."

Cole returns the cash to his safe and goes about his afternoon shift in the yard. A shunter calls out to him,

"Things are looking up Mr. Cole."

"What's that all about then?"

"Police, finally, been showing a bit more interest in our missing lamp." Cole's hairs stand up on the back of his neck and his mouth slips a trickle of blood as he bites deep into his already chewed at lip. Cole returns to his office leaving a trail of spat out blood stains across a light covering of snow as the wet start to the winter turns decidedly colder.

CHAPTER 17

THURSDAY JANUARY 14TH 1943

Sat in a barber's chair DI Clarke watches the snow falling outside in Northampton Street next to Northampton Square, itself not much of a square, used as short cut between Upper Charles Street and Granby Street. It's busy in the barber shop with two chairs and a steady flow of customers.

"Usual Mr. Clarke?" asks a barber smart in black trousers, a white jacket with what hair he has left greased and parted down the middle. He knows that DI Clarke's automatic nod means a short back and sides, as all policemen have.

It's a pensive Clarke that lets the barber with his gold rimmed spectacles perched on the end of a hooked nose get on with his job. The constant snapping of the razor sharp scissors is not heard as he thinks about the day in front of him.

The main item in his diary is a meeting with DCI Johnson of Special Branch on how to deal with Harry Cole and others who may be involved in a plot to destabilise the British banking system by contaminating it with counterfeit £5 notes. Before that meeting he has an appointment at Gilroes Cemetery and the funeral of Mary Frobisher, former bank clerk identified as the dead woman pulled out of the canal between Hitchcock's Weir and North Lock. A distant cousin has come forward and made the necessary arrangements for her funeral and cremation.

Leaving the barber shop DI Clarke slips on compacted snow, trodden to an icy layer by workers making their way to nearby hosiery and garment manufacturers ready to start the day shift.

"Steady now Mr. Clarke, we want to see you in a fortnight," calls his barber who by now is not so smart, smothered in clipped greying hairs.

"I'll try to be Christopher, I'll be back." DI Clarke acknowledges the barber's concern with a wave of the hand before pulling on a trilby and crossing the road to a police car parked outside a gents' underground public toilet.

The snow eases and the clouds break showing a few patches of blue sky.

"Morning, Jim. Busy day today, starting with this sad business."

Mary Frobisher's funeral service is attended by just two relatives, a bank manager, a neighbour and two policemen led by a local vicar. From arrival at the crematorium chapel to the committal for cremation, the whole affair is completed in just fifteen minutes.

"No sign of Markham, sir?"

"No and not surprising, it was an outside chance he'd turn up."

The policemen's presence is acknowledged by nods, knowing looks and softly spoken thank yous and a firm handshake from the vicar, who continually mutters,

"Sad business, very sad."

DI Clarke offers the neighbour a lift, as hearse and cars go their separate ways snow starts to fall. The journey back to Kate Street and Charles Street police station is painfully slow as the driver struggles to control the car; the snow gets heavier laying a thick white carpet across the city.

"Got what we needed in court yesterday, sir?"

"Yes, further remands and probably best now to just pursue burglary charges against our friend Charlie. The charge of attempted murder of a police officer against chummy involved in the armed robbery might make him think more about his predicament and make him talk a little more."

"Special Branch, MI5 or whoever is behind this afternoon's meeting will be happy, at least there was no mention of counterfeits. What are you going to do for Charlie?"

"No deals, no promises made but don't be surprised if at the end of all of this he is paroled for good behaviour, earlier than what might be ordinarily expected."

Behind the white façade of Leicester's main police station a secretary makes ready a room for a meeting. She lays out pencils and note paper, arranges six chairs and places a jug of water and a tray of glasses in the centre of a polished mahogany oval table.

The meeting will be chaired by the station's detective chief superintendent, DI Clarke's senior officer. He is not in the chair for his knowledge of Harry Cole, that's down to DI Clarke and DS Wilson to provide, but to put the meeting on an equivalent level of rank with DCI Johnson of Special Branch.

Others at the meeting include Captain Smythe, a specialist in radio message tracking from British Signals Intelligence SIGINT and a civilian boffin clever with crosswords and maths, recruited as a cryptographer; someone who can decode gibberish messages and can see hidden meanings that lie behind decoded messages.

The meeting starts promptly at two-fifteen and is expected to last up to two hours. The usual courteous introductions over the chairman makes a point that whatever is discussed or information revealed or any actions agreed there must be no communication with anyone outside of the meeting without DCI Johnson's or DI Clarke's approval.

The chairman announces that DCI Johnson will lead the operation against Harry Cole with DI Clarke being his second in command. Clarke is not concerned at his apparent demotion in the case of Harry Cole; he is fully aware of and used to rank protocol between His Majesty's law enforcement agencies. Clarke also knows that with his general knowledge of Cole, his habits, his recent movements and contacts he is best placed to manage the legwork. Johnson on the other hand with his connections and experience in all-round policing, including Special Branch's work where foreign agents are concerned is the right officer to be in overall charge.

The first hour of the meeting is shared between Clarke and Johnson, briefing the meeting on what they know or suspect of Harry Cole as a fence and now as it seems a German agent. An agent who has been supplied with thousands of pounds worth of counterfeit £5 notes and has somehow managed to get unknown totals of forgeries into the vaults of at least one Midland Bank.

DCI Johnson confirms that his colleagues have established that Cole has no record of existence prior to his last job working as a supervisor in a local foundry. Leaving the foundry he rented a plot of railway land near and started trading as a scrap metal merchant.

"Simply put, Cole is a non-person, next to no records, no history beyond working in a foundry. Our best guess is that he is a sleeper agent activated sometime before the start of the war, maybe even set in place as long ago as the end of the last war. Until you brought him to our attention we had no inkling that he ever existed."

The DCI explains that Cole, working alone as a sleeper would be managed by a handler, someone possibly responsible for several agents. The handler will most probably be a radio operator acting as a go between for messages to and from Germany's SS-foreign intelligence service, a Nazi led organisation heavily involved in covert operations and is a parallel service to that of the Abwehr, the German Military Intelligence.

At this point the up to now silent Captain Smythe of SIGINT joins the briefing aroused by the mention of a radio operator and its implication of a radio transmitter operating somewhere close enough for Cole to pass on or receive messages. He confirms that although some signals have been confirmed as being transmitted from or nearby Leicester he is sure Cole has no such equipment.

"He is a relatively static target, living and working in a short radius and if he were using a transmitter it would have been targeted before now."

DI Clarke points out that Cole is a cyclist and is known to travel outside the city limits, this suggestion is politely set aside as improbable owing to the size and weight of the transmitter power packs required for long distance signaling. He would need at the very least, a medium sized suit case, and it would be heavy.

DCI Johnson sets out what needs to be done. He informs the meeting that Cole, currently under 24 hour observation will be arrested on Sunday morning at his home and at the same time his scrap yard and site office will be raided.

The three days until Sunday will allow the SIGINT teams to establish in the first twenty-four hours two tracking stations at separate locations to support Beaumanor Hall and then track any messages and locate the radio operator up to and after the time of Cole's arrest.

"Can't the SIGINT boys work any faster?" asks the Chairman. DCI Johnson nods towards Captain Smythe to answer.

"Sir, we are developing our radio message tracking hardware all the time, for this operation I have requested the latest and best equipment. It takes a little time to put teams and equipment together and since enemy transmissions are very short or often just a series of electrical pulses, some only lasting for a few seconds, I want to be sure we have the best available equipment so as not to miss a thing.

Ordinarily we would use two tracking stations to obtain a cross reference but we will boost our chances by providing a third; we may only get one opportunity and the more accurate we are at locating the source of a transmission the better the chances of the ground teams hitting the target.

Beaumanor Hall is our lead station and arrangements are well in hand to set up stations at the new RAF Leicester East airfield near Stoughton and at RAF Bitteswell airfield. Twenty-four hours is the maximum to set up, we may be ready earlier."

"Thank you. We are also aware of two messages that are believed to be connected with the German operation now thought to be called *Kinder-B* or *Baby-B* delivered on the 17th before Christmas, do our colleagues from SIGINT have any other information?"

Again DCI Johnson nods towards the SIGINT officer to answer. Captain Smythe clears his throat with a nervous cough and sips a mouthful of water.

"Since being alerted about the possibility of enemy agents and counterfeits being air lifted into the Midlands we have re-checked our records at Beaumanor Hall and Bletchley Park. We have batched together four messages that we think are relevant to the so called Kinder-B. There are the two you know about already:-

Mother detached. On Course. On Time

Kinder-B delivered

These messages were tracked on the 17th from the same aircraft that took a detour after a bombing raid on York. It was making what was thought at the time a target run on our monitoring station at Beaumanor Hall.

The next message:-

Abort Kinder-B

Monitored on the 21st from a location in Germany.

The implications being it is an instruction to stop, close down or destroy Kinder-B or it may have been sent as disinformation aimed at confusing us particularly as it came just four days after the drop, the Kinder-B counterfeits may have already been deposited in the bank." Smythe takes another sip of water.

"Aye, you could be right there, bank records do show that Cole visited the safety deposit vault on Friday the 18th and again on Monday the 21st," adds DI Clarke.

"The fourth message was monitored on the 24th from the same location in Germany:-

Clean up Kinder-B

At the moment it is anybody's guess as to its meaning and like the third message is treated with some caution it could be another to confuse our thinking. We now know that by the time this message was sent there is the high probability that there were already large quantities of counterfeits in the bank."

"£24,000 identified in the bank with another £2,000 as part of the armed robbery making £26,000 in all," adds DS Wilson.

"Maybe a whole lot more unwittingly put into the public domain by the bank itself and it's anyone's guess how much," suggests DI Clarke who pours a glass of water and pauses to take a drink.

"Furthermore, it would seem that the Midland Bank has been dealt a double blow. Not only has it been hit with thousands of pounds of counterfeits, it has been confirmed that following an audit of its note ledgers, all are in order and tally meaning that an equivalent amount of bona fide cash has been removed and replaced by the forgeries. Our friends Mr. Cole and his associates have been clever and now have a fortune in their grasp making our robbers look amateurs."

The SIGINT cryptographer, chewing on a pencil end, breaks his contemplative silence to add to the discussion.

"Gentlemen, there is actually a fifth message that has been identified and passed to me last night and I've been working on it. Whilst it does not mention Kinder-B specifically I think it is relevant when one takes account of what has been said so far. The message was monitored on the 23rd December from a source somewhere in the Soar valley area of Leicester."

Using a blackboard he chalks up four bullet points, writes out each section of the message and adds his comments as he does so.

> *Half package collected.*
> "This is interpreted as being confirmation that just one of the two containers contents was successfully collected at Beacon Hill".
> *Virus planted and spreading.*
> "Seen as an indication that counterfeits, even if not all of them, have been deposited into the Midland Bank which unwittingly is spreading them out to its customers etc."
> *Recovery Impossible.*
> "A confirmation that Kinder-B is inside the bank and doing its job as a virus would infect a body and is not retrievable having been moved on to other banks and customers."
> *1809.*
> "A numerical reference that so far has not been decrypted, but may be as simple as an identifier as to who sent the message or needs to be referred to a code book to be interpreted."

Pausing to catch his breath the boffin continues,

"Gentlemen, though it does not mention Kinder-B the significance of this message is that it is seen as a report on the status of that operation.

It is believed to be a direct response to the *Abort Kinder-B* message which may now actually indicate that there was an instruction to stop the operation but it came too late.

This fifth message was monitored just a few hours before the *Clean-up Kinder-B* was intercepted in the early hours of Christmas Eve which may now indicate that the agents are to hold their position, stop any new activities and destroy any evidence."

The chairman thanks everyone for their contributions so far and identifies the main actions aimed at taking two German agents into custody.

> 1. To locate the position of radio operator and his transmitter SIGINT will provide and set up two additional tracking stations, one at RAF Leicester East and another at RAF Bitesswell to work in conjunction with Beaumanor Hall. Captain Smythe will be responsible.
>
> 2. To provide a rapid response and close in and arrest the radio operator additional officers from Leicester teaming up with Special Branch officers will be posted in radio equipped cars or vans at strategic locations around the city and its sprawling suburbs for the duration of the SIGINT operation. DCI Johnson and DI Clarke have joint responsibility for this with DI Clarke in the lead.
>
> 3. Harry Cole suspected as being in the lead for introducing counterfeit five pound notes into the British banking system will be arrested on Sunday morning at his home. At the same time Cole's scrap yard and office will be raided and made secure for further investigation. The arresting Officer will be DCI Johnson, with the arrest facilitated by DI Clarke. DS Wilson will take care of the raid on the scrap yard.

The chairman goes on to say, "DCI Johnson will have overall responsibility for this operation. I propose to call it Operation Home Guard since we are taking on Germany in our own back yard and in recognition of and a tribute to the unfortunate private fatally wounded on Beacon Hill."

There are no dissenting comments, only gentle nods of agreement from those around the table.

"Meanwhile we keep tabs on the creature of habit Mr. Cole. How is this being done DI Clarke?"

DI Clarke explains that whenever Cole is on the move, not at home or at work, he will be tailed by three plain clothed officers who may be on foot, on a cycle or in motor transport: three teams of three rotating on a four hour shift on and eight hours off, 24 hours a day.

Whenever Cole is at home or at work he will be watched by static teams.

When at his home both the front and rear of the house will be kept under observation. The rear of the house will be watched from a van on the other side of the canal and at the front from a bedroom of an empty property almost opposite Cole's front door.

When at work Cole will be under surveillance from windows in a tower, part of the Great Central Railways electrical and hydraulic power house. Observer teams will have an all-round view of Cole's yard and office.

Each observation post will have a minimum of two officers working eight on and eight off.

"Bit of a drain on manpower?" asks the Chairman.

"Has to be sir, can't have Cole twigging a familiar face as he goes about his daily routine."

"So as we speak, Cole is at his scrap yard with two of our men watching with binoculars with another three officers ready nearby should he make a move?"

"Correct, sir."

"Mmm… thank you."

The meeting closes with DCI Johnson following DI Clarke and DS Wilson into the canteen where rotas are checked and rechecked over a cup of tea.

"Jim do we have the phones in place at the house and the tower?"

"In and tested."

"What about contact with the teams on the ground?"

"We have two radio cars or vans patrolling just off Cole's usual routes and we can turn round messages inside as little as a minute. It may mean a bit of a sprint now and again by the lads but the teams have had a few trial runs and are happy with what's laid on."

"Let's hope Cole keeps to his regular pattern and we just have a watching game on our hands."

DCI Johnson is impressed with the way the provincial team has set its stall out.

"Carry on like this and I'll be out of a job, good planning and team work between the pair of you. Well organised."

"Nice of you to say so sir but I think your job is safe enough. We have plenty of policing to do without fighting the enemy here on our own doorstep."

"What we didn't discuss are any contingency arrangements?"

"Not discussed but what we have in place will cover two possible events. Jim, you have your say on this."

DS Wilson describes that in the event of the surveillance cover being blown there will be an instant order to arrest Cole. If Cole loses his tail there will be an immediate clamp down at railway stations and at bus depots. Road blocks will be established to slow down traffic flows and vehicles thoroughly searched particularly lorries and vans, no matter how long it takes or amount of disruption caused.

"As I said I'll soon be out of a job. My men will all be armed, I advise you issue as many guns as you can, what we don't know about Cole or any associate of his is what fire power they have. We must be ready for anything."

"We will be ready."

"Right since I'm here for the duration, can you first recommend a barber? Afterwards I'll take the first round early doors at your watering hole the Spread Eagle, care to join me for a drink?"

"Thanks for the invite; try Pinder's hairdresser across the road in Northampton Street, tell Christopher I sent you, chat about photography, it's his hobby."

CHAPTER 18

FRIDAY 15TH JANUARY 1943

It is six o'clock in the morning. The cold bedroom air rouses Harry Cole from a whiskey induced deep sleep. He feels the chill in the bedroom as he swings his legs out from under the warm woollen blankets and stretches out groping for his trousers slung over a nearby spoon backed chair.

With trousers hitched over his hips and braces dangling at his sides he straightens a well-worn vest that's overdue a wash. Standing at the window he takes a peek through the blackout curtains and sees a blanket of snow covering as far as the eye can see. Snowflakes are still falling making drapes in the corners of the window panes.

Cole lights an oil lamp and gingerly steps his way down a flight of steep and narrow stairs into the middle room and tip-toes across to the kitchen where he lights a gas ring and boils a kettle. Snow is steeped against the kitchen door; Cole doesn't intend to struggle to the outside privy, runs the tap and pisses into the low stone sink.

Cole's flickering oil lamp is spotted through a chink in the ill-fitting curtains.

"I think he's up and about. Time 06.06," calls one observer to his bleary eyed colleague watching with binoculars through the back window of a van, a window that is forever misting over. The unmarked van is beyond the railings at the bottom of Cole's back yard on the other side of the canal.

Cole is soon wide awake after a shivering wash with the usual carbolic and cold water. The house is cold all over; Cole warms his hands above the kettle as it comes to the boil ready to make a pot of tea. Sipping tea from his tin mug Cole gradually gets more movement into his body and pulls on a thick cotton shirt and slips his braces over his shoulders, he is almost dressed and ready for work. Almost ready for work he may be but Cole has a few things to do to be ready for his meeting with *Mercury* later tonight.

On the underside of his rickety dining table he tapes a stiletto dagger, in a coal scuttle by the fire he drops in a sharp carving knife.

Pulling open a sideboard drawer he takes out a bundle of rags, unwraps it to reveal an ageing Webley Mark 4 revolver. He snaps it open and checks the cartridge cylinder, it's fully loaded. He snaps it back together and carefully cocks then un-cocks the firing mechanism, it's in excellent condition and working order. The gun is laid on the drawer bottom and the rags are laid loose covering it, he closes the drawer.

Inside a cubbyhole under the stairs, between the living room and the front room, stands a cardboard tube, out of it he pulls a sawn-off shotgun, he checks if it's ready for use, it is. Cole has now set out his defences ready for *Mercury's* visit at nine o'clock that evening; he hopes he is ready enough.

"I don't know the man, trust no one."

Cole sets about a daily domestic chore as he first clears the fire grate and sets a fire ready for later when he gets back from what he expects to be a cold day. Working outside in the open at his scrap yard in winter is never a pleasant experience.

"No bike today, I'll be better off just walking."

Cole sorts out a woolly jumper to go over his vest and collarless shirt, he pulls on his overalls and boots, ties string around the leg bottoms of his overalls and reaches for his dark blue duffle coat and a scarf. It's seven-thirty as he tugs on a cloth flat cap and with some effort ploughs his way, knee deep, through the snow in his back yard, he has some temporary respite down his shared entry before turning right into the snow blanketed Heanor Street.

With a shuffling gait he sets off to find the tow path at North Lock and battle his way through the unrelenting snow to his scrap yard.

"Target's on his way, on foot. Time 07.22; first tail on the move," is called and logged in another cold bedroom almost opposite Cole's house.

In Charles Street police station there is an air of quiet satisfaction in the knowledge that whatever Cole does or wherever he goes he will have company, arranged courtesy of DS Wilson. After leaving his house the two observers in the van at the rear of the house and the two in the house opposite in Heanor Street are reduced to one. This is a move forced on DS Wilson as officers struggle to get into work on time and in some cases not at all, the wintry weather is proving irksome.

Its hard work getting through the snow before Cole finally climbs the steps up from the tow path to Western Boulevard. He trudges across the road to his yard gates where both of his labourers have managed to beat the weather and get into work. All three know that there is little chance of doing any useful metal sorting let alone loading. Braziers are lit and Cole instructs his lads to busy themselves around the open fires stripping cables and rescue the much prized copper cores.

Two police observers, watching from a tall metal framed casement window in the tower of the electrical and hydraulic power house, strain to see the yard through the falling snow and have little of note to report; they know that they are in for a cold miserable shift.

Moored on the downstream side of North Lock below the North Bridge Inn is the narrow boat Mercury. Inside the cabin lying under several blankets, its owner, the German agent and radio operator *Mercury*, begins to stir.

Captain Smythe of the Signals Intelligence Service, SIGINT, is at RAF Leicester East and making an early call to Special Branch officer DCI Johnson.

"Good news and bad news Johnson, good news is we have our tracker installed here at Stoughton and as we speak it is being tested. Unfortunately the bad news is that the equipment for RAF Bitteswell is held up, it's off the road after a road traffic accident. Silly arsed driver put the lorry into a ditch blaming the snow."

"But you can operate the monitoring with just Beaumanor and Stoughton, can't you?"

"Correct, sir."

"So when will you be ready?"

"Mid-day at the latest, but I don't think we will hear anything today."

"How come?"

"The weather old chap, we're having some bother moving equipment and staff in this damn snow, our transmitter friend will have the same difficulties. Receiving won't be a problem for him but he'll not want to transmit without knowing that he can pack up and move on to avoid being tracked and pin pointed."

"Thank you Captain Smythe, keep me posted."

In Charles Street police station DS Wilson has set up an incident room, he has manned it with uniformed officers to answer phones, collate and index surveillance reports.

In the adjacent room, with its door always open, a radio operator can be heard in constant contact with eight police cars and vans testing their radios. These rapid response cars and vans need to be in position in and around the city by mid-day when the additional SIGINT tracking stations are operational.

"We'd have been short on radio cars had we not been able to call in a few favours from Nottingham, sir."

"Aye Jim, and just as well they came down yesterday before this lot set in," replies DI Clarke watching snowflakes the size of pennies fall thickening the white blanket in the street below.

"Least while it snows I doubt Cole will move too far, makes our job a little easier."

It's three o'clock and DCI Johnson and DI Clarke are at a meeting to review progress on Operation Home Guard. They have been joined by DI Clarke's boss, the station's detective chief superintendent and the chief constable.

The chief constable is aware that those directly involved in Operation Home Guard are busy and he begs their indulgence and provide him with as a full as a report as they can. He has a meeting with the prime minister and the home secretary at a police review meeting in Downing Street over the weekend.

DCI Johnson informs the meeting that the signals intelligence teams have two of three tracking stations set up at Beaumanor Hall and RAF Leicester East monitoring for enemy transmissions from the Leicester area. SIGINT is certain that there is a German agent transmitting from the Soar valley area and that includes anywhere in or around the city. The River Soar flows through the city and is in parts a canal. The SIGINT team at Stoughton has been operational since mid-day and the third station at Bitteswell is expected to be up and running by 8pm.

In readiness to swoop on a pin pointed target there are eight radio fitted police vehicles spread about the city and its suburbs. However, it is an unfortunate detail all that vehicle test response times have so far been patchy with drivers constantly battling against the heavy snow fall.

DI Clarke takes up the review stating that the surveillance of Harry Cole is working well and the arrangements for his arrest Sunday morning are in hand, those directly involved will be briefed on the day at 6am. Another brief at the same time will target Cole's scrap yard.

The chief constable is grateful for Johnson's and Clarke's time. Making to leave he comments,

"All seems to be well under control, well done so far. However, your biggest problem is the weather, it's forecast for another heavy fall, there'll be no going home tonight for some of the chaps I'm afraid."

"You're quite right sir, with the weather in mind DS Wilson has brought in the WRVS to man a 24 hour feeding station under the main stand at the

Leicester City Football Club. That, plus the good will of Corah's and our own canteens, should keep the lads out there happy."

At about the same time as the Operation Home Guard review the German agent *Mercury* is off his boat and making his way down Heanor Street from the Pasture Lane direction carrying a holdall and heading towards Cole's house. Heanor Street is buried under six inches of fresh snow, *Mercury* walks on the cobbled foot path following in the well-trodden line of footsteps of others making a fist of either getting to work or to secure what rations they can buy at Lottie's or from the ribbon of shops in North Gate Street.

Ahead of him and to his left almost opposite Cole's front door he sees a man in a rain coat with the collar turned up enter an empty house, a *To Let* sign is pasted over the front room window. Suspicious, *Mercury* quickens his pace and walks straight on by Cole's house and keeping his head low shields his face with his muffler against the snow or anyone who may be watching.

Moments later he sees an opportunity as a large van struggles in the snow as it turns out of Craven Street into Heanor Street and slowly makes its way towards him. *Mercury* turns and walks alongside the van's rear wheels and out of view. As soon as the van is alongside Cole's entry to the back yard he is down it like a sewer rat.

"Big van passing, 15.20," is logged. "Got to log something, this is bloody boring," a shivering policeman mutters to himself.

Mercury is confronted by a waist deep snow drift as he forces the back gate open just enough for him to squeeze through. Working quickly and quietly he slides a long bladed knife between the upper and lower halves of the living room's wooden framed sash window and eases the brass catch open. He lifts the window and in a matter of seconds he is on the inside with the window shut. Being on the inside is one thing but he knows he has a long wait for Cole before he comes home from work.

Mercury checks out the kitchen and leaves his holdall under the sink. Back in the living room he takes off his boots placing them out of the way to the side of the fireplace. A prepared fire is set in a grate supported by brass knobbed andirons within a decoratively moulded cast iron fire place with an oak mantel piece above. On the mantel piece stand two brass candle sticks and a small round faced oak cased clock. Unnoticed next to a candle stick, blown flat by the draught as *Mercury* opened the window, is a picture postcard.

In his stockinged feet *Mercury* carefully checks every cupboard and every drawer in every room of the house; he moves about silently and without any light. Coming back to the middle room on the ground floor, Cole's living room,

Mercury places a sawn-off shotgun, a revolver and two knives onto the table: he has laid bare Cole's defences. Under Cole's bed he had found a suitcase and a battered leather briefcase, he stuffs the weapons into the suitcase and stuffs it behind a copper boiler in the kitchen.

At the scrap yard Cole finally gives into the weather and calls it a day still with half an hour to go. He has not even made his usual trips to the slipper baths or the bank and pays his two labourers out of his pocket, giving them a fiver each.

"Sorry lads, no bank and no change today and with the weather as it is don't bother coming in tomorrow I won't be opening up, it's not worth it. Come back Monday; see what we can do then." Cole has a wry smile to himself as he locks the office door.

"Not been to the bank? Got a bank of my own now."

Cole sets off and is tailed on the return trudge along the canal tow path back to North Lock and calls at Burberry's in North Gate Street, then it's home to light the fire. Lying in wait for him is *Mercury*.

Arriving at North Lock Cole is picked up by another tail and on seeing Cole leave the fish & chip shop follows him through the jitty into Harding Street and towards his house in Heanor Street.

Mercury, still in stockinged feet, moves silently about the house and is now in the front room waiting for Cole.

"Target arrived house, 17.20 on foot."

Mercury can hear Cole going down the entry stamping and kicking his boots to clean off caked on snow. After a pause he hears Cole coming back along the entry.

"Target back in street, 17.22."

Cole is stymied by the back gate with its steep snow drift as high as the latch. Back in the street he fumbles with his key ring before eventually selecting a mortise key and unlocks the front door. He kicks his boots against the door step and is soon in the front room locking the door behind him.

"Target in house at 17.24."

The curtains and blackout are still drawn and the house is in darkness with everything appearing to be a different shade of black. In the gloom Cole's eyes adjust as he makes his way through the front room into the living room. He is instantly felled by a heavy blow to his right temple from a pistol butt, on his knees and groggy a second blow to the back of his head sends him sprawling to the floor and his parcel of fish and chips sent flying toward the kitchen door. *Mercury* stands above and astride his quarry apologising.

"Sorry about this 1809, it's just got to be done."

As sorry as *Mercury* may be, it means nothing to Cole who is dazed to a point of being unconscious. He hears nothing and is helpless and as limp as a wet rag as *Mercury* pulls off his blue duffle coat and slips a wire noose over his hands and binds his wrists tight together behind his back.

Leaving Cole almost senseless on the floor *Mercury* lights an oil lamp on the living room table. Picking up the lamp he deliberately walks around the house, upstairs and down as if he were Cole checking and tugging at the curtains and blackout making sure they were properly closed.

"Target moving about and now in kitchen at 17.43," is logged in the back of a van.

Mercury is making certain that if there are any watchers they will know that since Cole went through the front door all appears normal. He returns to the living room, pushes the rickety dining table to the side and places a chair in front of the set fire which he now lights. In the kitchen he lights a gas hob and puts the kettle on.

"Smoke from chimney, 17.50" is logged, "Looks as though target is settling in for the night."

Cole with his face pressed hard against the stone floor comes round and calls out,

"Who are you? What the fucking hell do you want?"

"Wait and you'll see."

Cole receives a kick to the kidneys and creases in agony. *Mercury* gets him by the scruff of his neck, drags him to his feet and manhandles him into the chair in front of the fire that now crackles and spits as the kindling sticks catch light, flames dance around lumps of coal and lick at the chimney flue.

"What do you want?" asks Cole again.

"I said wait and see," is the terse answer that came with a bone cracking thump to Cole's ribs.

Cole is beginning to hurt all over and bites his tongue as *Mercury* ties his body to the chair with rope to hold him firmly in place, each leg is tied to a chair leg.

Cole is totally disabled with his boot toes resting on a fender just inches away from the fire and is completely at *Mercury's* mercy. *Mercury* works feverishly to complete his task and with one of Cole's rolls of the newfangled duck-tape wraps the sticky material round the back of Cole's head and across his mouth to prevent him calling out again. Cole can hardly breathe as the tape covers his mouth and shoves his nose to one side.

Mercury has Cole where he wants him, he is in no rush, has a job to do and will only get one chance. He picks up the by now cold parcel of fish and chips and lays them close to the fire to warm up and feeds the fire with a few more lumps of coal adding a little slack. A pot of tea is brewing and *Mercury* takes a seat and devours Cole's evening meal. Cole strains to look sideways at him.

"No point in wasting these."

Cole has wriggled and twitched his nose about and gets his nostrils above the tape and is breathing a little easier and wonders what the burglar wants with him. It's not long before the penny drops and he realises that this is the same man who splashed soapy water into his eyes at the slipper baths, it is *Mercury* and he has come early.

Cole thinks about his two knives, sawn-off shot gun and revolver but that's all he can do. He is in a dire situation with his arms going numb tied behind his back and tied to the chair. His legs fare no better and are immovable, there is no slack in the rope ties.

Mercury is grateful for the fish and chips.

"Thanks 1809 not bad at all. Tea not bad either, but then I did have to make it myself."

The helpless Cole is not amused and can do nothing about his situation; he thinks that he must get a chance at some point to talk and maybe reason with his assailant. *Mercury* chucks the fish'n chip papers on the fire and pokes at it stirring the flames and leaves the poker in amongst the red hot coals.

Mercury picks up the lamp and leaves Cole alone in the dark. He repeats his walk around the rooms still suspicious that the house is being watched. Upstairs he leaves the front bedroom and walks through a second bedroom to the small box room at the back of the house. Here he leaves the lamp on a chest of drawers and returns to the front bedroom closing doors behind him.

Now in total darkness he gently eases the curtains apart and concentrates his gaze on the house up for letting. Sure enough, in the darkened bed room almost opposite he makes out the outline of a seated figure that hardly moves but is definitely there, waiting and watching. Carefully he closes the curtain, retraces his footsteps to collect the lamp and returns downstairs to the living room and Cole.

Mercury has been instructed to *Clean up Kinder-B* and although he knows he is at considerable personal risk of being captured he gambles that whoever is watching does not know he is in the house and that they will not move on Cole just yet. Better to wait and take him after he has gone to bed and during the early hours in the morning or even out in the open, if in deed taking Cole is part of their plan.

Taking a seat alongside Cole *Mercury* and sits in silence for about thirty minutes; the waiting raises the tension in the air as the mantel clock ticks and ticks time away. The silence is broken.

"1809 we need to talk, we have to talk. I will ask the questions and you will answer, understood?"

Cole, still with his woolly jumper and overalls on is uncomfortable as he feels the increasing heat of the open fire; he is puffed faced and sweats profusely as he nods in agreement.

"Ah, a good start, but now let's assume you don't answer or I believe you are lying and messing me about, what can I do? Don't bother to try and answer, I'll show you."

Mercury pulls the now white hot poker from the fire and without hesitation stabs it into the side of Cole's leather boot. The cured and work roughened hide smoulders and burns as the poker point passes through into Cole's ankle, the torturing searing heat is instantaneous as the flesh is burned and pierced. In an atmosphere of burnt leather and flesh Cole rocks about in agony fearing what is to happen next. *Mercury's* torture is over in a matter of a few seconds, he pulls the poker away and returns it to lie again among the red hot embers.

Waiting a few minutes more *Mercury* leaves Cole to suffer excruciating pain, to think about his predicament, to worry and become more fearful of what's to come.

"So 1809, that's a taste what will happen if you don't co-operate? If I have to reach for the poker again it will be one of your nostrils followed by one your earholes that will next feel the heat. Understood?" Cole who has no choice violently nods his head.

"Good 1809, now we can be a little more civilised."

Cole is still kept tied rigid to the chair, his body is overheating in front of the fire and his vision is becoming blurred as sweat now runs off his forehead and washes through his bushy eyebrows and curling eyelashes, he continually squints hard and shakes his head trying to clear the sweat to see what is happening around him.

Mercury still won't rush; he is deliberately debilitating Cole to a point that any question asked will bring a correct answer at the first time of asking. He stokes the fire making sure Cole continually feels the heat then runs the water tap in the kitchen; it runs a few minutes before he fills a tin mug full to the brim and places it on the table where Cole can just about see it.

"Want some?" Cole nods repeatedly until *Mercury* moves to stand behind him. Cole's bulging steel blue eyes flick from side to side not knowing what's coming next and suddenly gives out a contorted squeal of pain as duck-tape is ripped off of his face, instinctively he stretches his stiffened jaw and tries to lick his lips. *Mercury* offers the mug to Cole's lips but before he has a chance to even take a sip the mug of water is chucked at his face.

"Now is the time for some questions not water."

For the next hour Cole is asked questions, repeated questions, questions that are rephrased and asked over and over again until *Mercury* is satisfied he has all the answers he needs.

He is satisfied that Cole was working with two others, Mary Frobisher and William Markham who helped him to plant counterfeits into the Midland Bank and who are now both dead. Frobisher killed and dumped in the canal by Markham and Markham killed and buried by Cole somewhere he will never be found.

Mercury is sure Cole is telling the truth when he says only £50,000 of the £100,000 worth of counterfeit notes were collected at Beacon Hill and since deposited into the Midland Bank. Cole wasn't pressed as to how the counterfeits got into the bank's vaults and *Mercury* is unaware of the existence of the £40,000 genuine fivers in a safe beneath Cole's scrap yard office. *Mercury* must have assumed the forgeries were just a normal transaction and despite his deteriorating condition and state of mind it is a point not missed by Cole. *Mercury* pushes a mug of water at Cole's lips, he is allowed a few sips, just enough to help sustain consciousness.

Dehydrated, debilitated and at the point of losing consciousness Cole summons up strength enough to try to talk and make a deal with *Mercury* for his life. Barely audible, it's an exhausted man that mumbles through cracked and swollen lips trying to buy his way out of a situation that he knows is by now a death sentence.

"Release me, let me go and I'll make you a rich man."

"How? How can you do that?"

"I've done well at the scrap metal trade. This war is a big payer. I've got £10,000, let me go and it's yours. You got what you came for, let me go."

"Where is it?"

"Untie me and I'll take you to it."

"You must think I'm a fool. Where is it?" He lays a left hook into Cole's face, blood seeps from his broken nose, a right upper-cut to his jaw bursts a lip and more blood drips onto the floor. Cole is almost done for.

"Where is it?"

Cole's will is broken and he looks to the chimney breast and with a croaking voice,

"It's in the chimney... in the chimney, please let me go."

Mercury checks the chimney all-round and soon finds the dummy flue cover and pulls it off revealing a small safe.

"The key, the safe key where is it?"

Cole is unable to answer, *Mercury* realises it must be on his key chain. He easily finds it and is soon wafting wads of five pound notes in the air and under Cole's nose. Cole is resigned, knowing he is almost a goner but has a little comfort knowing he has probably done his best to take *Mercury* with him by feeding him £10,000 worth Kinder-B counterfeit fivers, hoping he will be caught out when he tries to spend it.

For the last time *Mercury* stands behind Cole who is by now in a state of delirium, the room is spinning. Feeling in his holdall *Mercury* pulls out a length of wire fixed with wooden toggles at each end and with his knee in the back of the chair he steadies himself. He carefully crosses his hands and slips a wire noose round Cole's neck, pulling harder and harder on the handles garrotting his helpless prisoner. Cole's blood-shot eyes bulge even more to the point where they must soon burst; he can't call out, not even in pain and is soon throttled to death. *Mercury* releases his grip patting Cole's shoulder.

"Sorry, 1809, I had to do it, just carrying out orders to *Clean up Kinder-B*."

So tight are the ties that *Mercury* tied around Cole's body to restrain him to the chair ensures that his lifeless body is held still upright in a sitting position, his head flops forward with his chin almost in his chest. His body lets out a last breath, a gurgling death rattle, he has breathed his last.

Mercury covers Cole's bloodied head with a tea towel and makes another pot of tea and calmly sits with his victim and considers his own situation.

"What to do now 1809? Done my orders, done my duty and now it's time to somehow save myself."

CHAPTER 19

FRIDAY NIGHT 15TH JANUARY 1943

Even as the lifeless Harry Cole is sat tied to a chair with a tea towel over his bloodied head, *Mercury* calmly finishes another mug of tea while he works out what he has to do to get away from the house in Heanor Street and safely back to his narrow boat.

Mercury keeps up the pretence that all is well in the house as he again walks from room to room carrying the oil lamp keeping the sharp eyed police observers busy.

It's nine o'clock and he decides to continue his charade by leaving the house audaciously disguised as Cole and head for a local pub and make good his escape from there. It is a daring plan but *Mercury* knows he has no alternative since there isn't any possibility of him leaving the house unseen.

The snow that started falling two days earlier has left a white blanket up to six inches deep and deeper where it has drifted. The snow clouds have cleared away and the temperature is dropping below freezing point. Snow becomes crusty and glints reflecting the bright moonlight making it impossible for anyone in Heanor Street to move about unnoticed.

Mercury pulls the briefcase from under Cole's bed and neatly packs in the ten £1,000 wads of Kinder-B counterfeit white fivers. Taking one of Cole's ties he threads it through the briefcase's handle and ties the ends together making a loop. He slips it over his head letting the briefcase rest snugly on his chest. He forces his stockinged feet back into his warmed up boots and slips on his jacket, he stuffs his muffler into one pocket and his gun into another. Cole's extra-large blue duffle coat is easily pulled on as an overcoat and the collar turned up. He picks up and tugs on the scrap dealer's trademark flat cap.

Before unlocking the front door *Mercury* stands straight checking if the duffle coat is buttoned up and the cap is on tight. Taking in a deep breath of the cold night air he is soon on the outside, turns quickly on the step and locks the door. All the police observer can see is the hunched back of a man wearing a duffle coat and flat cap.

"Target leaving house on foot at 21.10. Tail has him in sight."

In the crisping, glistening moonlit snow *Mercury* soon senses he is being followed. He trudges through the snow crossing Heanor Street into Craven Street and then into Harding Street where at Lottie's sweet shop he diagonally crosses the road and steps into the Freemans Arms public house. His tail holds back and from the steps of Lottie's sweet shop watches the pub from the corner of Johnson Street and Harding Street.

Inside the Freeman's Arms *Mercury* passes by the Tap Room and the Off-licence sales hatch and goes into the back yard looking for the toilets. He quickly takes off Cole's duffle coat and cap and wraps his muffler round his neck and half covers his face. The briefcase with its £10,000 is still hung around his neck and under his jacket. As he leaves the toilet Cole's coat and cap are thrown amongst the empty beer barrels in the snow covered yard.

Leaving the pub are a man and his wife, *Mercury* follows them out into the street. He deliberately walks and pushes in between them putting his arms around their shoulders feigning to make out they are all friends together. Not to cause any alarm, he quickly removes his arms and softly apologises for his mistake but stays in between the man and woman.

"Sorry about that folks, thought I knew you, do you know the way to the North Bridge Inn?" His ruse works as he gets the reply he was hoping for.

"Come with us mate, through the jitty and we'll soon be there."

Mercury's overtly friendliness is enough to convince his tail that they are three friends out for a night's drinking, he remains on the corner rubbing his hands and stamps his feet to keep warm waiting for Cole to come out of the pub.

Once through the jitty into Northgate Street the trio of drinkers turns right and heads for the canal and the North Bridge Inn. *Mercury* leads the couple into the public bar and before they realise it he is out through the back smoke-room side door and down the canal steps unseen onto his narrow boat moored just clear of the lock.

Outside Lottie's sweet shop a boy aged about twelve brushes past the tail who reprimands him with a threat to cuff him around his ear.

"Sorry mister got to fetch Mr. Cole."

"You say Cole, why?"

"His bloomin' house is on fire at the back. Police already called the fire brigade, fire engine on its way." The boy scampers off into the Freeman's Arms public bar shouting,

"Fire, fire, Mr. Cole are you in here, your house is on fire?"

"Not in here tonight laddie, not seen him at all. Now you get out," is the sharp reply from the landlord. The boy rushes out and falls into the arms of Cole's tail.

"Sorry again mister, he's not in there, most probably at the Heanor Boat, someone else gone to fetch him from there."

The pub starts to empty as drinkers hear the boy's news and set off to watch or if still capable lend a hand. The tail goes into the pub finding it all but empty.

"No Mr. Cole tonight?"

"No, who wants to know?"

"Have you a back gate?"

"Out the back with the toilets but it's locked and only used for deliveries. Who are you?"

The policeman doesn't answer and races to check the back yard where he finds Cole's abandoned duffle coat and cap.

"Damn it."

In the incident room at Charles Street police station DS Wilson takes a call, not only has Harry Cole slipped his tail but his house is now on fire. A fire engine is struggling in the snow to cross town from its station in Lancaster Road.

The air of satisfaction at the police station has evaporated, the police assume Cole had changed his appearance and has done a runner. DI Clarke orders railway stations and bus depots to be watched and road blocks to stop and search what little traffic there is leaving the snow bound city. DCI Johnson is initially livid,

"How on earth did we lose him Clarke?"

"Suckered by the quick change of hat and coat routine. Cole's duffle coat and cap found in the pub yard. He never even stayed long enough for a drink."

"Well he won't get far tonight. Few trains and even fewer buses, road traffic is light enough for us to handle, luckily this damn snow is as much a hindrance to him as it is to us. Also, we've got search patrols out within a mile radius of the pub but unfortunately there are plenty of maybes but no actual sightings of him as yet. My guess is that if we don't pick him up by midnight he'll have gone to ground."

"What puzzles me sir, is why tonight in this weather as you say it's a hindrance to us all?" asks DI Clarke.

"Maybe he spotted his tail earlier or maybe Markham tipped him off. Anyway, don't worry about it Wallace these things sometimes happen to the best of us." DI Clarke is grateful for DCI Johnson's comments. Johnson continues,

"Even the best laid plans can foul up, and I've had a few. We've been rumbled by Cole and constantly stuffed by the weather so what we need to do now is to regroup, rethink our strategy and redouble our efforts, I suggest we meet at eight in the morning. I'm off to my room, call me at the Grand if needs be."

"Right, eight o'clock it is and thank you, sir."

Mercury is safe on his boat, least that is what he hopes. In the clear night air he can hear the pandemonium surrounding the fire at Cole's house where he'd left Harry Cole, agent 1809, dead. Cole's body had been cut free by *Mercury* who pushed it onto the floor rolling it face up and doused it with petrol. Next he set a device with a slow burning fuse that would erupt into a ball of flames intent on causing a distraction and later confuse the police as to a corpse's identity found among the debris.

Mercury had filled a balloon with petrol and suspended it over the table using a length of jute string twine from a hook in the ceiling rose. The string was then run around a second hook on the picture rail above the fire place its tail end tethered to a nail hammered into the middle of the table. The balloon was suspended two feet above several drawing pins set pointing upwards; a candle had been placed below the string where it made an angle with the table. *Mercury* lit the candle just before he left the house.

A yellow flame licked at the twine and *Mercury* reckoned he'd be about five or so minutes clear of the house before the string is scorched, set alight and burnt through releasing the balloon to drop onto the pins bursting and spraying its flammable liquid about the table and onto the floor and ignited by the candle flame ensuring the room erupts into an all-consuming fire.

First sign of a fire was when the next door neighbour taking a pee in his outside toilet heard the living room window's cold glass panes crack and shatter having been suddenly subjected to the immense heat of the fire.

Soon at the chaotic scene are many neighbours doing what they could to quell the flames before the Fire Brigade arrives. In Heanor Street the front door has been kicked in and a human chain passes bucket after bucket of snow or water to a man standing at the living room door holding the fire at bay by wetting the walls and dousing the creeping flames.

Another dare devil neighbour has climbed a ladder into the front bedroom and hurls buckets of water onto and down the steep narrow staircase and walls preventing the fire spreading upwards towards the bedrooms. The two pronged attack stops the fire spreading to the first floor but the living room and kitchen are well alight and cannot be entered.

A third human chain is made in the back yard lifting and passing buckets of water out of the canal to add to the attack on the fire.

The goodwill of the neighbours in breaking in at the front of the house has unwittingly added to the fierceness of the fire as they create a flue effect between the front and back of the house. A strong flow of air blows through the living room and kitchen feeding the fire it with a plentiful supply of oxygen ensuring an almost total incineration of anything in the two rooms.

The Fire Brigade finally arrives and takes control, hoses are connected to a hydrant in Heanor Street and more water is pumped from the canal. The Fire Brigade provide a welcome respite to the by now knackered neighbours who mop brows with sweated handkerchiefs or cool faces with a hand full of snow.

Thanks to the quick thinking and fearless neighbours the front room and bedrooms are saved but the living room and kitchen are gutted and are blackened caverns with tables, chairs, sideboard and cupboards almost burnt to a cinder with doors and windows badly charred and paintwork blistered. Every pane of glass is broken either by the searing heat or by the neighbours attempting to try and douse the flames. Parts of the living room's plaster ceiling and its ornate rose have collapsed onto what's left of the furniture and floor. Walls affected by years of rising damp have sheets of plaster lifting and breaking away from the solid brickwork. In front of the fire place and buried by the debris is what remains of a badly burned body waiting to be discovered.

Cole's house is now watched by a different set of watchers, the men of the Fire Brigade who with the tremendous effort raised by the neighbours have contained the fire, put it out and will until daylight keep spraying and dampening down to prevent hot embers reigniting.

In the police canteen DS Wilson catches up with his DI.

"Why do a runner now and in this weather, did he latch on to us, what's the house fire all about, what do you think sir?"

"Plenty to answer there Jim, let's see what DCI Johnson has to say tomorrow morning. Oh, you'd better bring Cole's bike in, let's take a closer look at the badge and see what's missing."

CHAPTER 20

SATURDAY 16ᵀᴴ JANUARY 1943

The search for Harry Cole, suspected German agent, gains a fresh impetus as day breaks over a snow bound Leicester. DS Wilson has re-organised plain clothes CID and special branch officers to support the uniformed constables searching for Cole. Homes and businesses, within a mile radius of Cole's last known sighting at the Freemans Arms public house in Harding Street are paid another visit.

Cole's scrap yard is surrounded by drifts of snow with no recent sign of it being entered and just in case he returns it is kept under surveillance from windows high up in the Great Central Railway's electrical and hydraulic power house.

Captain Smythe of SIGINT rings Beaumanor Hall and the two new message tracking stations at the Stoughton and Bitteswell airfields. The stations have nothing to report, there have been no unaccounted for transmissions in the Soar valley and surrounds.

The fire at Cole's house is out and dampening down completed. Breakfast for the weary firemen is a mug of tea and a bacon sandwich supplied by a WRVS mobile canteen. A senior fireman checks the living room and kitchen for the cause of the fire, later a building surveyor will check if the building is structurally sound or if it requires partial demolition or temporary support to make it and neighbours' homes safe.

At the first hint of daybreak *Mercury* is up, stove lit and a kettle of water is almost boiling as the boat's steam engine powers the boat into the North Lock ready to be lifted to the upper level.

Mercury is heading up stream and moor between the spur to the Old River Soar, just by the Walnut Street Bridge and the next lock at Freeman's Meadow. The air is cold and the sky a clear blue, it's going to be a bright sunny day.

On the canal tow path and banks the snow has crisped up and as the sun rises it has a pretty Christmas card look about it. Pretty it may be but *Mercury* is glad to be out of it and sipping tea in his warm cabin. Despite his present precarious situation he thinks of warmer climes that will now be available to him being £10,000 richer.

In Charles Street police station the incident room is still staffed. The radio operator next door is in contact with the eight police cars and vans waiting to race to a pinpointed location identified by SIGINT and apprehend a German radio operator.

DCI Johnson of Special Branch has held a review meeting about what's to be done following the previous night's fiasco when, as he has conceded, Cole cleverly slipped his tail.

Owing to the well organised Leicester CID the review is little more than a rubber stamping exercise, DCI Johnson has agreed with DI Clarke that for the next twenty-four hours DS Wilson's search pattern is to be continued and widened, Captain Smythe has been instructed to keep the highest level of concentration at the tracking stations, monitoring for any message out of Leicester and the surrounding area, searching for any message that can be linked to Kinder-B. DI Clarke's boss has abandoned the need for rank matching at any meetings with DCI Johnson and is happy to allow DI Clarke to get on with it provided he is kept informed of progress.

DI Clarke stands at the top of a flight of stairs chatting with his DCS when he hears the heavy stamps of shoe leather on stone treads. It is DS Wilson with an urgent message.

"Excuse me sir, I think DI Clarke should see this," the DS passes a pre-printed form used by the radio operator; on it is a scribbled out message from the Fire Brigade in Heanor Street.

Heanor Street fire is out.

Body found during clean up.

Police attendance requested.

"Thanks Jim; excuse me sir I'd better get over there. Jim you get a message back to stop any more cleaning up till we've had a chance to have a look, go and get the car I'll tell DCI Johnson on the way out."

In Heanor Street there is a tinge of burn in the air, a mortuary ambulance waits as firemen wash down and roll up lengths of hoses. The two policemen go down the entry to the back gate where burnt pieces of what remains of furniture litter the slush covered blue bricked yard. A fireman is collecting fire buckets and is tidying up.

"Is it safe to go in?"

"Yes, it's safe but be careful of your footing. The body's in there." The fireman points through the rectangular hole that was once the living room's sash window. The crumpled outline of a body can just be made out in a rounded heap of ashes and broken chunks of ceiling plaster lying in front of the fireplace.

"It's not a pretty sight."

DI Clarke calls for a torch to better light his way and taking great care not to disturb any possible evidence he goes through the kitchen into the blackened living room.

Moving towards the body he can see it is an adult and probably a man. The torch is held nearer to the head and Clarke winces at the sight of flesh having been burnt off and exposed skull bone has been charred by the fire. Turning away he looks around at the total destruction of what was once Cole's living room.

The oak mantel piece above the fire place is charred and what remains clings precariously to the damaged plastered wall, on it a clock is just a blackened dial with its brass dial and movement laid bare. Two brass candle sticks stand in patches of re-set candle wax. Close to one candle stick under a protecting layer of broken bits of plaster and soot blackened dust is a post card.

Curiosity gets the better of DI Clarke and using his pocket penknife teases the card free of the fire debris and gently tips it up to stand against the wall, it is a picture postcard of a granite strewn hillside.

"Here Jim, take good care of this and then call for a photographer and the rest of the forensic team. I'll inform the coroner and organise a post-mortem, we'll be treating this as a crime scene till we know anything different."

"First Miss Frobisher, could this be Markham and another murder, sir?"

"Who knows, let's get what we can find here, wait for the post-mortem and see then what we are dealing with. Meantime get word out to the lads that if Cole is found he must be approached with extreme caution."

What remains of the partially cremated body is carefully lifted into a tin coffin and removed to the police mortuary and a post-mortem.

Moored at Freemans Meadow Lock *Mercury* is satisfied he has *cleaned up* Kinder-B; those involved on the British mainland are dead. William Markham has killed his bank colleague and would be lover Mary Frobisher who had wished for better things with Markham who is also, according to Cole, dead and buried.

The unfortunate Cole who played his part in operation Kinder-B so well has found himself on the wrong end of an order from Walter Schellenberg, Head of SS-foreign intelligence.

Mercury now needs to inform Schellenberg that Kinder-B has been *cleaned up* and is no more except for the £50,000 worth of counterfeits he is certain Cole and his two helpers managed to get into the banking system before the abort command was received. He prepares his message and encodes it for transmission later, he keeps it short:

Kinder-B. Cleaned Up except for half of virus.

Mercury is becoming increasingly worried that the net cast by the British police is closing in on him; he has noticed the increased police foot and motor patrols either side of the canal particularly near to Cole's house and now at his scrap yard.

Wary of his transmitter being tracked *Mercury* has it in mind to make his next message to Schellenberg his last before going to ground for some time, probably forever. He still has Cole's keys and he decides on another audacious plan, he wants to move his transmitter to Cole's scrap yard office.

To check how he can best move his heavy suitcase of equipment unseen by the increased patrols *Mercury* reconnoitres the route from his boat to the scrap yard gates. He walks the tow path from Freemans Meadow Lock to the Walnut Street Bridge and climbs stone steps to Western Boulevard, a tree lined road that stands about twelve feet above and parallel to the canal. Just as he reaches the top of the steps he sees, to his left and high off the ground, a flash of reflected sunlight, a reflection from a window high up in the tower of the Central Railway's electrical and hydraulic power house. He recognises it as probably someone with binoculars; he instinctively knows the scrap yard is being watched more carefully than just a passing police foot patrol.

Mercury tugs his cap down, pockets his hands and hunches his shoulders, crosses the road and continues on as though he has seen nothing and keeps close to the railings. He catches up with a wretch pushing a pram full of coal slack scavenged off the snow covered railway sidings for the price of a tanner paid to the sidings foreman, a tanner he regards well spent. *Mercury* keeps the poor sod company till he is past Cole's scrap yard gates and out of the watcher's line of sight below the power house tower. He crosses back over the road to the canal bridge at Mill Lane.

Quickly down the steps and back onto the tow path and under the road bridge *Mercury* engages in a conversation with a passing boatman. A narrow boat is steered towards the path and *Mercury* jumps aboard for a lift back to Freeman's Meadow Lock. At the Lock *Mercury* repays a favour and helps with the lock paddles and gates before boarding his own boat to reconsider where best he can transmit his message from.

Mercury forgets about using Cole's office and intends to move his boat to a position opposite the scrap yard gates reckoning that if his transmission is tracked it will be at best be the yard and office or at worst a vehicle on Western Boulevard that will be targeted; no one, he hopes, will suspect a narrow boat.

Following the transmission the radio set and all its trappings, including aerial and power pack, will be ditched in the canal and *Mercury's* boat will be just one of several already moored on the wide straight between Walnut Street and West Bridge.

DI Clarke and DS Wilson attend the police mortuary to hear at first hand the post-mortem results on the body found under the ashes and fire debris at Cole's house.

"Good afternoon gentlemen I've completed the gory bit and you've missed something special. However, this will interest you, we started with an apparent victim of a fire, but it is actually a murder. A messy one at that and were it not for the body being partially protected by plaster off the ceiling and walls much of the evidence would have been lost."

The police surgeon talks in plain English, the medical terms will follow later in his report. The cadaver, as Clarke suspected, is male about five foot nine inches and was dead before the fire started, there being no signs of smoke inhalation or soot particles found in what's left of the mouth, nasal cavities or lungs. It has several broken ribs, one puncturing a lung, a broken nose, a deep burn hole into an ankle, two depressed skull fractures and what's left of the skin is pretty well bruised all over. The coup de grace was death by garrotting determined by the clear signs of a wire cutting into the neck's skin compressing muscles and blocking the windpipe: cause of death is asphyxiation by throttling.

"Now what do you think about that?"

"Another murder, but who is he?"

"Well it can't be Markham, too short by five or six inches," says DS Wilson.

"Well. It's got to be someone, any finger prints?"

"Just a thumb and part of fore finger, fortunately the body must have been rolled over partly trapping the right hand under its back protecting part of it from the fire, forensics are working on it."

Saturday afternoon is proving to be quiet, too quiet, at Charles Street police station where the incident room is taking fewer and fewer reports, there are no definite sightings of Harry Cole.

"DI Clarke, there's no point in carrying on with the full team; I'm going to withdraw the extra uniform lads and my chaps off the search, any comment?"

DI Clarke is still smarting at Cole slipping through his fingers but is in full agreement with DCI Johnson's proposal.

"You're right, sir. He could be anywhere by now. He'll need to break cover sometime and we'll need a little bit of luck when he does."

DS Wilson is instructed to withdraw the additional uniformed constables; some go home well pleased with overtime coming to their pockets while others return to their beats keeping the City of Leicester safe. DCI Johnson pulls in half of his team allowing them to catch the next train back to London. He keeps the remaining officers to help man the eight radio vehicles for another forty eight hours.

On the canal *Mercury* moors his narrow boat in the failing light, tying up almost opposite Cole's scrap yard gates. He settles in and with hours to kill he sets about making a hot meal of a small piece of boiled bacon, boiled potatoes and a carrot. Beverage is a can of tea without milk or sugar, he doesn't have any.

DI Clarke and DS Wilson are at RAF Leicester East airfield at the invitation of Captain Smythe who is treating them to a plate of sausage and eggs; a feast of a meal in wartime Britain and is the first decent meal either man has had in the last two days.

"Now then chaps how about a drink, a tot of whisky before I show you how we operate?" On duty or not DI Clarke likes a drink and nods his approval, he and DS Wilson are presented with a good measure of a Glenfiddich single malt scotch, a Christmas present to Captain Smythe from his mother.

"A rare treat captain: thank you."

"Surely is," adds DS Wilson.

It's another cold clear night as the three well fed men make their way across a snow covered field. A radio truck is parked in a secluded corner some distance away from the airfield's control tower and purposely sited to reduce the amount of radio interference. Above the truck its direction finding aerial is arcing rhythmically left then to the right and back again as the operator scans the airwaves. Inside the operator with head phones on concentrates on identifying unusual signals passing through the ether, searching for that signal which is not from a recognised direction or source.

Once a signal from an unknown source is picked up the operator will take control and manually pan the aerial to locate the line and direction of greatest signal strength and read off a bearing along which the rogue transmitter is located. This bearing when combined and crossed referenced geographically with bearings from Beaumanor or Bitteswell or both will pinpoint the target to an accuracy of 30-50 yards.

"We are refining our equipment and target accuracy all the time. Soon we will be spot on," boasts Captain Smythe.

The tracking operator raises a hand to shush the background conversation, she has picked up a rogue transmission and is scanning for the direction of the strongest signal, it's a coded Morse signal.

"Sir, I have a strong signal and a bearing."

A phone rings, it's Beaumanor Hall and it too has tracked the same transmission, the two bearings are plotted on a map and a crossing point identified. A third reading from Bitteswell confirms the location as a pin is stuck into the Great Central Railway's sidings on Western Boulevard, Leicester. Police radios crackle into life and the race is on to hunt down the transmitter and catch its operator.

"Look where it is Jim, it's got to be Cole's scrap yard." DI Clarke is almost right and *Mercury* would be smug if he knew the policeman's thinking.

Mercury rubs sweat away from his eyes and works feverishly to complete his transmission. He dismantles the radio equipment and ditches everything into the murky canal well before the struggling police reach Western Boulevard and Cole's scrap yard.

The scrap yard on Western Boulevard is approximately half way between bridges at Walnut Street and The Newarke and opposite to the intermediate canal bridge at Mill Lane. Police cars and vans block access to the road at the three bridges while two other cars travel along Western Boulevard towards each other looking for anything suspicious as they close in on Cole's yard.

In his boat, behind closed cabin doors and curtains, sitting in silence in total darkness *Mercury* watches and listens for any police activity on the tow path. Resting on a knee he holds a Luger in his right hand and caresses its barrel with his left, he is tense and sweating, hoping all the time he is safe.

On the road above the two police cars come together outside the scrap yard gates, nothing suspicious has been found; a parked lorry and car have had their bonnets felt and were stone cold, none the less they were broken into and checked over just in case.

By the time Western Boulevard had been checked and nothing out of the ordinary found DI Clarke and DS Wilson have arrived closely followed by the alerted DCI Johnson. Harry Cole's scrap yard is immediately surrounded by uniformed police posted at twenty yards intervals. DS Wilson orders a burly officer to cut the chain securing the gates.

"What's your plan Clarke?" asks DCI Johnson.

"Sir, we'll go in at first light, too dark to do a thorough search. If he's in there he's going nowhere, DS Wilson has the place surrounded."

"Can you be sure you have him?"

"No, and if he were in a car or truck we've already missed him."

"What about the canal?"

"Five boats, no sign of life and all tucked in by the look of it. Man posted nearby."

"Alright, but if Captain Smythe reports any more transmissions you go in and whenever you go in just be careful, I want him alive," are DCI Johnson's last words before returning to his room at the Grand Hotel.

DI Clarke leaves DS Wilson at Cole's scrap yard gates and returns to his office intent on getting a few hours sleep. In his in-tray lay a sealed envelope marked urgent and had been delivered by hand from the Forensic Department. Opening it he reads a simple message identifying the body found following the fire at Cole's house in Heanor Street, pursing his lips he carefully folds the message and places it back in the envelope. Taking an easy chair he loosens his tie and cat naps.

In Berlin, *Mercury's* decoded message to the SS-foreign intelligence is passed to Walter Schellenberg bemoaning his waking.

"This had better be worth it." Schellenberg reads the message.

Kinder-B. Cleaned Up except for half of virus.

"Excellent news, pity about the £50,000, still it can't be traced back to me."

Schellenberg returns to his bed and wakes his whore for the night, he is well pleased with his efforts to recover a situation that could have seen him and Major Krueger posted to the Russian Front or even suffer a worse fate.

CHAPTER 21

SUNDAY 17TH JANUARY 1943

I t's eight o'clock Sunday morning and even at this time the blocking off of Western Boulevard by police vehicles and posted constables has attracted a few curious onlookers. On the adjacent canal, life stirs among the boatmen and a flotilla of five narrow boats set off heading downstream, down the long straight towards West Bridge and beyond Hitchcock's Weir, North Mills and into the North Lock.

Mercury on board Mercury steers his boat stern faced looking straight ahead ignoring the enquiring glances of the uniformed policemen standing on the tow path or looking down from bridges above.

At Cole's scrap yard gates there is an air of anticipation as adrenalin levels begin to rise.

"Ready, Jim?"

"Yes sir, we have fresh men all-round. Six armed officers with me going through the gate to take the office, another twelve armed men to scatter and search the yard."

"Good, that's good but before you go in look at this." DI Clarke hands over the message from the Forensic Department. DS Wilson's eyes lock onto two lines of words.

Heanor Street house fire: Body identified as a Mr. H Cole of the same address.

"Shit. Frobisher dead, Markham missing and now Cole is dead too. So who have we been chasing, who's likely to be in here?"

"I think it's fair to assume by now that Markham is also dead and that Kinder-B has been *cleaned up.* We are certainly chasing a bigger fish than all of those three put together, the agent who has been transmitting and receiving messages from Germany and likely the one responsible for the so called cleaning up of Kinder-B.

He's someone of interest to us in the murders of Miss Frobisher and Cole and probably Markham as well, but he'll be of even greater interest to DCI Johnson of Special Branch and others in MI5, you can bet your week's wages on that."

"That's right gentlemen" is barely off DCI Johnson's lips when the tranquil cold, crisp and clear air of Sunday morning is shattered by a tremendous explosion of noise, followed by a screeching and clattering of metal and timber being torn, twisted and tortured. Instinctively, policemen of all ranks duck in unison fearing it to be a bomb.

"What the fuck?" is the question muttered on just about every ones lips.

In the railway marshalling yard a shunting engine driver has misjudged the speed of his train as he set back to couple up a loaded coal wagon and ended up propelling it along the siding. The freewheeling wagon crashed through the scrap yard's rear railway gates and smashed through a stop block before slamming into the side of Cole's office.

The wooden structure is almost demolished, pushed off its ground pillar supports and the whole of the shattered building is shoved some ten yards towards the railway's electric and hydraulic power house.

Underneath the building its wooden floor joists act as a series of small dozer blades that pick up and push along a concoction of scrap yard rubbish, coal slack and sodden earth. The padlocked access hatch to Cole's homemade air raid shelter is buried under a compacted layer of muck as the building and railway wagon judder to a stop.

DS Wilson gathers his wits about him and along with his six armed officers are quickly through the gate into the yard surrounding the stricken office. Another twelve constables scramble among the scrap cars and buses and heaps of sorted metal: there is no sign of an enemy agent or a transmitter. Harry Cole's now trapezoidal and partly demolished site office is still to be checked.

"Nothing found so far, sir."

"Well if he's in there he's had a rude awakening for a Sunday morning Jim."

DS Wilson calls out, announces his presence asking anyone in the office to come out with hands up. He calls again warning that it's the police who are armed and ready; he gets no reply and apart from the creaking of loosened corrugated fence sheets that flex in the slight breeze the yard falls eerily silent.

DI Clarke wastes no more time.

"Come on Jim, we'll take a look inside, any sign of it collapsing and we are out of it double quick, any sign of any one in there and we take him alive, disable him if needs be but we must have him alive."

DS Wilson tugs at the twisted door, it falls off its hinges. Gingerly he steps inside the distorted office and is immediately confronted by the bruised buffers of a railway wagon with its dislodged leading axle and set of steel wheels embedded deep into the wooden floor, axle oil drips onto a ragged carpet covered in lumps of coal. There is no sign of an agent or a transmitter and the office is a complete wreck apart from Cole's school ma'am's desk that stands untouched taking centre stage chaotic scene of smashed windows, furniture and splintered wood and spilt coal.

DI Clarke's attention is drawn to the desk, lit by a shaft of light bursting through the split roof, and reads the scratched message *Abort Kinder-B* that has been encircled and initialled HC with the C a little below the H.

"Ok Jim, at least we now have a definite connection between Cole and the SIGINT's Kinder-B decoded message. Not much here yet for DCI Johnson I'm afraid, so take this place apart, plank by plank if necessary, be careful."

DS Wilson sets about clearing Cole's office. First out is the school ma'am's desk still in one piece followed by everything else including all that's been damaged or broken. Every drawer and cupboard is checked for any sort of clue that may shed light on Cole's handler, a German agent thought to be using a transmitter, nothing is found. An oily and coal dusted carpet is removed and a trap door is lifted, again nothing is found.

The intact school desk is stood to one side, away from the growing heaps of broken or splintered timber ripped apart by the violent arrival of a coal wagon. Watching the proceedings DI Clarke takes the weight off his feet and leans, arms folded, on the school ma'am's desk.

"Jim, do you still have that postcard we found at Cole's house after the fire?"

"Yes sir, still in my pocket and forensics already cleaned and checked it over."

DI Clarke carefully takes the postcard from a buff envelope and places it on the desk slope, holding it in position with the tip of his fore finger, and compares the encircled initials scratched into the table and the same letters similarly written on the back of the postcard.

"Jim, let the lads have a breather and come and look at this, quick."

"Sir?"

"Take a good look at the encircled initials, on the card and those on the table, what can you see?"

"Capitals H and C, Harry Cole?"

"I don't think so; I think Harry Cole has left us a message. Whether he has done it purposely or, as we all sometimes do, subconsciously he has read the messages and then he's doodled, adding the identity of the sender." DS Wilson's response is another questioning look.

"Sir?"

"Look again and forget Harry Cole, what else can you see?"

"Capital H and capital C, with the C set slightly below the H."

"Almost right, look at the C again, is there a tail at the end of the bottom curve?"

"A small one but that would make it a G. If you are right, who the devil is HG?"

"Not who? But what, then who."

"Now you are really losing me, sir."

"Bear with me Jim. HG, usually written with a small *g* is the chemical symbol for Mercury, a heavy metal in fluid form. Mercury is also a winged messenger in Roman mythology and happens to be one of the planets in the universe.

Yes, I believe Harry Cole has left us a lead and our lucky break is them boys chalking up a list at the North Lock."

DS Wilson is struggling to take in what he is hearing.

"Sir, where is all this leading?"

"Jim, I realise I may seem to be off my rocker but consider this. What is the connection between an initialled postcard recovered from Cole's house, a desk at his site office bearing the same initials and a school boy's chalked up list of planets?"

"Sorry sir, now you've completely lost me."

"Jim, sometimes we concentrate too much on one thing and fail to see what is staring us in the face. We have concentrated all our efforts on Cole so let's look at this case from a slightly different angle. HC may be Harry Cole but if I'm right and the initials are HG for Mercury, then the connection is Mercury as the winged messenger of the Roman gods.

The initialled postcard found at Cole's house is a message of some sort with a picture identified as Beacon Hill; the desk in his office carries a definite message to *Abort Kinder-B*. I believe both messages were sent or delivered by a German agent whilst cruising or working the canal on a narrow boat named Mercury."

"Sir, you are suggesting that we are wasting our time here and that we ought to be looking for a narrow boat, identified as one of several floating planets by some kids, named Mercury and that it is actually acting as a base for a radio transmitter-receiver between here and Germany?"

"You've got it now Jim."

A constable close by overhears DS Wilson's comment about a narrow boat, he stubs out a Woodbine and steps forward.

"Excuse me sir. A narrow boat named Mercury left here this morning not an hour ago and heading down stream."

"Downstream on the canal, on the River Soar, it all ties in with SIGINT's tracking of rogue messages in the Soar valley area. Not an hour ago you say constable?"

"Correct sir, tail end of five boats we'd checked last night and again this morning, nothing found untoward and we let them go."

"Tail end of five probably means he's not through North Lock yet. Jim, pull your team together, constable fetch your sergeant please."

DI Clarke sets in motion a plan to capture whoever is aboard the narrow boat Mercury, speed is paramount if a surprise attack at the North Lock is to be successful. He briefs and checks that plain clothed officers and constables understand what is required of them.

"Remember, we need to take this boatman alive."

At the North Lock four boats have already gone through in pairs and Mercury is waiting for the lock to fill before the gates can be opened.

Unseen at the road bridge adjacent to and above the lock the crouching DS Wilson assesses the situation, behind him and a little down the road parked outside Burberry's fish and chip shop are two police cars each with four plain clothed Special Branch and CID officers. Behind the cars is a police van with six uniformed officers including two rifle carrying marksmen. The normal traffic across the canal bridge has been stopped at a safe distance in both directions.

"Sir, all is quiet and the boat with one man aboard is about to enter the lock ready to drop to the lower level. However, we have a problem; two young boys are assisting with the opening and closing of the lock gates."

"Right, this is what I want. Let the boat drop fully to the lower level and just as the boys start to open the gate our friend on the boat will be busy and that's when we will make our move."

DCI Johnson arrives and watches the drama unfold with a clear view from a bedroom window in the North Bridge Inn.

The two young boys are working well; they've done it before and expect to earn a penny or two for their efforts. The upstream gates are easy to open after the waters come level and Mercury steers his narrow boat Mercury into the lock, the boys close the wooden lock gates behind. Mercury checks the upstream paddles are fully closed and moves to open the downstream paddles allowing a rush of bubbling water to sluice through into the lower level. Slowly the narrow boat starts to sink below the level of the tow path; *Mercury* jumps aboard his boat Mercury.

As the waters level out and the downstream gates inch open under the boys exertions a police car turns at speed out of North Gate onto the road alongside the tow path and out jump four armed officers. Four more officers crouched behind the bridge parapet race to line the tow path above the narrow boat: one officer grabs hold the nearest boy and hauls him to safety, another shouts at the other boy on the far side to lie down straight away, no second shout is needed.

Mercury feels for his Luger as the boat's bow end breasts through the lock gates and is confronted by two police marksmen, standing on the stern of the last boat through the lock. With marksmen's rifle sights trained on him and more armed police on the tow path shouting to put his gun down *Mercury* realises his position is hopeless and makes a move to put his gun to his head. A rifleman opens fire and *Mercury* is hit in the right shoulder knocking him backwards; he drops the Luger into the swirling waters of the lock, officers pounce and handcuff the boatman. DS Wilson leads the injured man to the police van to be taken under armed escort to the Royal Infirmary for speedy treatment and transfer to Leicester Gaol.

"Well done DI Clarke, just a single shot fired, all in all a slick operation."

"Thank you, sir. I'm sure he's our man and if truth be told I thought our chance had gone."

"I've said it before; good team work with good organization with bit of luck is all we need. This time we got our break with that sharp eyed constable who latched onto DS Wilson's remark about a narrow boat named Mercury. Yes, good work all-round."

While agent *Mercury* is having a flesh wound treated the narrow boat Mercury is moved further downstream to the public wharf on Belgrave Road and is kept under armed guard awaiting a thorough search.

Captured enemy agents are afforded little time to recover from wounds before they are questioned by the police or interrogated by MI5. It's just a couple of hours since *Mercury* was shot and the only concession to his wounded right shoulder is that his first interview will be in the secure accommodation of the hospital wing in Leicester Gaol.

DCI Johnson of Special Branch is champing at the bit to get at *Mercury* but has agreed that DI Clarke will have the first go at getting some answers and formally interview the German agent. DI Clarke knows that this is his one and only chance to get some answers since an armed guard has already been arranged to take *Mercury* to London and further interrogation by MI5.

Mercury sits propped up by pillows in a hospital bed, his injured shoulder supported by an extra pillow. Either side of the bed sit DI Clarke and DS Wilson who has his notebook and pencil ready. Standing at the door is DCI Johnson listening in on the interview.

It's a relaxed but firm in voice DI Clarke who looks straight at *Mercury*, who looks around the room avoiding eye contact.

"Who are you? You won't talk, how are we to progress? I need just a few answers and if you refuse to talk all you will achieve is an earlier train ride to London for more interrogation and whatever follows that. Let's talk, shall we?"

Mercury breaks his silence.

"Who are you and what do you want?"

"As I've said I am Detective Inspector Clarke and this is Detective Sergeant Wilson, ordinary policemen and the gentleman at the door is just observing."

"MI5?"

"Not quite, but he has dealings with that organisation."

"What do you want DI Clarke? I will talk to you."

"I have two bodies and a missing person, all of whom knew each other, was friends or colleagues and all were alive and well on December 17th last year when operation Kinder-B dropped out of the sky at Beacon Hill. Since then a woman has been murdered, her body dumped in the canal, a man has gone missing and another man murdered before being left in a burning house."

"So what's all this got to do with me?"

"I have three open cases that I think are related and would like to close them before you leave for London. Purely speaking from my point of view I like to keep things neat and tidy and with your help I can tidy my desk. Co-operate now in helping me to close out two murders and a possible third and who knows what leniency may be shown later? By the way I don't make promises or do any deals, I just do my job."

"I still can't see what it's got to do with me; I'm a simple boatman selling bits and pieces, here and there along the canal."

"I'll continue and if I get something wrong feel free to interrupt and correct me.

You own the narrow boat Mercury, named after a Roman god, a winged messenger. Since you will not tell me your name I will call you *Mercury* and I believe you to be Harry Cole's handler and messenger for passing messages between him and Germany.

Your radio transmitter-receiver has been fished out of the canal and we've found your £10,000 in your secret compartment aboard your boat. Not many boatmen have German radio equipment or are rich enough to carry so much cash around with them.

So you can see that even without your help I am beginning to think you are someone different, someone not entirely what he appears to be allowing me to build up a picture of who you actually are and speculate what you are about."

Mercury sucks in and chews on the inside of his cheeks as DI Clarke goes on to relate a tale of one German agent operating a radio set informing another agent Harry Cole, a sleeper agent, by sending him one or more postcards to give him the date and time of delivery of Kinder-B and its drums of counterfeit white five pound notes.

DI Clarke believes that only half of Kinder-B was collected by Cole and successfully switched for genuine notes with the help of his accomplices Mary Frobisher and William Markham, colleagues at the Midland Bank. The switched fivers would be circulated into the banking system causing alarm amongst the banks owners and customers with confidence the pound sterling being lost at home and abroad.

Mercury's eyebrows raise a little then he faintly frowns when he hears DI Clarke mention that the counterfeits were actually switched. The observant DS Wilson looks across at DI Clarke who nods approval for a question to be asked.

"You seem surprised that the counterfeits were switched for genuine notes?"

Mercury with a sharp intake of breath through gritted teeth talks a little more.

"Alright, yes I am a radio operator; I admit that, that's all. How Cole managed the operation, what he did or didn't do was for him to deal with, nothing to do with me."

"That doesn't answer my sergeant's question?"

"I've nothing more to say."

DI Clarke continues with his hypothesis suggesting that at some point, shortly after the parachute drop a decision was made that Kinder-B was to be stopped, not proceeded with and in another word *aborted*; this order came too late for the industrious Cole who had already switched the counterfeit fivers.

As for Cole's accomplices, Miss Frobisher's destiny had already been decided before the switch as had the disappearance of William Markham. Whether or not it was Markham alone who killed Miss Frobisher, though there is strong evidence linking him to her final moments, may never be known and the disappearance of Markham is most probably down to Cole.

"That is unless you tell me different *Mercury?*" *Mercury* remains silent.

"You can see from what little information I have I can't close the cases on the dead woman or the missing man from the bank, not unless you can help me." DI Clarke pauses for a few moments then looks *Mercury* directly in the eye,

"However, I do believe that you killed Harry Cole; the final message from Germany, *Clean up Kinder-B*, was an order for you and a death sentence for Cole and anyone else you could identify as being involved with the operation."

"Fantasy, pure fantasy, even here in England your courts will not convict on such a colourful story line."

"I agree with you on that and that is why the files on Mary Frobisher and William Markham may never be closed but as for the brutal killing of Harry Cole I know I am looking at his killer."

DI Clarke goes through the evidence that links Cole to Kinder-B and *Mercury.*

To begin with he has sufficient evidence to identify Cole as the cyclist with a limp collecting the Kinder-B counterfeits at Beacon Hill. A railway guard and booking clerk will testify as to the timings and description of a cyclist cutting short his journey to Nottingham.

There is the matching piece of a broken Heron's head from the maker's badge on his cycle that cut into a Corporal's hand following a collision on the downhill from Beacon Hill.

There is a postcard on the mantel piece at Cole's house with its picture of Beacon Hill and its coded message and encircled capitals HG.

There are Cole's visits to the bank the day after the air drop and again the following Monday.

Finally there is the scratched message on his office desk *Abort Kinder-B* similarly encircled and including the capitals HG.

DI Clarke catches *Mercury's* eye again and stares intently at his prime suspect.

"Let's go back to the night Cole was killed. I believe you first tortured Cole to make sure you had all the information as to who was involved with him Then, as you allowed him to think he could possibly buy his way out of a desperate situation and fearing for his life, I've already mentioned we've found £10,000 hidden on your boat, you strangled him before setting the house on fire.

You certainly made a mess of the house and by burning the body you initially confused us but fingerprints are marvellous and unique things and Cole was soon identified."

DI Clarke pauses, the room is silent, and a pin dropping could be heard. He continues,

"As well as Cole's finger prints and even a month after being posted and surviving the fire, we have a thumb print taken off the king's head on the blue tuppenny ha'penny stamp on a postcard of Beacon Hill: you will know whose thumb print that is, won't you?

While you take in what I've said so far I have more bad news for you; the £10,000 you took from Cole is all counterfeit. You may have cleaned up Kinder-B but Cole has made sure that you too were infected with the same bad money that someone thought would be a good idea to infect the British banking system with. That is until for whatever reason Kinder-B was to be aborted. I think I could get a conviction on that story line, don't you?"

Mercury sees his situation as being hopeless, having the radio equipment is sufficient to get him hanged as a spy and although you can't hang a man twice, a murder conviction will serve to endorse a death sentence. He now insists he was only carrying out orders and in an attempt to gain some leniency he gives the answers DI Clarke is looking for. He confirms that Cole told him it was Markham who killed Miss Frobisher and it was Cole himself who killed and buried Markham but has no idea where the body is. Finally he confesses to killing Cole as ordered to do.

"I was only doing my duty; I was simply carrying out orders."

"Thank you."

"But how did you know it was me working with Harry Cole?"

"Cole initialled your Beacon Hill postcard HG and did it again next to the *Abort Kinder-B* message scratched into his desk, telling us who sent the card and who scratched out the message, you!"

"I don't understand; he doesn't know my name. HG are not my initials."

"He knew you only as *Mercury* and the chemical element symbol for the metal Mercury is HG, admittedly it should be a small *g* but he can be forgiven for making me think a little harder, I cottoned onto his lead which led me to think about *Mercury* as a winged messenger. I reckoned that Cole had given a clue, inadvertently or otherwise, as to the identity of his radio operator and messenger."

"Ah, I see, but what of my boat how did you know about that, without a connection there you only have a supposed name, how did you find me and my boat?"

"You were spotted by a couple of schoolboys looking for planet names on boats working on the canal. They already had Mars, Neptune and Jupiter chalked on a factory wall then they found you and added your boat Mercury to the list; probably the same two lads who helped you into the lock."

There is a pause; no one says a thing till *Mercury* repeats his defence.

"I was only doing my duty, I was carrying out orders."

The interview is over, DI Clarke can now close the file on Mary Frobisher but the file on William Markham will remain open but no further enquiries made unless a body is found. The file on the murder of Harry Cole by *Mercury* will be added to the evidence and any charges that Special Branch and MI5 may bring once they have finished interrogating the German radio operator.

DCI Johnson shakes hands with DI Clarke as he stands with his prisoner *Mercury* and two armed guards on platform 3 at Leicester London Road railway station waiting for the next train to London.

"Good result Wallace, it all came right in the end, a result made possible by some good detective work and that odd break we all need. Don't forget to give my offer some consideration; you will fit in well in my team."

"Thank you, I will. What happens now?"

"I'll have to hand him over to MI5 who are specialists at interrogation and if he is co-operative they may decide to turn him."

"Turn him?"

"Get him turned into a double agent; we get to know about other German agents over here and maybe in Europe. Also, we can send back any amount of disinformation to confuse the enemy and that will prove especially useful as and when we get the chance to go back into France."

"And if he chooses not to co-operate?"

"A closed trial and execution, death by hanging is certain."

DI Clarke and DS Wilson return to Charles Street police station and share a half bottle of Scotch with the station's DCS before going onto the Spread Eagle for bit of a celebration with other ranks at beating Germany in their own back yard.

"Well Jim, you've made a good start, thanks for all the leg work and I know you've done the maths."

"Yes sir. Two bodies, one missing person presumed dead, two murders and a probable third not to mention a German agent whisked away by Special Branch.

Finally, there is the not so small matter of £40,000 in genuine white fivers still to be found; just what did Harry Cole do with it?"

EPILOGUE

BERNHARD KRUEGER

Survived the war and returned to his home in Dassle, near Hanover. In November 1946 he gave himself up to the British occupation authorities who had prepared a charge of *Forging Foreign Currency & Passports*. The British held Krueger for a while before handing him over to the French without ever charging him; forging currency was not a war crime.

The French tried to recruit him for their own secret service by bullying and threatening him with a charge of murdering four prisoners who fell ill and were killed at Sachsenhausen. Declaring he had had enough of counterfeiting he refused to work for the French who eventually released him, also without charge, in November 1948.

He took a job as lowly store man and following a denazification process he joined, as a salesman, the Hahnemuhle paper factory, the same factory he used to supply the paper for Operation Bernhard.

Pursued by the East German communists in the 1960s he survived another attempt to have him charged with four murders.

Bernhard Krueger died in 1989, aged 83. He went to his grave unrepentant and claiming, as he often did, that he was only a technical consultant doing as he was ordered to do. He showed no remorse for being part of an organisation that put the world on hold as Europe was being brought to its knees with millions losing their lives and he, like so many Nazis, worried only about how he would survive the war.

WALTER SCHELLENBERG

Gaining promotion through the ranks to be a Brigadefuhrer (a general) he continued to oversee operation Bernhard as part of the SS-foreign intelligence which eventually took over the Abwehr, the German military intelligence in 1945.

Also, in 1945 he acted as an intermediary for discussions Himmler had with the Western Allies in an attempt to negotiate peace. Once the talks failed he tried to negotiate his own surrender knowing he would be a valuable asset to any of the Allies' intelligence services.

Whilst in Stockholm in April 1945 he was taken into custody by the British who used him to testify against the Nazis at the Nuremberg Trials in 1946.

In 1949 before an American court he was sentenced to six years imprisonment. He was released in 1951 on health grounds and died in 1952 of cancer.

THE COUNTERFEITERS

Continued to mass produce the high quality counterfeit English pounds to be laundered across Europe, they deliberately slowed the perfection of the American one hundred dollar printing plates, often wondering if Major Krueger knew what they were about but without him ever admitting it. They managed to survive the war though it was a close run thing. They arrived at Ebensee concentration camp, only two days before liberation, fearing the worst.

Released from captivity some went away to write about their experience, some provided affidavits in support of Krueger who managed to get them through those difficult years. All went away with unseen mental scars and managed the best they could.

THE OLD LADY OF THREADNEEDLE STREET

Governor Sir Montagu Norman and Chief Cashier K O Pepiatt maintained their stiff upper lip and ungenerous attitude and never made public the full effect of operations Bernhard and Kinder-B on the English pound.

The Old Lady was certainly worried about the loss of confidence in sterling and the falling value of the pound, particularly in Europe. Shortly after the failed Kinder-B and Bernhard and with more and more instances of forgeries cropping up all over the place, such as front line American soldiers finding boxes full of millions of counterfeit pounds, notably in Austria and Germany, the printing of new five pound notes and denominations above was stopped.

Printing resumed after the war only when a new five pound note with a metal strip was introduced, as the bank insisted, to assist in flushing out the counterfeits. The white five pound note was taken out of circulation in 1957.

DETECTIVE INSPECTOR WALLACE CLARKE

Remained at Charles Street police station, Leicester, until the end of the war continuing to work with and mentor DS Wilson. He eventually succumbed to DCI Johnson's repeated requests to join him in Special Branch.

He spent the post war years in Europe seconded to MI5 working alongside the American Army Counter Intelligence Corps (CIC) and the newly formed American Central Intelligence Agency (CIA) tracking down and interviewing suspected Nazi war criminals. He took over from DCI Johnson and managed covert operations against the Russian diplomats and other consular officials in the post WW2 Cold War. He retired to a village in Suffolk in 1958.

DETECTIVE SERGEANT JAMES WILSON

Proved to be an able detective in his own right and continued to live in Uppingham Road, Leicester, where he completely redecorated the family home twice. He never forgot Mary Frobisher, his first murder investigation, and laid flowers in the garden of remembrance at Gilroes Cemetery each Christmas Eve for ten years till 1953 before moving away from Leicester.

He moved on successive promotions to be a detective inspector in Manchester and a detective chief inspector in Norwich before retiring in 1983 still wondering what happened to William Markham and the £40,000 pounds Harry Cole had stashed away.

MERCURY

The German agent was successfully turned by MI5 on a promise of his life being spared and being given a new identity after the war. In the months before D-Day he transmitted disinformation messages to Berlin on the movement and boarding locations of Allied troops as they prepared for the invasion of France.

He was given a new identity and set free on May 10th 1945 two days after the war ended in Europe. He moved to Scotland and lived alone as a crofter. He died in 1972 having got drunk on whisky and in a fretful stupor he recreated the circumstances that started the fire that burned Harry Cole's house and body. He lit a slow burning fuse, sat in front of his hearth and fell asleep, the croft and his body were consumed by fire.

OPERATION KINDER-B

The operation came to an end when Harry Cole was murdered leaving no indication as to the whereabouts of either the switched genuine £40,000 or the body of William Markham.

The operation may have ended but the effects of infecting the British banking system with a counterfeit virus were more profound than Krueger or Schellenberg could ever have expected and had Hitler not been forced to change the objectives for Bernhard the outcome of the war may have been a different one.

FINALLY

Harry Cole's air raid shelter with its safe and Markham's tomb buried beneath his scrap yard was never found. The rented scrap yard and siding transferred back to the Great Central Railway before being leased out again to another neighbouring and entrepreneurial scrap merchant.

The Great Central Railway, having been nationalised and transferred into the Government's stewardship in 1948 as part of British Railways, was closed to passenger traffic in 1969 and to all traffic in the 1980's and the land sold.

The enlarged scrap yard was relocated and the site cleared for residential development. The location of Cole's former site office is now a public square surrounded by shops and is still overlooked by what remains of the railway's former electric and hydraulic power house, since converted into a public house and a convenience food store.

ABOUT THE AUTHOR

John R Dean was born in 1948 into a working class family in Leicester, England. As a youth he played rugby for his school and represented his county. Leaving school he sold books in a department store and worked in buildings maintenance before embarking on a lengthy career with British Railways designing and maintaining permanent way. Now retired, he pursues his passion for writing and currently resides in 'the country of my heart', Nottinghamshire, England.